D0356630

FRINGE
SINS OF THE FATHER

ALSO AVAILABLE FROM CHRISTA FAUST AND TITAN BOOKS

FRINGE

THE ZODIAC PARADOX

THE BURNING MAN

CHRISTA FAUST

FRINGE

SINS OF THE FATHER

TITAN BOOKS

FRINGE: SINS OF THE FATHER
Print edition ISBN: 9781781163139
E-book edition ISBN: 9781781163146

Published by Titan Books
A division of Titan Publishing Group Ltd
144 Southwark Street, London SE1 0UP

First edition: August 2014
1 3 5 7 9 10 8 6 4 2

A CIP catalogue record for this title is available from the British Library.

Printed and bound in the United States.

PART ONE

PROLOGUE

LONDON 2008

Richard McCoy nursed an overpriced lager in an appropriately generic Red Lion pub in Charing Cross. It had sprung up in the last month to take advantage of increased tourist trade, and had all the trappings one would expect from an "authentic" English pub—wood paneling, darts in the corner, a long bar with row upon row of taps, and a fat, balding barkeep behind it. He'd read somewhere that Red Lion was the most popular pub name in all of England. Something like six hundred of the damn things throughout the country.

In his early fifties, McCoy had thinning salt-and-pepper hair and an aquiline profile that might have once been described as regal, but now just seemed pinched and bitter. His tall frame was slump-shouldered and defeated, with an unfortunate paunchiness around the middle that would probably tighten up if he laid off the lager and put a little more effort into exercise.

But he just couldn't be bothered.

He had just come off a performance of an atrocious dinner theater production of *HMS Pinafore* at the nearby Charing Cross Hotel, where he'd had the pleasure of entertaining a room full of gluttonous tourists as "the Rt. Hon. Sir Joseph Porter, KCB, First Lord of the Admiralty," who sang such unforgettable songs as "When I Was A Lad," "For I Hold That On The Sea," and the ever-popular, "Here, Take Her, Sir."

He'd never felt more broken in his entire life.

"Pour us another," he said to the barkeep, banging his empty pint glass on a bar that was disgustingly devoid of water rings. *A pub should be grotty, lived-in,* he thought bitterly, *not like this mass-produced, plastic tourist trap. A pub should be like a woman, experienced, real, slightly used.*

The barkeep placed a fresh glass in front of him, wearing the same sour look he'd worn since McCoy had walked in. McCoy wondered if maybe the man was as plastic as the rest of the place. He couldn't even remember what his lager was. Some pretentious micro-brew passed through the kidneys of a monkey in the Venezuelan rainforest, no doubt.

He drank it, anyway.

How had it come to this? From a stint with the Globe theater twenty years ago, where his Romeo and Lear were raved about internationally, to doing three shows weekly of Gilbert and Sullivan for a room full of fat housewives who wouldn't know talent if it reared up from the depths and bit them on their enormous, pimpled asses.

But he knew the answer to that question. He was drinking it.

"Excuse me," someone said behind him. American accent. Woman. McCoy cocked his head to the side, only just realizing that he'd somehow managed to slump down onto the bar. How many lagers had he had? No more than two, certainly. Maybe three.

"Are you Richard McCoy? The actor?"

Somewhere in the back of his alcohol-shrouded brain something like self-respect asserted itself, and he sat up straighter on the barstool, stifling a burp.

The woman wasn't quite forty, trim and attractive with blond hair, a blue silk scarf around her neck and—he couldn't help but notice—rather ample breasts. She had a quirky, sardonic smile and trouble in her eyes. At least it looked like trouble to him.

His kind of woman. Experienced, real, slightly used.

"I am," he said as clearly and regally as he could, silently tacking on a "Who wants to know?" He owed money to more than a few unsavory types, and just because this American woman didn't look the sort to truck with those types, it didn't mean she wasn't a spotter for some leg-breaker lurking out in the alley.

"I *knew* it," the woman said, so delighted that she bounced in a thoroughly distracting way. "I saw you when you were in San Diego, touring with the Royal Shakespeare Company. Oh, ten, fifteen years ago? You were *wonderful*."

McCoy thought back on that time.

"*Twelfth Night*," he said. "Yes, I remember. And it was a few more years than fifteen."

"You haven't aged a day," she said, and he laughed.

"Kind of you to say so—"

"Miranda," she said. "Miranda Stallings." She put her hand out, and he grasped it in his own meaty paw, bringing it to his lips and giving it the gentlest of kisses.

"Miranda," he said, smiling at her giggle. "A beautiful name. From *The Tempest*. I played Prospero once, you know. Here in London. Oh, so many years ago. I'd say there's a sight more gray in my hair since you saw me on the stage last."

"Oh, I like the gray," she said. "It's very refined."

"Thank you very much, Miranda," he said. "You take years off just by saying so. Please, allow me to buy you a drink. What would you like?"

"Oh, I wouldn't want to trouble you, Mr. McCoy."

"Please, call me Richard."

"Okay," she said after a pause. "Richard. What should I get? I'm not much of a drinker."

That was the best news McCoy had heard all day.

A few cosmopolitans later and McCoy had sweet-talked Miranda into allowing him to accompany her to her hotel, the nearby Corinthia on Whitehall. She had been part of a tour group, she said, who had left that morning to head to Bath. She'd fallen in love with London, and wasn't interested in going to see some stodgy Roman ruins.

"They're not coming back for another three days," she said, sliding the key card for her room, getting it into the slot the third time. She leaned into him, unsteady on her feet, eyes bright.

"That sounds very lonely," he said.

"It is," she said, giggling. "Very."

McCoy gave a low whistle as they stepped inside. Miranda's suite was enormous, an expensive room in an already expensive hotel. Well appointed, with soft blue carpet, chrome-and-glass lamps, and modern, sleek furnishings. He made a beeline for the minibar, figuring she could afford a few tiny bottles of expensive vodka on her hotel bill.

He stopped when he saw a device sitting on the table next to the bar. It was a small black box with an odd knob on the top and two ribbon cables, each ending in a flat plate with three small, sharp prongs. McCoy picked up the device, and turned it over in his hands.

"What's this, some sort of sex toy?" he asked, hoping he didn't sound *too* hopeful. He touched his finger to one of the prongs. Too sharp for his taste. Americans were all into weird sex stuff—came from all that pent-up repression in the Bible Belt. But even so, this seemed a bit extreme.

Miranda came up behind him, wrapping her arms around his waist.

"It is," she said in his ear, her voice a husky whisper. "Do you want to try it?"

"Oh, you're a naughty girl," he said. "I'm not really into toys, though. Make a man feel inadequate."

"How about a little bondage instead," she said, tugging the silk scarf from her neck and wrapping it playfully around his own. "I'll let you tie me up. Have your way with me." She slowly pulled the ends of the scarf tighter, tugging playfully at the ends.

"Now that," he said, turning to face her, "is something I can get into."

"So glad you approve."

"I do, though it's a bit tight there, luv. Loosen up a tad, would you?"

"Where's the fun in that?" she said, yanking hard on the ends of the scarf, making him gag. The silk bit into his throat, and he pushed at her—tried to knock her away—but she wouldn't budge. It was as if she was made of stone.

He clawed at the scarf, kicked at her, tried to pull away, but nothing he did helped. She pulled the ends of the cloth tighter and tighter, shrugging off his blows as if they were puffs of air.

He slumped, and she followed him down to the floor as he went to his knees, holding tight onto that damned piece of silk, which was choking the air out of him. His vision fuzzed, going black at the edges until soon there was nothing but her face.

Then even that disappeared. A final thought passed through his mind as the blackness took him.

At least there won't be any more goddamn Gilbert and Sullivan.

FRANKFURT 2008

He'd had many names before today. Miranda Stallings, Evan Beetner, Nathan Wallace, Jaclyn Herera, and on and on. He changed identities the way some people changed their clothes, each new name bringing a new face along with it.

And now he was Richard McCoy, a British citizen in his mid-fifties, late of the London theater scene. A has-been actor, publicly disgraced. Well known in certain circles, but not too well known outside of them. A man with a face and a history and a paper trail.

Just the way he needed to be.

The abandoned factory outside Frankfurt had been used to manufacture dolls, an irony he was never quite able to wrap his mind around. Was it a joke? A metaphor? A flair for the dramatic? He was never sure, and it had always bothered him.

He stepped past broken porcelain limbs and cracked plastic heads left half-painted on rusting machines in the outer rooms. High-vaulted ceilings let in sunlight through shattered skylights, illuminating the drab, gray walls, the piles of concrete dust and rat and bird droppings that littered the floor. He made his way through the bleak corridors and down rusting stairs, flicking on a flashlight as he descended into the basement levels. He'd been in the factory many times before, but never as Richard McCoy.

He stopped at an aging fuse panel next to some

unused steam pipes, flipped a convoluted sequence of switches and waited for a long spike to pop out of a recess. He hated this part. But the automated security didn't know him on sight, not in this body, and if he didn't verify his *bona fides* they'd cut him down with machinegun fire.

He put his hand in front of the needle and it shot forward, puncturing the skin and drawing a small amount of what passed for blood in his body. He waited for the process to complete, a green light indicating safe passage, and then used a handkerchief to wipe away the silver liquid from the prick in his hand. He closed the panel and continued on his way.

He followed the steam pipes to a room with a series of large, industrial boilers, rusted hulks that were barely worth the cost of scrapping them. Behind one of these he found a metal trapdoor set into the floor. He wondered—as he always did when he came down here—if the automated systems actually had recognized him.

Moment of truth. He pulled on an iron ring set in the trapdoor. It popped open on oiled hinges. No gunfire. No hail of bullets. He'd passed.

Then he let out a breath he hadn't realized he'd been holding. Of course he'd passed. He *always* passed. He'd been spending so much time in these skin suits he'd started picking up their damn neuroses. He went down the steps deep beneath the factory, the trapdoor closing behind him as banks of LEDs sprang to life, illuminating his passage into a thoroughly modern laboratory facility.

His mission was going to be active the minute he got through decontamination and changed into his chemsuit. Once the airlock opened, he was confronted with gurneys loaded with body bags, lining the hallway outside the main lab.

Several technicians were pulling a dripping body from one of a dozen clear, horizontal cylinders filled with a cloudy liquid. It was the last one. The rest were all empty. From the state of the body, this experiment had failed, too.

The corpse looked half-formed, sexless. The skin was barely there, a thick slurry that sat on top of the muscles like the jelly in a can of Spam. The veins were visible, but where blood should have pumped through them, they were clear, with no sign of activity.

"Ah, Richard is it?"

"It is, sir," McCoy said, turning to see the man he took his orders from, David Robert Jones. Even in a chemsuit, the man had presence. "Richard McCoy. As you asked."

"Excellent," Jones replied. "I saw him on the stage in Brighton some years ago. He had a modicum of talent. Where did you find him?"

"Doing dinner theater. Gilbert and Sullivan, of all things."

Jones shuddered.

"Poor man. Did him a favor, then. Well, he's perfect for our uses. A bit of theater is exactly what we'll need."

"Are we on to Plan B, then?"

Jones said nothing for a long moment. He watched the technicians hauling the corpse into a body bag, ready to join the others in the hallway. As the techs lifted it out of the cylinder, the right hand separated at the wrist and dropped back into the pool of cloudy slime with a loud plop.

"Yes," Jones said. "We're on to Plan B."

1

BANGKOK, THAILAND 2008

Peter Bishop sat on the edge of the creaky double bed in his cramped box of a room at the Sweet Orchid Hotel. There was a pervasive smell of mold and cigarettes in the claustrophobic space, and every surface was damp and slightly sticky. The cheap mattress felt like a bag of soggy boiled rice beneath him.

The old, asthmatic air conditioner was struggling valiantly, but it was no match for the humid swelter. Tied to the air conditioner's dirty grate were three pink plastic ribbons that fluttered listlessly in the ineffective breeze. When Peter had complained to the apathetic maid that the air conditioner wasn't working, she had pointed to those ribbons as a silent rebuttal before going back to vacuuming the hallway without further comment.

The room itself was barely large enough for the double bed, rickety desk, and padlocked bar fridge—key available for an extra fee. A bulky television the size of an old-fashioned toaster offered a rotating selection of adult movies, also for an extra fee. Peter had easily picked the padlock and liberated several bottles of Chang beer from the fridge, but the TV wasn't worth the effort.

In a cheap frame above the bed was a photograph that looked as if it had been cut out of a magazine, of a purple *Phalaenopsis* orchid. On the bedside table there was a "gentleman's guide" to the local red-light districts, translated into seven different languages. The crude map on the back and the vaguely Thai design on the polyester bedspread were the only clues to what city he was in this week.

Well, those and the girl.

She'd said her name was Katy. She was petite and slender, with a feathery bob haircut that had been dyed an odd reddish brown. Her face was wide and heart-shaped with a tiny, thin-lipped mouth. Earlier in the evening, she had used fuchsia lip liner to make that anime mouth twice as big, but it had quickly worn off over the course of their… encounter. Her heavy makeup didn't quite cover the scatter of acne on her cheekbones and forehead.

She'd looked a lot better under the multicolored bar lighting.

"Finished?" she asked, sitting up in bed behind him.

"Yeah." He ran his fingers through his sweaty hair. "Finished."

He watched her squeeze into her colorful scraps of clothing and jam her blistered feet into plastic platform heels. When she was dressed, she shrugged, slung her glittery purse over her shoulder, and left without saying goodbye.

Alone again, Peter found his mind wandering. He had been with a lot of different women from all over the world, but had a hard time making anything resembling a real, lasting connection with any of them. The few times he'd actually tried, it had inevitably gone wrong—sometimes horribly so. Eventually, he'd given up trying and resigned himself to perpetual bachelorhood.

With the occasional temporary company as needed, of course.

Most of his relationships had been so brief that he had little memory of them at all. With one exception—a girl he had met when he was just a kid. A blond girl who'd had something to do with his father's research in Florida. Even she was a blur, but he remembered her green eyes, and her drawings, and how she didn't really seem to fit in. *That* was something he could understand.

And something about tulips, a field of white tulips...

Where did that come from? he wondered, shaking his head as if that would dismiss the fleeting memory. Peter stood and padded over to the bathroom. It was cramped, windowless, and fully tiled—including the ceiling, which made it look kind of like a combination shower and toilet stall. *Or a tiled coffin.* There was a drain in the middle of the floor and a shower nozzle sticking out of a seemingly random spot on the wall.

If he angled that showerhead correctly, he could wash his hair while sitting on the john.

Instead, he opted for a more conventional, standing shower, his third since around noon, local time—when he'd awakened with a brutal hangover. It didn't seem possible to take enough showers in Bangkok. Before he could finish toweling off, though, he was already sweating again, the gritty, toxic breath of the city settling back into his pores like a houseguest who wouldn't leave.

He grabbed his knock-off Rolex from the nightstand, slipped it around his wrist and checked the time. Just after 1 a.m. He had a little over an hour and forty-five minutes to get everything in place, and get his ass where it needed to be for the 3 a.m. meet.

Once he was dressed in respectable but comfortable, unrestrictive clothes and his favorite high-end running shoes, he slid a pair of identical briefcases out from under the bed and set them side by side. He checked the contents of both cases several times and made a few minor adjustments to the weight, then snapped them both shut and headed out into the steamy Thailand night.

The Sweet Orchid Hotel was located right around the corner from the Soi Cowboy district. As he hit the street, Peter's brain was blasted with euphoric multi-sensory overload. Visually, it was a fever dream of throbbing neon signs and mirror-ball glitter, painting exposed skin and leering faces in eye-searing, unnatural colors.

His ears were assaulted by a dozen competing Thai and American pop songs all playing simultaneously, warring against the thumping, bass-heavy dance music that was blaring from the doorways of bars.

A miasma of clashing scents filled his lungs, sweat and perfume and spilled beer mingling with the meaty smoke and exotic spices, wafting from mobile grills serving late-night street food.

As he passed, bar girls in skimpy club wear tried to lure him in, waving English signs advertising cheap beer. Flushed and grinning Caucasian men reeled from bar to bar with their sunburned arms slung around each other's necks. Competing club touts called out in a variety of languages while stone-faced, silent bouncers broke up a sloppy, half-assed drunken shoving match and gave the bum's rush to a pickpocket who should have known better than to mess with the geese that laid the golden eggs.

Because Soi Cowboy was, for all its lurid tease and titillation, really just a sanitized and benign amusement park for foreign men. If you wanted a real walk on the wild side, there were plenty of sleazier, more dangerous areas in Bangkok where you could get your freak on. This place was relatively safe and non-threatening—an utterly artificial environment created solely for the purpose of separating tourists from their baht, yen, euros, or dollars.

Peter loved it.

He'd been travelling constantly, ever since he was a teenager—picking up odd jobs, engineering a variety of scams, and then moving on. Everywhere he went, he always found himself most attracted to the flashy, lurid, tourist-filled areas of the bustling cities. Because he felt inexplicably at home in places like this. Places that were no one's home, where everyone was a stranger from somewhere else. Places like this made him feel paradoxically at ease. Unnoticed.

Conversely, he hated small communities and rural areas where he was easily spotted as the blatant outsider. They reminded him far too much of the strange period of his childhood in which he'd found himself feeling like an alien in his own hometown.

As he walked the gaudy length of Soi Cowboy, he was just another big Caucasian guy from somewhere else, towering over gaggles of glammed-up farmers' daughters from backwater villages in the rural interior. Some of the bar girls he'd met were from as far away as Laos or Cambodia. After more than a dozen visits to this district, he'd met only one person who was actually born and raised in Bangkok, and that was Jaruk.

Jaruk was sharp and fiercely intelligent. A crackerjack hustler who could con a dollar out of the devil with one hand tied behind his back. He always had multiple schemes going at any given time, and was always willing to cut Peter in on a juicy setup. In exchange, Peter lent his American credibility to the pitch.

They'd met at the Classy Lady two years ago, and

had been trying to run numbers on each other for about ten minutes before it had dawned on them that they were kindred spirits. Now Jaruk was Peter's local fixer, his go-to guy for any kind of action in Bangkok.

And Jaruk was going to be pissed when he realized that Peter wasn't going to cut him in on this latest deal. Sure, Peter was throwing his friend a healthy fee for the loan of a motorbike, a couple of cell phones, and a few discreet arrangements. But he'd been extremely squirrelly about the exact nature of the transaction in question. He told himself that he was looking out for his friend, that he didn't want to expose Jaruk to the very real risks that were involved. But he knew better. It wasn't about that at all.

It was about the money.

It was about Big Eddie Guthrie.

If Peter cut Jaruk in on the deal, he wouldn't have enough left over to pay off Big Eddie. And if he didn't pay off Big Eddie soon, well… that wasn't something he wanted to think about. He had to stay focused on the job at hand.

"Here comes trouble."

Jaruk was standing at the back door of the Classy Lady, and spoke as Peter walked up, setting the two briefcases down on the pavement between his feet. A nearby pile of trash smelled like fish.

His English was flawless, with a slight British accent. He was short and wiry with a tousled, bed-head haircut and intense dark eyes like those of a peregrine falcon. He looked like a former teen idol gone bad, his good looks marred by years of hard living and a missing front tooth that had been knocked out by an angry Muay Thai champion.

But he more than made up for it with wit, charisma, and charm.

"How's it hanging?" Jaruk asked, reaching out a scarred brown hand and slapping palms, then bumping fists with Peter.

"To my knees," Peter replied with a smile.

"That's not what I heard," Jaruk said with a wink, extracting a cigarette from a crumpled pack and lighting up.

"Aw, man," Peter said. "Your mom swore to me it would be our little secret."

"My mother has been married six times," Jaruk replied. "She would eat you alive."

Peter laughed.

"How's life at the Classy Lady?" he asked.

A topless girl in a pink, zebra-striped G-string staggered out through the back door, wobbling on her clear plastic heels and nearly crashing into Peter before she started throwing up into an overflowing trash barrel. Then she slumped down into the trash.

"Classy as ever," Jaruk said, with a dryly raised eyebrow. He took a drag from the cigarette pinched between his forefinger and thumb. "But enough about me," he added. "I want to talk about this big deal of yours. You're not holding out on your old friend Jaruk, are you?"

"Trust me," Peter said, fishing a cash-filled envelope out of his pants pocket. "The less you know about this one, the better."

"When a guy like you says 'trust me,'" Jaruk replied with a skeptical squint, "That usually means I shouldn't."

"Fair enough," Peter said, holding out the envelope. "It's just that I'm taking a hell of a risk on this one. I don't want to put you in any more danger than you already are."

He attempted to shore up his less-than-total sincerity by letting Jaruk see just a little bit of fear in his eyes. But once he allowed himself to think about how dangerous this deal really was, that fear started to feel real.

He dropped his gaze and looked away.

"Are you sure about this?" Jaruk asked, taking the envelope and making it disappear.

Am I? Peter wondered.

It didn't matter. He didn't have a choice.

"Sure I'm sure," he said, looking his friend in the eye.

"Because if anything bad happened to you in my city," Jaruk said, shooting him a look of stern warning, "then I'd be forced to admit that I actually care what happens to you."

"*Chiew-chiew*," Peter said with what he hoped was a relaxed, bemused smile on his face. "It's not that big a deal."

"So which is it?" Jaruk asked. "Too dangerous for me to know about, or not a big deal?" He laughed, and shook his head. "You know what, don't answer that. You're right, I don't want to know." He tossed a ring of keys, which Peter caught one-handed out of the air.

"Motorbike is there, at the end of the alley," Jaruk said, pointing. "Cell phones are in the left saddle bag, clean, charged and ready to go. Also, I left you a little something extra. A present. Sounds like you're going to need it."

"You're in my will," Peter said, hand on his heart.

"Good," Jaruk said. He pitched his cigarette butt into an oily puddle and turned to help the semi-conscious drunk girl back into the club. "At least I'll get something out of this mysterious scam of yours."

The motorbike was an orange-and-black Honda Click with hard, locking saddlebags. There was a holographic skull sticker on the left one. Peter unlocked it with a small key on the ring Jaruk had given him, and surveyed the contents.

As promised, three disposable cell phones—and the extra gift Jaruk had mentioned. Unsurprisingly, it turned out to be a Kimber 1911 Ultra Carry, and it came with a spare clip. Peter took out the pistol and two of the phones. He checked the gun, found it loaded, then reached around his back and stuck it down the sweaty waistband of his pants, covering it with the tail of his loosely fitting shirt.

He put the extra magazine and one of the two phones in his pockets, and used the other to make a call. Someone picked up immediately.

"*Moshi moshi.*"

The man on the other end spoke Japanese with a distinct Korean accent. They had compromised on Japanese because the man on the other end didn't speak English. Peter had always had a gift for picking up languages, but his Korean was limited to a few amusingly off-color slang phrases that were good for making bar girls giggle—rarely useful during serious negotiations.

He confirmed the location of the meet, and assured the man on the other end of the line that everything was going according to plan. Then he ended the call and dialed a second number, switching to Russian. His Russian wasn't as fluent as his Japanese, but he understood it better than he spoke, and he could speak well enough to get the message across.

"*Privet,*" a voice said. The person on the other end had a Chechen accent, and spoke with whispered, barely contained urgency, like a man making an obscene phone call. Talking to him made Peter's skin crawl, but he kept his tone calm and friendly, telling him the same thing he'd just told the Korean.

When he ended the call, he dropped the phone to the

ground, crushing it under his heel. He closed and locked the saddlebag, and then stacked and used a bungee cord to secure the two briefcases onto the package carrier. He took a moment to center himself, and let the surging adrenaline cycle through his system.

Then he mounted the motorbike, strapped the half-helmet under his chin, and keyed the machine to life, heading out toward the mouth of the alley.

As far as he was concerned, riding a motorbike was the only way to get around Southeast Asia, for a variety of reasons. It was easier to squeeze through narrow streets and zigzag through congested, erratic, and generally dangerous traffic. But for Peter, he just loved the raw *realness* of it. The feeling of independence, of the wind on his face and the olfactory overload of exotic scents both delicious and repulsive. Being in a limo or a car was like riding around in a fish tank, isolated in an air-conditioned bubble. Being on a motorbike made him feel alive, and he wanted to savor that feeling, drink it in.

Considering what he was about to do, he might never get another chance.

2

The Infinity Towers Hotel was located in the upscale Embassy Row neighborhood, surrounded by shopping malls, five-star restaurants, and exclusive nightclubs. A far cry from Soi Cowboy. The conjoined oval towers were designed to look like the infinity symbol, when viewed from above, but from Peter's lowly point of view as he pulled the motorbike around to the service entrance, their double-barreled shape was more reminiscent of an old side-by-side shotgun pointed into the starless sky.

He dismounted, took the cases off the package carrier, and handed the motorbike over to a twelve- or thirteen-year-old boy who was there waiting for it. The boy acknowledged him with a silent nod. Peter pressed a sweaty handful of baht into the kid's outstretched hand and told him in halting Thai not to park too far away.

A brace of young men in cooks' whites squatted against the wall by the service entrance, smoking and talking smack. They ignored Peter completely as he entered as nonchalantly as he could manage.

The door led into the narrow offshoot of a long, cement corridor that cut through the center of the west tower like an artery, providing stealthy access to all areas of the ground level. It allowed service personnel to appear—seemingly by magic—any time one of the esteemed guests knocked over a drink, or needed help finding discreet company, or asked for advice on where to buy cocaine or overpriced designer handbags.

To the left was a double door that led into the spicy sauna of the kitchen. To the right was the employee locker room, and as Peter passed, a trio of pretty young girls emerged, having just traded their drab maid uniforms for flashy club wear.

Once he reached the junction with the main corridor, Peter was greeted by a tiny, obsequious older man with a glossy black toupee and an immaculate cobalt-and-black Infinity Towers uniform. He flashed clearly fake white teeth in a smarmy smile, unleashing a cloud of strange breath that smelled as if he'd been drinking the blue liquid from that jar where the barber puts his combs.

"Good evening, Mr. McClane," the man said. "So glad to have you with us again."

Peter was going to have to kick Jaruk, and tell him to lay off the *Die Hard* movies. But if the little man had a clue, he didn't show it. He just reached out, offering a heavy, embossed envelope. Peter set the cases down and accepted it.

"Inside, you will find the key to your usual suite," the man with the toupee said. "As you are a preferred platinum member, that key card will also allow you access to the Black Pearl Lounge, the spa, the gym and"—he leaned in, sparse eyebrows lifting significantly—"the rooftop garden."

There was no rooftop garden at the Infinity Towers.

"Thank you," Peter said, checking the unmarked key card inside the envelope and then stashing it in his pocket and picking the briefcases back up. "Keep your people off the top floor until 4 a.m."

"Use the service elevator," the man with the toupee replied, tipping his chin toward a large steel door down the hallway on the left. "And enjoy your stay, Mr. McClane." Was that a hint of sarcasm?

He turned and slipped away into the bowels of the hotel, leaving Peter to his fate.

"Yippee-ki-yay, *ai hee-ah*," Peter muttered to himself, checking his watch.

Two-fifteen. Right on schedule.

He walked down to the elevator and pushed the button.

When the massive textured steel doors slid open there was a waiter with a rolling cart stacked high with dirty dishes. He gave Peter a knowing nod, and then rolled the cart out of the elevator and down toward the kitchen.

Peter stepped in. Unlike the showy exterior glass lifts that ferried guests up to their luxury suites, this one was dull and utilitarian. The floor was textured rubber and the walls were scratched and dented steel. It was large enough to stable a bull elephant, and there were doors on two sides. When Peter got in, he pushed the button marked 30E, so that when the elevator arrived on the thirtieth floor, the rear door would open, discharging him into the east tower.

As the elevator rose, he closed his eyes, breathing slowly and trying to relax the bunched up muscles in his neck and shoulders. He had everything planned down to the millisecond. Clockwork. It was going to be perfect. No worries.

When the elevator reached the top floor, the back door slid open, letting Peter out into a service area. It was a stubby white hallway with a supply closet, an employee restroom, and a holding area used to stash housekeeping carts between shifts. At the end of the short hallway there was a doorway that led into another world.

Whereas the hidden service areas were unremarkable and strictly functional, the areas of the hotel which had been designed for guests were all sleek, subtle luxury. The hallway Peter entered had that velvety, cocoon-like hush shared by expensive places all over the world. It was as if the vulgar bustle and noise of the city below had been muffled by an insulating layer of hundred-dollar bills. Subtle, recessed lighting spotlighted minimalist, monochromatic flower arrangements in angular, ultra-modern blue glass vases. The immaculate cobalt-blue carpet was thick as quicksand, silencing Peter's footsteps completely.

The suite he'd selected sat directly in the middle of the wasp waist that connected the two towers. It was precisely equidistant from the places where he had arranged for each group to wait while the deal was in progress. There were two such suites—one in each of the conjoined buildings, located at the narrowest point. The door to his suite pointed east, and its twin faced west.

His payoff to Jaruk had insured that both suites would be unoccupied that night. The eastern facing door was pivotal, because he would need to make his escape from the roof via the eastern staircase.

He used the key card to let himself into the suite, but didn't turn on the light. Relative darkness was essential—both inside this suite and its western facing twin. If the lights were on, the glow would shine upward through the skylights, illuminating the area of the roof where his most crucial sleight of hand needed to occur.

He stood for a moment in the semi-darkness, letting

his eyes adjust. Although the lights were all off, the room was *far* from pitch black. It was indirectly illuminated by the candy-colored *Blade Runner* skyline which filled the floor-to-ceiling windows. It was a hell of a view. Guests who paid the exorbitant fee to stay here expected nothing less.

In the dim glow, the room seemed even more seductive and appealing than it would have been with the lights on. Its lines were stark, modern, and minimalist. Understated in a way unique to things that are outrageously expensive.

Crossing to the window, he stood there, drinking in the view. He saw the Grand Palace in the distance, its needle-like pointed rooftops glowing gold in the nighttime. Peter couldn't help but wonder how much longer he was going to have to keep hustling before this kind of lifestyle came within his reach. Luxury hotels, fast cars—the entire world at his fingertips. No matter how hard he worked, he just couldn't seem to get ahead.

It didn't seem fair that the whole take from this potentially fatal caper would go to pay off his debt to Big Eddie. It seemed like he really ought to get *something* extra for his troubles. Danger pay, so to speak.

Yet that kind of thinking was what got him into this mess in the first place. His "take" from this job was his life. Period. And, given the way he'd been jerking Big Eddie around for the past few months, he ought to be damn glad to have it.

Enough with the daydreaming, he decided. *Time to go.*

He checked to make sure the empty suitcase was there, and found it sitting on a folding rack beside the bed. *Thank you, Jaruk.* It was a generic black roller bag, exactly like a million others that passed through any given airport on any given day, and it was exactly the right size to fit both briefcases.

Check.

Then he looked up at the large, multi-paned skylight. There was an automated shutter that could be controlled using a bedside button, for travelers who hadn't yet adjusted to local time, or just wanted to sleep in without the interference of daylight. The shutter was fully retracted, revealing the thick, milky frosted glass of the skylight. There were five long, rectangular panes in a row, and the one closest to the door had been removed, allowing a brisk, exhaust-scented breeze to waft into the room.

Check. Everything was as it should be. *Time to head for the "rooftop garden" to put the final pieces into place.*

He stuck the key card into his hip pocket, grabbed the two briefcases, and left the suite as he found it. Out in the center hallway he headed for the fire stairs at the far end.

Inside the stairwell, there was only one way to go, and that was down. Unless you had the key to the door on the right, which was marked AUTHORIZED PERSONNEL ONLY.

Peter did.

He swiped his key card through the lock and it beeped its acquiescence, accepting him as suitably authorized. He pushed through the heavy door and onto the narrow stairs that led up to the roof.

At the top of the flight stood a second door that also required a swipe of the card. He had to push hard to open the door against the wind.

Once he was able to squeeze out, he found himself at the far eastern end of the infinity-shaped roof. This high above the city, the wind kept the stifling heat and humidity at a reasonable level. The 360-degree view was breathtaking—the owners of the hotel had missed out, he decided, by *not* installing some kind of garden, sun deck, or lounge.

Then again, he thought, *if they had, I wouldn't be able to pull this off.*

Turning so that he faced west, across the roof, he saw a lot of empty space with very minimal cover. Each tower boasted a tall, thin antenna with a blinking red light at the top to warn away aircraft. There was a slight zigzag in the middle of the rooftop, created by the two knee-high, raised skylights that stood above those twin suites. That was the critical spot—the one where he would make the switch.

Peter had never been particularly afraid of heights, but he kept to the center of the oval-shaped eastern tower as he walked toward the wasp-waisted spot where the twin buildings joined. The spindly metal railings around the edge didn't do much to instill a feeling of safety—upright posts with steel wires strung between them, more like an afterthought, really. Barely crotch-high when measured against his six-foot-two frame, and thin enough that he was pretty sure they would buckle under a person half his weight.

Still buffeted by the wind, he arrived at the middle of the little zigzag. He turned and looked back at the door leading to the eastern stairway. It was visible, but dimly lit in the ambient glow from the city.

Checking its twin to the west, making certain there was no one there, he stashed the two briefcases next to the raised steel framework of the skylight that looked down into his suite, on the side away from the missing pane of glass. The height of the framework was perfect—almost exactly the same as that of a briefcase, standing with its handle up, ready to grab.

With the cases positioned right where they needed to be, Peter peered toward the western stairwell to the west. He envisioned all of the players, in place and ready.

Koreans to the west, and the more temperamental and unpredictable Chechens to the east.

He'd gone back and forth on the placement, trying to determine who should be where, and who could be counted on to react appropriately when the time came. The Chechens were the clear winners, he decided—the most likely to shoot first and ask questions later. The downside, however, was that in order for Peter's plan to work, the more potentially dangerous group had to be placed on the same side as his escape route.

All he could do was hope that they didn't decide to shoot the messenger.

He checked his watch.

Showtime.

3

Peter took the other cell phone from his pocket, pressed the "talk" button and dialed the second number he'd been given—this one by the Koreans. His call was answered on the first ring. He told the man on the other end to meet him by the entrance to the western staircase, on the thirtieth floor.

Then he hit the "off" button.

Taking a moment to breathe deeply, and arrange his face into the affable, trustworthy *I'm just here to help* expression that had served him so well for so long, Peter headed over to the western stairs. As he walked, he twisted his shoulders, rolled his neck, and shook out his arms. In deals where no one was speaking their first language, body language was crucial. He had to appear comfortable and relaxed.

Confident, but not cocky.

He had to look like a man who had everything under control. He just hoped that if he could make the Koreans believe he did have everything under control, maybe he would be able to convince himself.

He opened the door to the western stairwell and

headed down to the thirtieth floor. When he arrived at the AUTHORIZED PERSONEL ONLY door, he heard Korean voices on the other side.

You got this, he told himself.

Then he pushed the door open.

There were four men waiting in the stairwell. Two were obvious muscle—bulky knuckleheads in tracksuits, with big hands and cold, stony expressions. The other two were a Mutt and Jeff pair. The taller one was handsome and lanky with a bleached, pop-star haircut, a mournful expression, and a briefcase just like the one Peter had hidden up on the roof. The shorter one looked like an accountant, with wire-framed glasses and a little bit of a belly under his unremarkable navy-blue dress suit. But the way the others silently deferred to him, it was clear that this was the boss.

"Mr. Park," Peter said, extending a friendly hand to the accountant. It was the name the man had given him on the phone, but "Park" was the Korean equivalent of "Smith." Not that it really mattered.

He'd told Mr. Park his name was Baker. It seemed more appropriate than "Butcher" or "Candlestick Maker."

Mr. Park eyed Peter's hand as if he suspected Peter might have failed to wash up after his last visit to the men's room. Reluctantly, he accepted it with a limp, moist handshake that felt like gripping a dead squid.

They had a brief exchange in Japanese, in which Peter explained that the seller was shy, and didn't want to meet directly with the buyer. To protect the anonymity of both groups, they would wait on opposite sides of the roof, with Peter acting as a go-between, ferrying the money to the seller and the product back to Mr. Park.

The Korean nodded with a wordless grunt of acceptance.

It was very hard for Peter not to pump a victorious fist in the air. Instead he did a little happy dance in his head, while maintaining a stoic expression. Turning, he motioned for Mr. Park and his men to follow him through the locked door and up to the roof.

When they stepped out into the wind, the tall, handsome guy immediately set the briefcase between his designer sneakers, trying and failing to fix his trendy hair. The muscle twins flanked the boss as he stepped forward and surveyed the roof. Park was frowning.

"Where are they?" he asked in Japanese.

"I will call them now," Peter assured him. "I wanted to give you the strategic advantage of being first to arrive."

Again, the nod-and-grunt combo. Peter smiled, took out the phone, and dialed the Chechens. The guy with the creepy voice picked up, sounding more eager than ever. Peter switched to Russian, telling him to wait at the eastern stairway on the thirtieth floor. The man on the other end went into elaborate detail about what would happen to Peter if he tried anything funny.

Peter made himself smile and nod for the benefit of the Koreans, and then ended the call.

"They will be here," he assured them. Then he showed the Koreans five fingers to indicate how long it would take to fetch the Chechens and get them set up on their end of the roof. With that, he headed over to the eastern tower.

The Chechens were waiting there in the eastern stairwell. There were five of them, and they seemed shockingly young—not one a day over twenty. They were all roughly bearded and underfed, clad in ill-fitting, brand new suits and cheap ties that made them look like hillbillies dressed up for a court appearance. They hadn't bothered to buy new shoes to go with the new suits, and were all wearing battered combat boots.

Two of them had brought baggage. One had the requisite briefcase, and the other had an unexpected duffle bag almost certain to be full of killing tools. He suppressed a shudder and hoped they would be pointed at someone other than him.

"Pozdravleniya," he said, then added, still in Russian, "Which of you is Umarov?"

To Peter's surprise, the one who stepped forward and introduced himself as Umarov in that now-familiar, creepy phone-sex voice was the youngest-looking of the group. He was of a slight build, with narrow shoulders and small hands, as if he hadn't received enough nutrition as a child. He had a sharp, Slavic profile and his light-brown beard was wispy and still baby-fine. He couldn't have been old enough for a legal beer in the US, but he had terrifying zealot's eyes.

A guy his age should be busy trying to start a garage band, or talk girls out of their trusiki, Peter mused. But the world was full of child soldiers, teen gang members, and lost boys of all kinds. There was nothing he could do to save them from the fate they chose. And it wasn't like he was planning to kill these guys himself—just point them at the Koreans. If they didn't want to start something, they didn't have to.

And if they *did* shoot first, they still might win and walk away unharmed.

Peter wasn't putting their fingers on the triggers. He just provided them with the opportunity.

That was what he told himself, anyway.

He turned and let the Chechens into the locked stairway. They followed him upward, their boots thudding on the stairs, and out onto the windy roof. As soon as they had emerged, they set themselves up in a precise, military formation. The guy with the duffle bag unzipped it and pulled out an AK-47, then stepped off to one side, his jaw clenching and unclenching as he chewed a wad of gum. He kept the barrel pointed down, but was bird-dogging the Koreans the entire time.

The others passed around a variety of firearms as if they were candy bars, while Peter stood there trying to look calm and relaxed.

Jaruk's 1911 against the sweat-slick small of his back no longer seemed like much of an asset.

4

He asked Umarov if they were ready. The Chechen nodded and gestured for the kid with the briefcase to hand it over to Peter.

This was it. His moment to shine.

Peter nodded. His palm was slick with nervous perspiration, and he had to grip the handle tightly to keep it from slipping while he walked toward the wasp-waisted center of the roof.

As he reached the skylight, he couldn't help but notice that the Koreans had also gunned up, and were scowling through the gloom at the Chechens. Although being in the crossfire made Peter feel like a mechanical duck in a shooting gallery, he also knew that all those guns would keep the two groups focused on each other, and not on him. Which was exactly the way he had planned it.

Nevertheless, it felt as if his heart was trying to beat itself to death against the inside of his ribcage, and the high wind was wicking the cold sweat away from his exposed skin, making him feel chilled and shivery. Yet he couldn't let himself think about any of it. He had to concentrate on the sleight of hand that was coming next.

When he reached the skylight with the missing pane, he dropped the Chechens' briefcase into the suite below, smoothly grabbing his own identical case, and never breaking his stride.

The Koreans were so busy giving the Chechens the stinkeye that they barely noticed Peter until he was right beside them, handing the case over to Mr. Park. The Korean nodded and passed it to the tall guy with the bleached hair, trading it for the one he was holding.

But Park didn't hand over the Korean case. Instead, he waited silently as the tall guy opened the one Peter had given them, and began to inspect the contents.

This was a tricky spot. The point where everything could go to hell.

Peter held his breath, and clenched his fists.

Inside the case was a device of Peter's own creation. He'd told both sides that he could deliver to them a device which would allow the user to hack and reprogram armed UAVS, also known as drones. In reality, the Korean was examining an old laptop motherboard and frame, grafted to a touch-screen tablet and the controller for a toy helicopter.

It only needs to be convincing for a few minutes, he reminded himself. He'd told each group that the other one was selling this technological unicorn. Both parties thought *they* were the buyers. Peter already had the Chechen money, which he'd dropped through the skylight. Now he needed to get the Koreans' payoff, as well, so that it could join the first case in the suite below.

On paper, it all looked simple.

Peter liked to believe that, after a decade of experience as a freelance "social engineer," he was able to predict human behavior like a veteran sailor could predict the tides. Along the way, however, he'd also learned to expect the unexpected.

Stay calm, he reminded himself.

To his amazement and relief, Blondie nodded his approval. Peter felt every muscle in his body turn to relieved jelly as he let out the breath he had been holding, trying not to be too obvious.

So far so good.

Mr. Park handed Peter the other briefcase, motioning with his weak chin, gesturing toward the antsy Chechens. Peter thanked him in Japanese, and started back across the roof.

When he reached the skylight, he made the second crucial swap, smoothly dropping the Koreans' case into his suite and grabbing his own. He could feel the Chechens' hard eyes boring into him as he cleared the final stretch, hoping all the while that the shadows had kept his secret.

By the time he reached the other side, he was clenched-up again. He handed the ringer case to Umarov. They were less than ten feet away from his escape route now, but one of the Chechen boys had positioned himself in front of the door. Peter's only hope was that when the *govno* hit the fan, the goon would leave his post to join in the action, giving Peter the opportunity to take a powder, unnoticed.

The kid with the Kalashnikov drew down on the Koreans with rock-steady hands. He spat his wad of gum off to one side, narrowly missing Peter's sneakers. Umarov opened the case, revealing its contents—several copies of the "Gentleman's Guide" to Bangkok's red-light districts.

Life would be so much better for this kid, Peter thought to himself, *if he spent his rubles on a hot soap massage with a happy ending*. Umarov swore and flashed a low hand signal. The kid with the rifle unceremoniously shot Mr. Park in the face. His aim was superb, considering the lighting, the high wind, and the distance of the target.

This couldn't be his first time.

Peter hit the deck and covered his head with both arms.

The Koreans returned fire.

Chaos erupted with so much noise that it was impossible to distinguish one sound from another. Bullets struck the rooftop and dislodged bits of concrete, but most of them flew by at a safe height. After a few seconds Peter pulled the gun from the small of his back and raised his head to check out the scene.

One of the Korean muscle twins was bleeding from his left arm, but still firing steadily from the cover of the western stairwell, while the other dragged his fallen boss around the back. Blondie had thrown himself down on his belly with the precious case under his chest, and was shooting wildly every which way.

Peter eyed the door to his eastern exit, wondering where the guy who'd been standing there had gone. He was about to make a run for it when his question was answered by a hand gripping the back of his shirt, and then hauling him forcefully around the back of the stairwell.

It was pretty much the only serious cover. All five of the angry Chechens were crammed there together, in the narrow strip that separated the structure from the spindly railing on the edge of the roof. Taking turns leaning around the corner and shooting at the Koreans, they were having some kind of unfathomable argument in Chechen, which Peter didn't understand at all.

What he *did* understand was that he was stuck on the wrong side of the stairwell—the side that didn't have a door. He needed to get the Chechens to cover him, while he made a run for the door. Otherwise he'd get plugged the second he stuck his head out.

But his brain was spinning, coming up blank, again and again.

He had to think.

Think!

Die Hard jokes notwithstanding, Peter wasn't an action hero. He knew how to use a gun, but he was an average shot under the best of circumstances. He wasn't particularly brave. Reckless, yes, but not because of courage.

He really wasn't a bad ass.

But he *was* good at manipulation. That was his super power. The ability to think on his feet, and talk his way out of any situation. Not that it was doing him much good.

Think, Peter!

Suddenly, it hit him. He knew exactly what he needed to say, and was retrieving the proper Russian translation from his adrenaline-addled brain when one of the boys took a bullet in the shoulder and reeled backward, spinning and slamming into him.

Peter let out an involuntary shout and fell into one of the slender railings that stood between him and the deadly thirty-story drop to the hot Bangkok street below. Unsurprisingly, the half-assed railing bent backward under his weight, and his feet slipped into the narrow gap between the railing and the edge of the roof.

He dropped Jaruk's gun and flailed for balance as both his legs followed his feet. He was narrowly saved from falling to his death by a flat metal post, which wedged between his legs and slammed into his junk, preventing the rest of his body from slipping through.

Bolts of pain shot through him.

Never in his life had he been so happy to be hit in the nuts.

The awkward fall left him balanced like a witch on a broomstick. Instead of its usual vertical position, the post was sticking horizontally off the edge of the roof at a 90-degree angle. It had been attached to the roof with four bolts, three of which had been torn loose by Peter's weight. The only thing holding him up was that one bolt and the two flimsy wires connecting the bent post to its wobbly neighbors.

Below his dangling feet lay the teeming nighttime city.

Concentrating on breathing through the nauseating pain and trying to recover enough to climb back up onto the roof, he forgot for a crucial moment what a bad idea it would be to look down.

He looked down.

Vertigo slammed into him harder than the wounded Chechen, and he swallowed an airless, terrified gasp, grasping frantically for the post. He could see dozens of tiny motorbikes and taxis flowing like glowing corpuscles along Wireless Road, far below. Ant-sized people swarmed around the brightly lit, multicolored fountain in front of the neighboring shopping plaza. It might have been a beautiful view, if he weren't about to fall into it.

His body told him in no uncertain terms that he shouldn't move an inch, under any circumstances. His arms and legs had the fence post in a boa constrictor's death grip, but dangling there—with his heart pounding and his eyes squeezed shut—wasn't going to accomplish anything.

Then he heard a rasping sound. The last bolt—the one thing standing between him and certain death—was starting to inch slowly and inexorably out of its hole.

He peered at the edge of the roof.

Just reach up with first one hand, then the other, he told himself. *Grip the edge, and then pull the top half of your body up. Raise one leg up, then the other and* voila*! You're home free.* Hauling himself up wouldn't take much effort. It'd be a piece of cake.

There was just one problem.

In order to reach up and grip the edge of the roof, he'd

need to let go of the post. Which didn't seem like much at all, really. Just a slight shift of one hand, a movement of about ten inches from the post to the edge. He'd still have his other hand and both legs holding on to the post.

No big deal.

So why couldn't he do it?

C'mon, just reach over...

Or he might just stay there, frozen and clinging to that post for the rest of his life.

The last bolt made the choice for him. It emitted a creaking, stressed-metal sound, and finally slid loose from its hole.

In that moment, all the air was suddenly gone from his lungs. He hoped whatever panicked, involuntary noise he made didn't sound too girly, but he couldn't hear it himself over the sound of the wind—and of his pounding heart.

He shot forward as if someone had jammed a branding iron into his ass. He caught hold with both hands and pulled himself up so that the sharp edge of the roof dug into his roiling belly. The post hung loosely between his legs, held up now by the wires that connected it to its neighbors.

If Peter's full weight had still been on it, the wires would have broken.

5

The shoot-out on the roof continued with undiminished vigor. When he managed to swing up and onto the roof, he lay there gasping for a handful of seconds, bullets flying all around him.

When he got his shaking legs under him and retrieved the shreds of a plan from the terrified Jell-O of his brain, he realized how little time had passed since he slipped off. It felt like a lifetime, but in reality it had been less than a minute.

None of the Chechens were dead yet, although one of the wounded was starting to look a little bit rough—icy-pale and breathing heavily through his open mouth. But he was still in the fight. Another was bleeding, but didn't seem to notice.

Umarov was intact, and looked almost happy, like a corpse-sniffing dog thrilled to be playing the fun game his trainer taught him. When the Chechen leader ducked back behind the stairwell to reload, Peter gripped his arm and spoke close to his ear.

"They've still got your money," he said. "You can't let them get away. Don't just hold your position—go on the offensive, before they duck out and take your cash with them."

Umarov's eyes widened as the words sank in. Suddenly the firefight was more than an enjoyable diversion. He started barking orders to his underlings, and they split into two groups of two, moving to the left and right of the staircase, while the badly wounded guy hung back and covered their attack.

Peter followed Umarov around the right side of the stairwell. The Chechen gave a passionate shout that didn't need translation, and charged toward the Koreans with his boys covering him on the right and left. Peter crouched low and duck-walked around to the stairway door.

He flinched as a bullet slammed into the wooden frame just above his head, spraying his face with paint chips and splinters. But he still managed to grab the handle. It took all the strength left in his shaking arms to pull the door open wide enough that he could squeeze into the stairwell.

The wind slammed it behind him.

Peter went down the steps two at a time, hitting the next door with his shoulder to shove it open. Once he was in the public stairwell, he took a moment to compose himself before opening the door to the hallway. The last thing he needed was to go tearing through the hotel like a maniac. Let the guys on the roof have all the attention. He had to look like just another unremarkable guest—preoccupied, maybe, but not in any rush.

He put on what he hoped was a nonchalant, slightly bored expression and pushed down the handle.

There was no one in the hushed hallway as he walked with a measured pace to his suite. Using the key card, he let himself in, and quickly shut the door behind him.

The racket on the roof echoed through the suite, and the smell of cordite wafted in through the missing pane. Shouting, and then more gunshots, but Peter did his best to ignore them, instead zeroing in on the two briefcases. One had fallen on the bed, and the other had bounced off to the left and landed on the carpet. He grabbed the one on the bed first and cracked it open. It was filled with stacks of greenbacks, exactly as promised.

He lifted a few of the banded stacks, to make certain the case was filled with money, through and through. It was legit.

The second one was similarly filled. Peter did an internal victory dance, but maintained an outward calm while he closed the two cases and put them into the empty suitcase. He zipped it up, set it on its end, and pulled out its telescoping handle. He was just about to leave the room when one of the intact panes in the skylight suddenly shattered, dumping a bloody rag doll onto the thousand-thread-count Egyptian cotton comforter cover.

Peter flinched away from the rain of glass, one arm thrown up over his face, the other hand locked in a death grip around the handle of the suitcase. Then he braced himself. He'd worked hard for this, and he was ready to fight for it.

But whoever had fallen though the skylight was in no shape to fight for anything. He was still alive, groaning softly, but so bloodied that Peter couldn't tell if he was Chechen or Korean. The figure reached out a shaking, broken hand, but there was nothing to do for him.

Nothing to do but get the hell out of there before anybody decided to look down through the ruined skylight to see what had happened to their buddy. He pulled the suitcase toward the door, its cheap plastic wheels crunching on broken shards. He didn't look back as he let himself out of the suite.

Out in the hallway, away from the skylights, the sounds of the gunfight seemed much more distant—they might be mistaken for construction, or even a large piece of machinery on the roof. As he pulled the door shut, he heard a scrabbling nearby.

What the hell...?

There was another guest, trying with some difficulty to enter a neighboring suite. The man was just a scant inch shorter than Peter, with thinning salt-and-pepper hair pulled back in a coarse ponytail, and a sharp, aquiline profile. He wore heavy, horn-rim glasses and an appalling Hawaiian shirt with pineapples and parrots. It gave him the look of a college professor on vacation.

He had a large carry-on bag slung over one shoulder, a laptop case, and a roller suitcase as innocuous as the one Peter was pulling. He seemed extremely nervous, fumbling with the lock on the door and trying the key card forward, then backward. He glanced up and eyed Peter with a furtive, almost embarrassed glance.

Peter gave him a casual nod and headed for the elevator. He was less than halfway there when the door to the stairwell burst open.

"Freeze!"

A group of Thai cops in SWAT armor came swarming out of the stairwell. The lead man yelled in flawless English as the men behind him drew down with an eclectic mix of handguns and rifles.

"Drop the suitcase!"

Peter felt a sick, helpless fury racing through his veins.

Goddamn, Jaruk—you swore that the cops had been paid off. Bastard probably kept the bribe money for himself, and left Peter with his ass in the wind. He'd been so close to pulling this off, too, and it infuriated him to think that his undoing would come from a trusted friend's betrayal.

Peter let go of the handle of the suitcase and slowly raised his hands, palms out. Then he heard a noise behind him. As he turned, the man in the Hawaiian shirt drew a massive Dirty Harry hand cannon and aimed it at the cops.

"You won't take me alive!" he shouted, revealing a rich, plummy, upper class British accent.

Peter was so dumbfounded by this astounding turn of events that he just stood there for a surreal handful of seconds—until the crazed Englishman rushed him and shoved him aside. The man tripped over the jumble of their combined luggage as he fired a wild shot into the expensive modernist chandelier. The gun was so close to Peter's ear that the sound deafened him.

He dropped to the carpet and rolled away, wedging his body against the wall and trying to will himself to become invisible as the trigger-happy Thai cops returned fire. Their aim was much better than the Englishman, and when Peter looked up, he saw that their quarry's ugly shirt had been enhanced by several large crimson blossoms.

Those were getting larger by the second.

The man staggered backward in a crooked zigzag, bouncing off the wall, and then threw himself onto his roller case. It was as if he was trying to protect it at all costs.

The Thai cops swarmed in, completely ignoring Peter and surrounding the bleeding Englishman. One of them cuffed him, while another wrestled the suitcase out of his weakening grip.

Peter was about to reach for his own suitcase and bug the hell out, when his previous mess came flooding out of the eastern stairwell. Two of the Chechens, neither of which was the kid calling himself Umarov, backed into the hallway, firing up the stairs at the pursuing Koreans.

They started down the hall as the first of their pursuers came into sight. One of the Chechens took a bullet in the hip and went sprawling on the carpet while a stray bullet from the Koreans caught one of the Thai cops in the shoulder.

That was enough to jolt the cops into action. One of them kicked in a nearby door, while another dragged the handcuffed prisoner and his precious suitcase out of the line of fire and into the hotel room. A third and fourth cop engaged with the Chechens, while the one who'd been shot grabbed Peter by the arm, shouting something unintelligible into his gun-deaf ear.

The cop who grabbed Peter was thickly built and moon-faced, with small, close-together eyes and a wide, flattened nose. He was wearing so much fake sandalwood cologne that it made Peter's eyes water. And even though the big man had just taken a bullet, he hardly seemed to notice it. He raised Peter up to a crouch, shoved his suitcase into his arms, and then duck-walked him to the elevator, using his Kevlar-covered body as a shield to protect them from the ongoing gunfire.

When the elevator door opened, Moonface thrust Peter through so hard that he nearly fell back on his ass, clutching the suitcase like a precious child. The cop reached into the elevator and hit the "L" button, pulling his arm back out of the car as the doors started to close. Peter tried to thank him before they shut all the way, but he could barely hear his own voice, and had no idea how loudly he was speaking.

Then it was too late.

As the elevator slid smoothly down, he noticed there was something wet on the sleeve of his shirt where the Thai cop had grabbed him. He touched the damp spot, expecting blood, but was surprised to find his fingers slicked with a strange silvery fluid. He stared at it for a moment, trying to figure out what it was.

Then he gave up.

He was lucky to be alive. As the car descended, a sort of euphoria swept over him. The fact that he'd made it out with the loot was like winning the lottery. This time, alone in the elevator with no one to see, his victory dance was on the outside.

6

Peter had rented three different rooms in three different generic franchise hotels near the airport, using three different names and three different creatively obtained credit-card numbers.

In each room he'd stashed a go-bag containing a change of clothing, basic toiletries, a gun, a wad of American dollars, a fake passport, a cheap laptop, and a poker hand of clean credit cards. Those were an essential part of his repertoire, and it had taken him years to set up a reliable source.

He staggered into the first one he reached, and collapsed on the bed for several blank, blissful minutes, just breathing and enjoying not being dead. Once he got his heart rate down to something not too far above normal, he hit the minibar like a typhoon, downing several tiny bottles of booze in a row without bothering to check the labels, and then cracking an ice-cold Singha.

He raised the bottle, toasting himself and the precious suitcase, and took a deep, heroic swallow. Simple beer had never tasted so good.

Flopping back down on the bed, he put the bottle

onto the nightstand, pulled the last of the disposable cell phones from his pocket, and dialed a number he knew by heart. A woman answered.

"Hello."

"Let me talk to him," Peter said.

There was a pause, a muffled exchange, and then the sound of violent, incomprehensible Scottish swearing starting on the other end of the line. It became louder and louder, like the leading edge of a nuclear blast. When it hit, Peter had to hold his phone away from his ear.

Finally the roar died down.

"Hello, Eddie," he said.

"That Peter Bishop?"

"Yeah, it's me," Peter said, sitting up on the edge of the bed. "I got your money."

"Oh, you *do,* do you?" Eddie's words became slow and condescending, as if he was talking to a child of questionable intellect. "And why should I believe you now," he demanded, "as opposed to the forty-seven *other* times you said you had my money?"

"Because it's right here," Peter said patting the suitcase and putting the phone between his ear and shoulder so he could turn it to face him. "I'm looking right at it." He unzipped the case.

There was a momentary silence on the other end.

"Tell me where you are, and I'll send someone," Eddie said. "And you'd best not be talkin' out your fanny flaps again, because I'm runnin' out of reasons not to kill you."

As he said it, Peter opened the suitcase. Then he stared, slack-jawed and disbelieving, at its contents.

There were no briefcases.

"Bishop?" Eddie said, his voice full of suspicion.

In place of the briefcases full of neatly banded stacks of American greenbacks, there was a custom-cut gray foam liner. It was shaped to cradle a Plexiglas cylinder clearly marked with a red biohazard sticker. Inside of that, there was a single pinkie-sized vial with an orange cap and black hash marks to measure volume.

It was a little less than a quarter full of cloudy pink liquid.

"Let me get back to you," Peter said. He disconnected the call before the Scotsman could launch into another wave of swearing.

Up in the empty suite on the thirtieth floor—the one that had been kicked open—Richard McCoy unbuttoned his stained Hawaiian shirt. Silence had descended on the otherwise empty floor of the hotel.

Nearby, Jones sat in a modern chair that was more stylish than comfortable. The "police officers" had gone back into the fray, leaving the two Englishmen alone in the room.

McCoy peeled off the shirt, revealing the squibs stuck to the skin beneath. He used a damp towel to wipe away the sticky fake blood and adhesive. A thin trickle of silver flowed from a slight nick just above his left clavicle.

"Good thing they didn't hit you dead on," Jones said, arching a brow at the superficial wound.

"I don't mind," McCoy replied, pressing the towel firmly against the small cut.

"I'm not worried about your welfare," Jones said with a dismissive wave of his hand. "I'm worried about the welfare of our little puppet show. If you had *really* started bleeding all over the place, Mr. Bishop might have noticed that something was rotten in Denmark."

McCoy nodded, dropping the towel and picking up

a clean shirt from the bedside table. He slipped an arm into one sleeve.

"There were a lot of moving parts in this little drama," he said. "Do you think he suspects anything?"

"No, overall I think it went well," Jones replied. "Even with that annoying intrusion at the last minute."

McCoy smiled.

"The game is on," Jones added.

Peter set the phone down on the bedside table, beside the half-empty beer he no longer wanted. The phone immediately started buzzing, demanding his attention and scooching itself across the surface of the table. But Peter ignored it until it stopped, squinting at the mysterious vial inside the suitcase. That crimson warning sticker made his skin crawl, even though he had no idea what could possibly be in there. Blood plasma? A virus?

Some kind of deadly bioweapon?

Instinctively he edged away.

Whatever it was, great pains had been taken to prevent the vial from being broken. Which told him that whatever was in there, somebody didn't want it to get out. Or maybe they didn't want the outside world to get in.

The phone began to buzz again, and his mind turned to a more immediate concern.

Big Eddie. There was no way the mobster was going to understand what had happened. He wouldn't even listen long enough for Peter to explain. No, he had to find a way to turn this around. Somehow…

He stared at the vial again.

How can I turn whatever this is into money, he thought, *and as quickly as possible?*

Peter considered himself to be a broad-minded entrepreneur, relatively unburdened by quaint, old-fashioned concepts like morality. It had been a gradual process, this erosion of the distinction between right and wrong. He'd progressed from harmless, penny-ante swindles—like faking an MIT degree—to identity theft and fraud, then to gray-market tech and smuggling.

Therein lay the answer to his current dilemma. He was sure of it. He was willing to sell pretty much anything to anyone—no questions asked—and was perfectly happy to rip off anyone dumb enough to let him get away with it. What was that old saying? *A fool and his money are soon parted.*

At least he hoped so.

He even was willing to sell someone a gun, knowing full well that if they were buying it from him, they weren't planning on using it for target practice. But if this vial really did contain some kind of bioweapon, chances were anyone who would want to acquire it wouldn't be using it to rob a bank, or teach a cheating husband a lesson.

No, if Peter went down that road, his carefully maintained, gray-shaded hat would go full-on bad-guy black.

It wasn't that he was a *bad* person. He just applied a sliding moral scale to each caper. Of course, the scale tended to tip in his favor, whatever the situation. Yet he tried to avoid ripping off people who couldn't afford to be ripped off. Fortunately for him, just about everyone in his world of shady dealings was just as selfish and "morally flexible" as he was.

But a virus wouldn't distinguish between innocent and guilty. It wouldn't even distinguish between the other guy and Peter. If it was deadly, and it was unleashed, it might kill him just as quickly and efficiently as Big Eddie.

There had to be another way.

Ignoring his self-preservation instincts, he made himself lean down close to the sinister vial, even though every inch of his exposed skin was screaming for him to stay as far away as possible. He didn't even realize he was holding his breath until his head started to spin from the lack of oxygen.

There was a printed label on the inner vial. The letters were tiny and difficult to read, so Peter practically had to press his nose against the outer Plexiglas cylinder in order to make them out.

VN11-H2.

Then below that, a name: DR. JULIA LACHAUX.

Peter reached into his go-bag, pulled out the laptop, and swiftly helped himself to the hotel's overpriced Wi-Fi, searching for "Doctor Julia Lachaux."

Bingo.

Lachaux was a scientist employed by the privately funded Center for Seizure Disorder Research. She was surprisingly photogenic for a scientist—a tall, leggy redhead with a curvy build and a warm smile.

And she was currently involved in a firestorm of controversy.

Doctor Lachaux was engaged in the development of a bioengineered retrovirus that supposedly held the key to a cure for epilepsy, a disorder from which she herself also suffered. There were several heartwarming stories about her tireless work to help kids with the debilitating condition they shared.

The controversy swirled around the rumor that the virus had been stolen. Reading that, Peter glanced at the vial.

"I think I can confirm it as true," he muttered. Then he returned to reading. The posts were all infuriatingly vague about what the virus actually did, but one claimed that it "had the potential to overwrite DNA."

He also found a post—about a week old—in which Lachaux denied the reports that her virus had been stolen, and assured the interviewer that even if it had been, there would be absolutely no danger to the public.

"Methinks the lady doth protest too much." The more he read of her vehement denials, the less believable they sounded. And with good reason.

He dug deeper, and found the official site for the Center for Seizure Disorder Research. Their facility was impressive—upscale and well appointed, with top-of-the-line equipment. A far cry from what his father had used at times over the years. It seemed to be funded primarily by some movie star with an epileptic kid. Most importantly—to Peter anyway—it looked as if they would have enough disposable funds to pay handsomely for the return of Doctor Lachaux's precious virus.

Maybe there was a way for him to profit from this mishap, after all.

Now that he knew *what* to do with his accidental cargo, Peter had to figure out the *how*. In essence, how was he going to smuggle a potentially deadly virus out of Bangkok and into the United States? Granted, it was less than three ounces, and would fit in a plastic baggie, but on general principle the Department of Homeland Security tended to frown upon that sort of thing.

He knew he wasn't a terrorist. They might not be so certain.

Of course, he might not have to bring it to Doctor Lachaux's doorstep. He just had to get it somewhere close enough that it wouldn't be out of the question for her to come meet him.

Still, he wanted to try to avoid getting the international agencies involved, if at all possible. So "close enough" still meant the States. He'd have to figure out how to slip in unnoticed, and in a situation like that, there was only one person he could think of who might be able to help him with this.

Peter dialed another number he knew by heart. She picked up on the first ring.

"Tess," he said, then quickly added, "Don't hang up..."

But she did.

Crap.

This was going to require some persistence and creativity, along with a healthy dose of charm. Luckily, convincing a hostile ex to do something dangerous was the kind of thing he did best.

7

PHNOM PENH, CAMBODIA

The Phnom Penh airport was pretty much like any major Asian airport. Really, like any airport anywhere.

Peter loved airports. Transitional places, full of strangers. Comfortable and anonymous. He could be anyone in an airport. And in that moment, anonymity was exactly what he needed.

He'd conveniently "forgiven" Jaruk, who'd claimed not to have known anything about the cops at the hotel. Whether it was true or not, Peter had leveraged his friend's chagrin, and enlisted his help.

He'd needed to slip out of Bangkok and across the border into Cambodia as discreetly as possible, just in case Big Eddie had been able to trace the call and narrow down Peter's location. So far, so good. He was feeling slick, on top of things. Like he might just be able to pull this off.

Using a fake credit card, he'd bought a ticket to New Zealand, but he wouldn't be on that flight. The ticket had just been used to get him through security. Instead, he was waiting by the gate for the arrival of Trans Global flight 177 from Heathrow.

He was waiting for Tess.

Her flight had been delayed by twenty minutes, and when it did arrive, they let off all the passengers first. Tired families with fussy children. Irascible businessmen. Dreadlocked backpackers. Peter watched the last of them wander through the gate with the now familiar squinty, bloodshot eyes and jet-lagged shuffle they all shared.

Must've been a rough flight, he mused. Finally, once all the passengers had deplaned, the flight crew followed, each with their own matching roller bag. Tess was last.

She was blond and petite with dark eyes and expressive hands. Her hair was slicked back and tied into a simple knot, and she wore the same dated and unflattering uniform as her fellow flight attendants—a scratchy navy-blue polyester suit and garish orange scarf printed with the Trans Global logo.

But to Peter, she looked beautiful.

She didn't see him. Instead, she turned toward her left, a warm, sultry smile blooming on her lips as she walked across the waiting area to meet a dark-haired Caucasian man in a flashy suit.

His back was turned toward Peter, so at first he didn't recognize the man. But when he turned to greet and embrace Tess, Peter saw his face.

Sonofabitch… Michael Kelly. His old partner in crime. Apparently Kelly had taken over more than the business after Peter had ducked out.

He watched as Kelly whispered in her ear, reaching down to grip a tight handful of her ass. Then he slipped something about the size of a playing card into her pocket and walked away.

She just stood there for a moment, watching him go with a closed, unreadable expression on her face. Then she put her hand into her pocket, feeling whatever he'd put in there, but didn't remove it.

As she turned to walk away, Peter double-timed his steps to catch up with her.

"Tess," he said.

She jumped without stopping, then turned to him, and her face went hard, eyes cold and narrow. She looked away and kept walking without answering.

"Please, Tess," he said. "Just five minutes of your time."

She stopped and looked at her watch.

"You have three," she said. "What do you want, Peter?"

"You..." Peter paused, tried a smile. "You look fantastic."

"I look exactly the same as I did when you tossed me away like an empty beer can. I've moved on. You should do the same." She looked at her watch again. "Now you have two and a half minutes."

"So, it's you and Michael now, huh?" Peter said before he could stop himself.

"That's none of your damn business," she said, turning again and walking away.

"That guy's a real piece of work," he replied, following her.

"He was there," she said. "Where were you?"

"Come on, Tess," he said. "I've seen how he treats women. You can do so much better than a loser like that."

She stopped dead in her tracks.

"Look," she said without turning. "You don't get to walk out of my life, with no explanation, and then suddenly turn up out of nowhere and start lecturing me."

To be fair, she wasn't wrong.

And he'd allowed himself to lose sight of his immediate goal—to get her to help him. Not to give her grief about her romantic choices.

So much for charm...

But it wasn't that simple. Part of the reason he'd run

away from their relationship in the first place was that he was having a hard time dealing with the way he felt about her. She did things to his head. And seeing her again brought all those complicated, contradictory feelings back to the surface.

"Look, I'm sorry," he said, backtracking as best he could. "You're right, I just... Is there somewhere we can talk?"

She looked back at him, eyes softening just a little. Something in his voice must have touched a nerve.

"I'm on the 6:45 to DC tomorrow morning, but I'll be at the Lucky Star for the next—" she checked her watch—"eleven hours. You remember the Lucky Star, don't you?"

He did.

"Thanks, Tess," he said.

She didn't reply, just walked away, pulling her little roller suitcase along behind her.

8

The bar in the lobby of the Lucky Star Hotel was a strange, schizophrenic knock-off of what a reclusive Asian entrepreneur had been convinced Americans would want.

In reality, it looked like something aliens might have come up with, based on a single blurry photo of an eighties-era franchise where the waitresses wore short shorts, and the menu was printed on a football.

Tess was sitting at the end of the bar, alone, drinking her usual Manhattan with two cherries. She had changed out of her frumpy flight attendant uniform and into a sheer, barely-there wisp of a white dress that floated around her lithe body like mist. All the other Americans and Europeans in the bar looked sweaty and rumpled, but Tess seemed perfectly at ease, despite the tropical swelter.

She had the knack. Supremely adaptable—a chameleon, able to pass as native wherever she went.

Seeing her dressed like that, he found himself hoping for... what?

"Hey," he said, easing himself onto the stool beside her.

"You want something," she said. "Other than my charming company, I mean." She held up a finger to the bartender, who brought Peter a Tiger beer. "So why don't you just get it over with. I don't have all night." There was a subtext to that, but he wasn't sure what it was.

"It's good to see you, too," he said, clinking his bottle against her glass and taking a much-needed slug.

He told her a heavily edited version of the bad deal and the encounter with the strange Englishman, trying to paint himself as an innocent bystander who'd wound up in the wrong place at the wrong time. He played up the helping sick kids angle, and how he just wanted to do the right thing by returning the virus to its rightful owner in the States. Though he didn't call it a virus.

He called it a "cure."

She listened quietly until he was done, then burst out laughing.

"What?" he asked, trying to look hurt.

"Sick kids?" she asked. "You really expect me to believe that? Come on, Peter. Come clean. What's the real angle? It's Big Eddie, isn't it?"

"Well..." He looked away.

"I thought so." She shook the ice in her glass and then, polishing off the last sip of her drink, continued. "Remind me how this is my problem?"

"Look," he said softly, taking her hand. She jerked slightly, but didn't pull it away. "I know you've got no reason to help me, after the way things went between us."

"The way things went." She rolled her eyes. "You say that like it rained, or your soufflé fell. Things didn't just go that way, Peter. *You* went that way."

"You're right, I know," he said. "I admit it, I was a jerk. Probably still am, but I'd like to stay alive, and maybe to try and make it up to you, if I can. If you'll help me."

He could see in her dark eyes that she was wrestling with herself over this, and the fact that she was even considering it felt like a major victory. He didn't want to push too hard, so he backed off and let her come around in her own time.

"What do you need me to do?"

He took the vial out of his pocket. He'd wrapped it in several layers of waxed paper and packing tape to hide the glaring red biohazard sticker. Nevertheless, the package was small—about four inches long. It could have been anything.

"I need you to get this to DC, that's all," he said. "It's the cure—and if the wrong people get their hands on it, it'll never make it back to the laboratory. They'll keep it to themselves, find a way to profit from it." He winced inwardly at that. "But it's fragile, so be careful." He pushed it toward her gently. "I'll meet you there. At Finley's, okay?"

"You really are a jerk," she said, taking the vial and slipping it into her purse. "You know that, don't you?"

"Tess," he said, pressing her other hand to his lips. "I owe you big time."

"Yeah," she said, smiling a little bit in spite of herself. "You do."

Suddenly she pulled away and stood, turning toward the entrance. Michael Kelly appeared in the doorway, frowning toward them with suspicious eyes. She moved quickly to him without another word to Peter, taking his arm and leading him out onto the street, all the while speaking softly near his ear. Peter had no right to feel jealous, and yet in that moment, he could have happily punched Kelly in the face.

But he squelched the thought. That kind of testosterone-fueled drama would blow the fragile truce he'd forged with Tess, and just then it was more important to get the virus back to the States, so he could score the payoff he needed to keep his neck out of Big Eddie's noose.

So he sat quietly and finished his beer. When it was done, he left a few crumpled bills on the bar and was about to head out into the bustling street when his latest disposable cell phone rang. There was only one person who had that number.

"Jaruk, you dog," he said when he picked up. "How's it hanging?"

The voice on the other end was female and hesitant, speaking in a heavy Thai accent.

"Sorry," the voice said. "I am Pim. Jaruk's wife. This is Peter Bishop?"

"Yeah," Peter said, frowning. "That's me."

"He want me tell you Little Eddie is coming," she said. "You run now."

"Jesus," Peter said, an icy dread congealing in his belly. "Let me talk to him."

"He in hospital," Pim said, her voice breaking. "He say he very sorry for telling. You run now, Peter. *Run now.*"

The line went dead.

9

Peter just stood there for way too long, staring at the dead phone, his mind blank except for a shrill, echoing fear filling his head like a car alarm.

Little Eddie.

Jesus, that was bad.

Physically speaking, there was nothing particularly big about Big Eddie Guthrie. He was pretty average in height, about five foot nine, with a stocky build and more wiry gray hair growing out of his large ears than on his shiny freckled head. But he was known as Big Eddie because he had a son, also named Eddie.

Unlike his dad, Little Eddie was big in every dimension. He was six foot four, broad-shouldered and thick through the middle. The kind of hard, heavy build that didn't come from working out at a gym. He was handsome in a thuggish, gangster-actor kind of way with dark hair and pale-blue eyes that were only pretty if you didn't look too close. He was a dog-kicker. Two hundred and fifty pounds of bad news.

And he was coming for Peter.

Peter sidled up to the door and peered down the

crowded Monireth Boulevard, first one way, then the other. Motorbikes and pedicabs jockeyed for position with cars and vans, and the sidewalk was bustling with pedestrians. Unlike his Bangkok accommodation, the Lucky Star was clean and modern, as was the section of town in which it stood.

He noticed Tess and Michael standing by a rickety food stall about a half a block away, talking to someone who had his back to Peter. Someone large, towering far above the dark heads of the bustling locals. He'd recognize those hulking shoulders anywhere.

Kelly, the rat bastard, was pointing back toward the bar. Tess was shaking her head and gripping Kelly's sleeve, until she spotted Peter. Her eyes went wide, silently warning him away with a subtle tilt of her head. But before he could heed her warning, Little Eddie swung around to face him, ham-hock fists clenching.

His pale, Scottish complexion was blotchy and pink from the tropical heat, and he was sweating through his tight-fitting shirt. His hair was damp and pasted to his forehead. The only part of him that didn't look overheated was the cold smile that spread across his thin lips when his gaze locked on Peter.

There was a strange frozen moment where the two of them just stood there, a tense tableau of tall, unmoving outsiders like rocks in a river, diverting the natural flow of the urban nightlife around them.

Then Peter broke and ran.

He tore down the crowded street, dodging buzzing scooters and curious bystanders. He faked to make it look as if he was headed toward an alley, and then turned the other way at the last second, running for a busy main drag that ran perpendicular to Monireth. He needed to stick with the crowds, use the urban bustle and chaos as cover, because if Little Eddie got him alone, even for a second, it would all be over.

After a few blocks, he risked a glance over his shoulder and saw that Little Eddie was rapidly gaining on him, shoving people out of his way as he came. Despite his size, his long legs gave him an advantage, and nothing slowed him down.

When Peter turned back again, he was too late to stop himself from crashing into a tiny old man who was attempting to dismount from a bicycle. It was so laden with stuffed animals that only half of the front wheel was visible.

"*Sohm toh*, Grandpa," Peter said, hoping that he'd pulled the right Southeast Asian apology out of his panic-addled brain as he hauled the terrified old man to his shaky feet and pressed some sweaty bills into his hand without checking to see if they were riel, baht, or American dollars.

Then Peter jumped on the bike and shoved away from the crooked curb, barely missing being sideswiped by a tour bus as he darted between two motorbikes. It was hardly ideal transportation, but he was all out of options, and if he didn't do *something*, Little Eddie would be on him like pissed-off rhino.

He felt a tug on the back of the bike, making it wobble to the left and when he looked back over his shoulder, he saw Eddie a short distance behind, holding a pink bunny rabbit the size of a small child and looking as if he was about to have a stroke from the heat.

But Peter couldn't keep his eye on his pursuer. He had to pay attention to the dangerous and unpredictable Phnom Penh traffic, or he was going to get creamed.

As soon as he turned away from Little Eddie, though, something bounced off the back of his head—the stuffed rabbit, no doubt. It didn't hurt, but it startled him and caused him to swerve slightly. It took his full attention to straighten out the overburdened bike while avoiding a large gaping pothole to his right and a taxi full of drunken tourists to his left.

Then the sharp crack of a gunshot shattered his concentration.

A puff of white polyester stuffing flew up from the blue teddy bear that'd taken the bullet intended for Peter. The fluff clung to his hair, stuck to his sweaty face, and got into his mouth. He spat out as much as he could and swatted at the clumps in his hair.

Then he took a header directly into the pothole, just as a second shot sailed through the humid city air where his body had been only seconds before. Peter flew over the handlebars and landed face down in a toxic puddle composed primarily of gasoline, rancid fish guts, and piss.

He rolled out of the street, spitting and gagging, just in time to avoid being flattened by two more taxi cabs and a pedicab with no passengers. Teddy bears went flying everywhere, the bike crashed off to one side, and Peter was drenched with filthy water as the taxis' wheels hit the puddle he'd recently vacated.

But he had more important things to worry about. Like the fact that Little Eddie was still shooting at him. He couldn't seriously be trying to kill Peter—not yet anyway. After all, if Peter were dead, his dad would never get his money. And it was a large enough sum that he probably wasn't yet ready to write it off. Of course, Little Eddie had notoriously poor impulse control, and really wasn't much of a thinker.

So Peter couldn't take any chances.

He scanned the street for options and spotted the big "Welcome" sign over the entrance to the sprawling Night

Market, about fifty yards away. If there were any place in this city where a big white guy could get lost, that was it. He ran for it without looking back.

The Night Market was a maze of cluttered stalls and vendors selling anything and everything, from cooked food and sweets to raw fish, fruit, and flowers. There were bootleg CDs and movies, religious items, and tacky plastic souvenirs. Tourists crammed the spaces between stalls, daring each other to try exotic delicacies and snapping photos and haggling over the price of Buddhas. Bare wooden two-by-fours held up cloth canopies, and the sound of music emanated from the large central stage.

Peter slipped easily into the flow of the crowd, eliciting little notice beyond a few grimaces at his wet hair, dirty face, and the aroma of urine wafting from his stained shirt.

He looked back over the heads of the shoppers, searching for one of the few people in Phnom Penh who was taller than him. He spotted Little Eddie back by the entrance, hung up like a Clydesdale horse trying to cut across a herd of stubborn, clueless sheep. The horse image was reinforced by the fact that he was all lathered up and drenched with sweat from the run, as if he'd been ridden hard by a heartless master. The tropical swelter was revealing itself to be Peter's ally.

If he was lucky, the burly Scotsman might just keel over from heat exhaustion.

He ducked behind a stand selling durian, hoping the sharp, powerful smell of the notoriously odiferous fruit would cover his own stink as he pulled his stained shirt over his head and used it to clean off his face and hair as best he could. When he was done, he tossed it into an open trash barrel that was already filled with the spiked empty durian shells whose pale gooey guts had been served to the more adventurous tourists. The pretty young girl in charge of the stand couldn't stop giggling at the sight of this large shirtless foreigner crouched behind her pile of spiky green fruit. It seemed kind of cute, until she started calling her friends over to look at him, too.

He waved his hands, shook his head and put a finger to his lips in a desperate universal pantomime for quiet. He cycled through the few Khmer phrases he knew and couldn't come up with anything useful other than the word for *please,* which he whispered over and over.

Too late.

Little Eddie had spotted him. And he was reaching for the small of his back, presumably to retrieve whatever he'd been using to shoot at his quarry out on the street.

Peter had less than a fraction of a second to decide what to do. He was all out of genius, so he grabbed one of the spiky, football-sized fruits and flung it at Little Eddie as hard as he could.

The durian hit Little Eddie square in the face and both his hands—including the one that now held a gun—flew up in surprise and shock. Without stopping to think about it, Peter picked up another fruit and then another, throwing them both in quick succession. The first bounced off Little Eddie's broad chest with minimal effect, but the second hit his gun hand, breaking open against the barrel and knocking the pistol from his grip.

The acrid, rotten-smelling pulp from the center of the broken fruit exploded all over Little Eddie's face and chest, clearing away the crowd faster and more effectively than the fact that he was brandishing a deadly weapon. While Little Eddie was knuckling the noxious mush out of his eyes and groping for his fallen gun, Peter made a run for it.

He dodged between stalls, ducked under curtains, and wound up in a small, open-air food court with colorful mats laid out on the ground behind the stage for customers to sit and eat, picnic-style. He stumbled over a row of shoes that people had taken off and left on the edge of the mats, apologizing in every language he knew along the way.

On the way out, he took a precious minute to grab a brown Tiger Beer T-shirt from a vendor near a side exit, and throw a random handful of money at the baffled, toothless old woman behind the table. He'd taken the largest one he could spot at a glance, but it was still laughably tight, and too short for his lanky torso. A good two inches of skin was visible between his belt and the lower hem.

Still, they wouldn't let him on a plane without a shirt, so it would have to do. Because he needed to be on a plane—any plane—and he needed to be on it five minutes ago.

He tore out through the side entrance and dove into the first cab waiting in the taxi rank. The driver was a cocky young guy with a hustler's smile and a kickboxer's lean, sinewy build under his loose pink tank top.

"Airport," he said to the driver.

"Luggage?" the driver asked with an arched brow.

Instead of an answer, Peter gave the guy money, and looked out the open window at the side entrance and the market beyond. He couldn't see Little Eddie yet, but he could see the leading edge of the commotion and chaos that meant his nemesis wasn't far behind.

"Yes, sir," the driver said. "Airport, right away, sir."

The kid floored the gas and peeled out. As the taxi merged into the flow of erratic Phnom Penh traffic, Peter glanced back through the rear window.

No sign of Little Eddie.

He'd made it. For now.

Covering his eyes with his forearm, he sank gratefully down into the seat.

PART TWO

1

Peter sat squashed into a narrow, economy-class middle seat with his knees up to his chin and his arms folded as if he were in a coffin. Which, to tell the truth, might actually have been more comfortable. But he wasn't complaining.

He'd had to hustle and sweet-talk and pull favors, but eventually was lucky enough to score the last available seat on this fully packed flight to Charles de Gaulle Airport in Paris. And he'd done so before Little Eddie had been able to hose off the durian stink and make his way to the airport.

Which didn't mean Peter was free and safe—it just bought him a little bit more time. So he had to use that time as wisely as possible. Once he was on the ground in France, he would need to finagle a flight to the United States, get his ass to Washington, DC, to meet Tessa, and figure out how to get that money from Doctor Lachaux.

But for the moment, there was nothing he could do but try to catch whatever meager shut-eye was possible in this torturously uncomfortable seat. And try not to think about anyone named Eddie.

He wasn't having much luck with either.

EDINBURGH, SCOTLAND 2007

It had seemed to him like a sure thing.

It wasn't his first visit to Edinburgh, but he never got used to the place. It still seemed to him like an elaborate set for some elf movie, with its curvy, cobblestone streets, quaint old buildings, and that big gloomy castle looking down on everyone like a disapproving maiden aunt. Glasgow was uglier and grittier, but felt more like a real city to Peter. It was harder to understand the accent, but easier to get lost and go unnoticed.

As with all cities he visited, Peter naturally gravitated toward the most touristy area, which in this case was the strip of shops along Princes Street. He'd chosen a bland, mid-range franchise hotel as his home base, but when he'd booked the room, he'd been unaware of a massive citywide construction project that had just begun tearing up the street right in front of the hotel.

Which, in retrospect, explained the deep discount he'd received.

So he was feeling hostile and running on too little sleep, up way too early and glowering at the noisy and seemingly pointless construction as he stood on the street and tried to get his head together. It wasn't quite raining—more like a foggy drift of floating moisture that clung to his hair and shirt, and made him feel like he was inside a cold humidifier.

When Micki Rose finally showed, she announced her presence by pretending to rabbit punch him in the back of the neck.

"Walk with me," she said, heading off down Princes

Street without waiting to see if he would follow. Even though she was a foot shorter than he was, he still had to walk fast to catch up to her.

She was a scrappy little spitfire, barely a hundred pounds and built like a twelve-year-old boy. She dressed like one, too, favoring expensive trainers, loose-fitting track pants, and video-game T-shirts that easily disguised whatever deadly weapons she inevitably was packing. At thirty, she still looked underage, and took full advantage of it. With her natural-blond ponytail, big, wide-set blue eyes, and upturned button nose decorated with a delicate spray of freckles, she was the dictionary definition of cute.

On the outside, anyway.

Micki had the words *Schemie Girl* tattooed in Old English lettering arching across her hollow belly, a local phrase Peter didn't completely understand. At first he thought it might be slang for a con artist, but discovered that it meant something more like "hood rat" or "white trash." She showed this tattoo often, with a kind of defiant pride. But trash or not, she was hands down one of the smartest operators Peter had ever met. Razor sharp and utterly fearless. Ballsy, but never reckless or impulsive.

Her scams always paid off, and paid off big. But if someone crossed her or got in the way of her score, she'd take them out without a second thought.

He would never act on it, or even admit it, but he had developed a serious crush on Micki. She certainly wasn't his type, physically, but there was something about her cold, ruthless brilliance that attracted him like a cat to a laser pointer. He could never resist her games.

"This is the setup, right," she said as soon as Peter caught up with her. "Been working this politician, a real pillar of the community by the name of Stephen Keith. Word is he likes 'em young and flat as pavement, so I reckon I'd better investigate. Find out firsthand, like. I was thinking straight-up blackmail, but then I learn that he's got a piece of a bantamweight champion called Lucky Munro. A big piece. So..."

"So you snap some candid shots of Mr. Pillar-of-the-Community," Peter said, swiftly catching on. "Use them to lean on him to have his boy throw the fight, and then clean up on an underdog bet."

"Close," she said. "Only it'll be video, not stills—and you'll be the one doing the filming. I'll be too busy being the star. Then, see, we each put down twenty-five thousand euros, and make it back times ten, easy. I take a ten-percent finder's fee off the top, naturally, but the rest is yours to walk away with. Only no one else can know about this fix, and I mean *no one*. If word starts getting around, it'll skew our odds, and then where will we be?"

"Where indeed?" Peter agreed.

"So." She stopped short, looking up at him with a sharp, appraising gaze. "You in?"

It sounded like a sweet setup. A sure thing. He knew it would be, too, because he'd known Micki for years and she'd never, ever laid a bet that hadn't paid off. She was too careful. Too thorough. Every contingency planned for, and every angle covered.

There was just one problem.

Peter didn't have twenty-five large in his hip pocket. It had been a real lean stretch, and it would be tough to scrape together twenty-five *hundred* on his own. But he knew a way to get it.

Normally he wouldn't even consider borrowing money from someone like Big Eddie Guthrie. But on a sure thing like this, he could turn the debt around in under a week, avoid the draconian vig, and still walk away with a healthy take.

Big Eddie's office was above a chip shop. It had been lavishly decorated with more money than taste, but the thick, oily smell that drifted up from below reminded Peter that the thin veneer of class was just that.

That went for Big Eddie himself, as well, sitting behind his ostentatious mahogany desk in his bespoke suit, diamond pinkie ring flashing, but you could still smell the rough, working-class sweat underneath the sweet miasma of his pricy cologne.

A bored Eastern European supermodel wrapped up in sparkling couture bandages that barely covered the legal minimum of her long, thoroughbred body was sprawled decoratively on a nearby sofa, chain-smoking and staring into her phone. Big Eddie shooed her out with a wordless tilt of his gray stubbled chin. She didn't even pout.

"Sit down, Bishop," he said in his thick Scottish accent, gesturing to the sofa recently vacated by the supermodel. "I must admit, I'm surprised to see you. Tell me, what dreadful misfortune has forced you to darken my door? Woman trouble, is it?"

"It's nothing like that," Peter said, taking the seat he'd been offered. The sofa was modern and very low, making him feel a little awkward. There wasn't enough room between it and the desk for him to stretch his legs out straight, so he had to bend them up so his knees felt almost as high as his shoulders. It had to be a deliberate move on Big Eddie's part, forcing him to scrunch into this undignified position and look up at the Scotsman in his tall desk chair.

"Well, then," Big Eddie said, leaning forward in a mocking parody of earnest concern. "What exactly *is* it like?"

"I need twenty-five grand," Peter said. "I can turn it around in five days."

"Pounds or euros?"

"Euros," Peter replied, shifting his uncomfortably bent legs.

Big Eddie nodded, taking out a small calculator from a desk drawer.

"Right," he said, punching buttons and scribbling in a leather-bound note book. "Collateral?"

Peter put a hand into his messenger bag, knowing that if he hesitated for a fraction of a second or showed anything but nonchalant confidence in this moment, he'd be screwed.

He extracted a slender file folder containing a sheaf of documents proving his five-year ownership of an upscale New Town property over on Albyn Place, and agreeing to transfer ownership to Big Eddie in the event that he was unable to pay back the loan within the agreed-upon time frame. Every page was a fake—and not his best work, given the time constraints—but he'd backed it all up by hacking into the local records and doing some creative editing, in case anyone decided to dig deeper.

He hoped it would hold up.

Then Peter sat back on the torturous sofa, slinging one arm over the back in what he hoped was a casual, relaxed pose while Big Eddie looked over the contents of the file. The Scotsman's weathered face was stoic, revealing nothing.

"Right," he finally said. "You'll have your money at..." He raised a hairy wrist, checking the time. Unlike Peter's, his Rolex was real. "Half-seven tomorrow night."

Then he stood, reaching out to shake Peter's hand. Peter lurched to his feet and took the offered hand. It was surprisingly large, and squeezed his fingers just a little too tight. Big Eddie smiled, his blue eyes bright and disturbingly merry.

Peter had a little twinge of doubt in that moment, wondering if he'd made a terrible mistake.

But he trusted Micki. She'd never let him down. It was a sure thing.

Nevertheless, he felt a lot better once he was out of Big Eddie's office—and out of range of that cheerful predator's smile.

2

The next step of Micki's carefully orchestrated plan involved wiring up her chosen love nest with hidden cameras. To that end, Peter paid a visit to a techie kid named Russel who could hook him up with all the necessary equipment.

Russel McNee was a tall, scrawny blond guy with glasses and a sardonic, gap-toothed grin. He was always home, day or night, and didn't seem to have any source of income that would pay for his historic apartment on the Grassmarket, or support his expensive hobbies of espionage tech and robotics. Peter figured he either had family money, or was living off the illicit information he was able to gather by spying on his wealthy neighbors.

When Peter arrived at Russel's cluttered bachelor pad, the kid was sitting cross-legged on the floor, eating Chinese food out of a take-out container and watching what had to be the single worst television program of all time on a massive flat-screen television. It looked as if it must have been shot in the late 1970s or early 1980s. There was goofy-looking guy with brown curly hair and what looked like a tiny middle-aged woman dressed up like a little boy. They were singing, badly.

Russel seemed to think this was the most wonderful spectacle of all time. When Peter walked in, the kid pointed at the screen with his chopsticks.

"You know what the best thing about the Krankies is?" he asked around a huge mouthful of some kind of slippery orange noodles.

"The fact that it's not available in America?" Peter guessed, shaking his head at the painfully unfunny antics on screen.

"No, it's the fact that they're married."

"Married?" Peter frowned. "What, the guy and the woman in the school-boy uniform?"

"Not only are they married," Russel said, raising a thin, white-blond eyebrow, "They're swingers. A couple of nasty perverts, they are. I'll bet she wears the Wee Jimmy costume in bed."

On screen, the man bent over and the woman kicked him in the ass, laughing and hamming it up for the camera.

Peter shuddered.

"I really didn't need to know that, Russel," he said, prying his eyes away from the television. "Have you got my order?"

"I surely do," Russel replied, unfolding his long legs and leaving the box of Chinese food on the floor. "Right this way, sir."

A large black cat appeared from between two boxes and headed over to investigate the abandoned noodles while Russel started digging through the piles and clutter.

"Ah, yes," he said triumphantly, lifting a cardboard box that used to hold bottles of Irn-Bru. "Here's everything you requested, plus extra cable and batteries which I've included out of the goodness of my heart."

"You're a saint," Peter said, extracting a manila

envelope full of clean credit cards under a variety of fake male names. "It's a pleasure doing business with you."

Russel took the offered envelope in exchange for the box, checked the contents briefly. Then gave Peter a big hammy grin and a thumbs up.

"Fan dabi dozi!" he said.

The next stop was the Lambshead Inn—a small boutique hotel that Micki had chosen for her command performance. It was perfect, tucked away in Newington apart from the tourist throngs along the main drag. The room she'd chosen—the one her accomplice at the desk would insist was the only one available—sat on the top floor. Directly above it was a low attic space that ran the length of the building.

That would allow Peter to install the main camera in the central light fixture, and then run a cable to the room next door—where he'd be set up with his laptop, monitoring the action. He had two other small, wireless black-and-white cameras he would install as backup, but the image quality wouldn't be quite as sharp. It was important to Micki that the mark's face be crystal clear and unmistakable in the footage.

The room was girlish and romantic, decorated in a flouncy Victorian style that did nothing for Peter. Lots of lavender and ruffles and chintz. On a pink velvet settee across from the bed was a stuffed toy dog, bearing a label proclaiming it to be a replica of the famous Greyfriars Bobby. Peter couldn't resist enlisting the faithful canine's assistance in this caper.

He made a small incision in the dog's belly and pulled out few handfuls of acrylic filler. Next, he carefully removed one of the black plastic eyes, slipping it into his pocket. He pushed the rectangular body of the wireless camera into the dog's belly, arranging it with the camera lens set into the hole where the eye had been. Then he used the complimentary sewing kit to stitch up the incision and set Bobby back at his post.

From where he sat, the pooch had a clear view of the bed.

"Good boy," Peter said, patting the stuffed dog's head.

Once that was done, he installed the second wireless camera in the ornate headboard to give him a reverse angle. That way he'd be sure to catch the mark's face at some point, no matter which way he was positioned.

Then he headed up into the stuffy claustrophobic attic to work on the installation of the final camera and the audio feed. That was cramped, grubby, miserable work, and once it was done he had to take a long hot shower in the neighboring suite to get all the cobwebs and dust out of his hair. Clean and fresh, he synced the three cameras to his laptop, and set everything so it would be ready to roll as soon as the talent arrived.

He sent Micki a text to let her know all systems were go. She responded instantly, letting him know she and the mark would be there in thirty minutes, as planned.

Peter pocketed the phone and smiled. There was something about the giddy, electric feeling of a caper that was running smoothly, tasks clicking off like clockwork and everything going exactly the way it should. It was like a kind of drug to him. A high he'd been chasing for years, and so often failed to catch. But when he did, it was better than anything else he'd ever felt. He'd never actually been in love, but he imagined that it would feel much the same.

⅄

There were footsteps in the hall, and the sound of a door opening and clicking shut. Then Peter heard giggling through the wall, and Micki appeared in triplicate on his laptop screen. From the front, from behind, and from above. Twice in grainy black-and-white, and once in color.

She was dressed in a disturbingly childish fashion—a short pink skirt and glittery sneakers, and a T-shirt with a butterfly on it. The shirt was tight and short, showing off a slice of her pale, concave belly, and Peter was surprised to see that she'd covered her tattoo with some kind of concealer. She didn't just look underage, she looked almost prepubescent.

He couldn't help but feel a little queasy, considering the performance he was about to witness. But he reminded himself that it was all part of the act.

Her companion was a chinless older man, portly with a florid complexion and thick, bristly hair the color of steel wool. He was dressed in a conservative navy, double-breasted suit and striped tie. There was a wedding ring on his fat finger. He was clearly nervous, his paranoid gaze bouncing all over the room, and when it settled on the stuffed dog, Peter felt a hot flush of adrenaline. His fists clenched involuntarily as the man leaned toward the lens hidden in the dog's eye.

"Isn't he so cute?" Micki asked, scooping up the stuffed animal and causing the image to blur into a vertigo-inducing whirl. *"Ruff ruff."* The camera settled as she held the dog steady, facing the mark. It was the perfect close-up of the man's frowning face. "Oh, Stevie, you must buy him for me. Say you will."

"Sure I will, pet," the man said, his scowl melting into a foolish smile.

"You're the best!" Micki said, kissing the man's cheek,

and then setting the stuffed dog down on a side table that actually gave Peter a much better view of the bed.

Atta girl, Micki.

Peter did his best to ignore the rest of the performance, briefly checking the screen every so often to make sure he still had the best angle on the action. The two wireless cameras were stationary, but the one in the light fixture could pan and zoom, so he made occasional slight adjustments when needed.

Micki was so good at her part of the job, he barely had to bother. She led that poor bastard around the room like a circus animal, making sure he was always positioned for maximum exposure, just the way she wanted.

When it was over, Peter uploaded the footage to her private server and backed it up on his own for safekeeping. Then he shut everything down and got the hell out of there.

3

Micki wanted to handle contacting the mark and laying out the terms on her own, so Peter had to sit tight for the rest of the night and the following morning, waiting for a text that would let him know it was a go.

The night was easily wasted in a large, flashy pub full of boisterous foreigners and ambitious local girls looking for a ticket abroad. While he'd had several passes thrown his way by females smitten with his "exotic" accent, he wasn't really in the mood for company, so he just nursed his pint in a quiet corner and people-watched until he was tired enough to sleep.

The construction clamor woke him bright and early the next day, so he headed up the Royal Mile to lose himself in the slow-moving tourist hordes snapping photos of each other buying cheap, scratchy kilts and mealy shortbread. None of them gave Peter a second glance. He was leaning against a red phone box and contemplating whether or not he should check out the inside of the castle, when his phone buzzed in his pocket.

It was Micki.

The hook was in.

The mark had agreed to her terms without hesitation. They were on. She texted him the address of the bookie where she wanted to meet at eight o'clock that night, and told him to bring the cash.

He responded, letting her know he'd be there.

After killing the rest of the day wandering around Edinburgh castle and its grounds, he grabbed a quick steak-and-ale pie in a quiet pub, and then steeled himself to swing by Big Eddie's and get the money. Once that was done, he'd head over to the bookie joint where he would be meeting Micki to place their bet.

When he arrived back at Big Eddie's office, a hulking bruiser was there to greet him. He identified himself as Little Eddie, shook Peter's hand like he was planning to take it home with him, and gave him a colorful, expletive-filled earful about how he'd better pay up on time.

"I see you've met my son," Big Eddie said, appearing through a side door and clamping a heavy paw on Peter's shoulder. "Trust me when I tell you that you don't want to be meeting him again."

He was carrying a large manila envelope, which he handed to Peter. It was heavy for its size, and when he looked inside, he saw that it held a fat, banded brick of purple 500-euro notes. He knew he didn't need to count it, but the solid, unquestionable realness of that money felt ominous in his hand. Not just the physical weight of it, but the invisible yet no-less-real weight of what it meant to be accepting it.

"See you in five days, Bishop," Big Eddie said, flashing that wide sunny grin that made Peter's blood go cold.

The bookie joint was in the back of a barbershop on Leith Walk. Big Eddie preferred to fly "under the radar," so to speak.

It wasn't a rough neighborhood or anything, but Peter still felt nervous about the lump of cash weighing down his messenger bag. The sooner he could get it out of his hands, and on its way to becoming a fresh crop of zeros at the end of his offshore bank balance, the better he would feel.

Inside the barbershop it looked like a movie set for a period film set in 1935. Black-and-green checkered floor, with a small heap of gray hair swept into one corner. Walls covered with old photos of boxers. A long, low counter strewn with various grooming products for which the packaging hadn't changed in seventy-five years. Two pale-mint barber chairs, one with black cushions and the other white.

One occupied, and one empty.

No one in the room but Peter was under seventy. There were two customers. One was having the silver bristles shaved off his wattled neck with a straight razor wielded by a stooped and lanky barber with a full, lustrous head of white hair that had been slicked down and sharply parted on the left. The other sat off to the side, snoozing under a tented newspaper that flapped gently with the tide of his rumbling snores.

When the barber heard the bells above the door ring, he looked up at Peter then tipped his chin toward a curtained doorway in the back. Peter nodded, crossed the room, and pushed through the curtain—into the modern world.

The back room was lined with glowing screens, each flashing up-to-the-minute results of a variety of sporting events all around the world. There were several long steel tables covered in computer equipment and money-counting machines.

The humans in the narrow, crowded room were equally divided between brains and muscle. There were a couple of hard bastards in track pants and wife-beaters, one by each of the two doorways. The one nearest Peter was a ruddy-faced ginger pug with a missing front tooth and tattoos that looked as if they had been perpetrated by blind, malicious children. The one by the far door was tall, fat, and grim, with a shiny bald head and a wiry lumberjack's beard.

Both were ostentatiously armed.

Seated at the center table was a nerdy pair who seemed utterly absorbed in the flow of information on the screens in front of them. The older of the two looked as if he could be Harry Potter's dad, with messy salt-and-pepper hair and round glasses. The other was maybe Indian or Pakistani, with a ninety-eight-pound weakling physique and a nervous, bird-like demeanor.

The fifth person in the room, the one who didn't fit so neatly into either of the two categories, was Micki.

She'd shed her fake cutesy girl drag and was back in her usual baggy sweats and trainers. She looked sleek and self-satisfied, like a cat that had proudly deposited an eviscerated mouse on your pillow.

"That was some prime camerawork, Bishop," she said. "Way to go." She glanced at his messenger bag. "You got the money?"

Peter nodded, patting the bag.

"Right," she said. "Let's do this, then."

He handed the brick of cash over to the Indian kid, who unbanded it and ran it through a counter. Twenty-five grand exactly. The older guy with glasses started tapping away on a keyboard, while Micki handed over an identical stack of money for the younger guy to count. Same number popped up on the little screen. Twenty-five thousand.

"You sure about this?" the older guy asked.

She nodded, then winked at Peter. He couldn't help but smile in return.

He gave his account information to the older guy, and Micki did the same. The guy handed them both printed receipts. Peter tucked his into his hip pocket, feeling giddy.

"Come on," Micki said, taking his arm and leading him out through the back door. It let the two of them out into a skinny, crooked cobblestone alley. Peter wasn't sure which way to go, but Micki just stood there for a minute, looking up at him with a kind of intensity he'd never seen before. He was trying to figure out what that look really meant when she put her arms around his waist and pressed her tense little body against him.

"You were perfect," she said, rising up on tiptoe to kiss his cheek.

"Um... thanks," he replied, feeling a hot blush creeping up from his collar. Was she coming on to him? She'd never displayed anything beyond cool professional interest before, but the way she was looking at him in that moment, he could have sworn she was about to tear his clothes off and have at him right there in the alley.

"Meet me at the Port O'Leith tomorrow night, to watch the fight," she said with that little satisfied-cat smile. "Eight sharp."

She let go of his waist and turned on her squeaky rubber heel, stalking away down the alley before he could come up with an intelligent reply.

When he arrived at the Port O'Leith, she wasn't there. Surprising, since she was always on time, but he just ordered a pint and took a seat at the far end of the bar.

He sent her a text, then waited through several unremarkable undercard fights and several pints, but there was no sign of her. He was about to send her another text when the Munro fight came on. The pub patrons were galvanized around the television, crackling with excitement and friendly wagers. Everyone rooting for the hometown boy.

It took less than a minute for Peter to realize why Micki wasn't there. Munro knocked his opponent out cold in the first round.

At first he wanted to believe that something had gone horribly wrong with the caper, that Micki had been hurt or even killed. But when he rushed back to the bookie joint to see if anyone had heard from her, he realized that the caper had actually gone horribly right.

He was the mark.

The quaint old barbershop was gone, leaving nothing but an empty storefront. When he questioned the woman in the neighboring kebab shop, she explained that there had never been any barber there, that some kids from the university were just using the unrented space to shoot a student film.

He set up his laptop in a nearby café, and started searching around for any information on a local politician named Stephen Keith. There was nothing, nor did any of the local politicians he did find look anything like the man he'd filmed at the hotel with Micki. Also, none of them owned an interest in any fighter. Lucky Munro was sponsored by some wealthy London socialite who was rumored to like a little blue-collar roughhousing in the sack.

How could he have been so stupid? He knew all the angles, all the scams and yet he'd fallen for this like some rube who'd just tumbled off the back of a hay truck. He should have done his homework, and if it had been anyone else, he would have. It was just that he *trusted* Micki. She'd made more solid, consistent money for him than any other partner.

He couldn't help but wonder if she'd just decided to turn on him recently, or if—more disturbingly—she'd been working him all along. Slowly, meticulously gaining his confidence. Making him believe she was solid, all the while grooming him to play this role in her big score.

As angry and terrified as he was, he couldn't help but admire her audacity. He certainly wouldn't have had the patience to run a long game like that. But reluctant admiration wasn't going to help him deal with his infinitely more pressing problem.

Big Eddie.

Peter woke from a fitful doze to the announcement, in French and English, that they were about to begin their descent into Charles de Gaulle Airport. He couldn't get out of that cramped middle seat soon enough. Unfortunately, he still had a long way to go before he was back in the States.

A long way to go before he had a hope in hell of finally getting his hands on the money he needed to pay his debt.

4

WASHINGTON, DC 2008

Finley's was a dive bar like any other anywhere in the world. The dank, hoppy smell. The cheap pleather booths. The irascible bartender. The weekday drunks.

Same shit, different country.

What wasn't there was Tess. Not yet, anyway, so Peter ordered a beer and took it over to a small, rickety table by the door. He was antsy, tightly wound despite the jetlagged exhaustion that weighed down his shoulders and eyelids. He checked his watch, waited a moment, then checked it again.

Finally, she appeared, looking annoyingly fresh and chipper compared to how he felt. She was dressed in her traditional American garb of jeans and a plain T-shirt, hair down and smiling. Sexy in an easy, unselfconscious way that was impossible to fake.

She walked up to him, took a large, sparkly purple vibrator from her roomy purse, and plunked it on the table in front of him. The bartender looked over at Peter and raised a bushy white eyebrow.

"Um..." Peter managed, but then he trailed off. He could feel himself blushing, and knowing just made it worse.

"That's your package, silly," she said, leaning in and lowering her voice. "No one ever wants to look too closely at a sex toy. Most of the time, they won't even touch 'em."

"Thanks," he said. "But how am I supposed to carry this? I can't just walk down the street holding it like a light saber."

"Not my problem," she replied with a smirk. "You asked me to get your package through customs, and I did. The rest is up to you."

He stood, trying to block the bartender's view of the vibrator while casually slipping it into his hip pocket. It was way too large, and protruded by several inches.

Tess put a hand over her mouth, quietly cracking up.

"Is that a serum in your pocket," she asked, "Or are you just happy to see me?"

Peter couldn't help but laugh, tugging at his shirttail to cover the end that was poking out of his pocket. It didn't do the trick.

"This is ridiculous," he said. "Don't you have, like, a plastic bag or something?"

She shrugged and shook her head.

"Take care, Peter," she said, her smile slowly fading and replaced by a thoughtful frown. "And be careful. Remember, Big Eddie isn't the only one gunning for you."

"I'll be okay," he said, hoping it was true.

"Somehow you always are, aren't you?" She touched the left hinge of his jaw. "Not that you deserve to be, but you are."

She turned to leave.

"I'll make it up to you someday, Tess," he called after her. "If you'll let me."

She waved a dismissive hand without turning around, and walked out the door.

⅄

NEAR HARTFORD, CT 2008

Sitting in a room of a yet another generic franchise hotel, Peter felt keyed up and anxious. It was funny that he was so nervous, considering the fact that he was doing something that could almost be construed as altruistic.

Well, maybe if you squint and ignore the eighty-thousand-dollar payoff thing, he mused. But given that he could have sold this little bug for quadruple that amount to some terrorist, it *felt* pretty damn altruistic. Altruistic for him, at least.

When he heard the soft knock on the door, he jumped a little, startled. He used the fisheye to make sure it was Doctor Lachaux, and that she was alone.

It was, and she was.

She had her head tucked down, so all he saw was the top of her head, covered in red hair. He opened the door and motioned for her to enter, stealing a quick glance up and down the empty hall before shutting and locking the door again.

Getting a good look at her now, he noticed several things at once. First, that she was gorgeous in person—more so even than her photos or video. Second, that she had a fading black eye.

Third, that she looked absolutely terrified.

"Wow, are you okay?" he asked, immediately regretting the words before he even finished the sentence. He'd meant to come off brusque and businesslike, leaving no room for sympathy or negotiation. Ready to take the money and run. But instead, he'd managed to blow any hope of hard-ass credibility with one involuntary outburst of motherly concern.

At this point, he might as well get her a sweater and make her some nice chicken soup.

"I'm fine," she said, her voice soft and halting. She had a very slight Boston accent. "I just..." She paused. Looked away. "When those men broke in and stole the virus, I was alone in the lab. We don't have much in the way of security, because we never thought anyone would want to steal a cure for epilepsy. Science nerd tunnel vision, I guess. I did my best to stop them, but..."

She shrugged, trailing off.

Looking closely, Peter saw marks and bruises all over her long, pale arms and neck, some of them disturbingly hand-shaped. There was a deep cut on her hairline that had been stitched closed. He couldn't help but feel like a jerk for extorting money out of her, after all she'd been through.

That's when he noticed that she didn't have any kind of bag large enough to hold eighty grand in cash. All she was carrying was a small, unfashionable beige canvas purse.

"Did you bring the money?" he asked, trying for tough and getting something more like cranky.

"Yes, of course," she replied, fumbling for a moment in her purse and then pulling out a checkbook.

"Are you kidding?" Peter asked. "What am I, the power company? I can't take a check."

"What did do you expect?" she asked, looking hurt. "A briefcase full of cash?"

"Well, actually..."

"I don't have that kind of money lying around," she said. "I have to pay you out of the foundation's account." When he didn't reply, she continued. "I can authorize an electronic transfer, if that would be better for you," she offered.

This was going from absurd to worse. Like an idiot, Peter had expected this naive, nerdy—albeit attractive—

scientist to have a clue about conducting underworld business. And the more time he spent with her, the more flummoxed and unsure of himself he became.

The next thing he knew, there was the harsh sound of fists banging on the door.

5

"Oh, my God," she hissed, gripping Peter's arm. "They must have followed me!"

"They?" Peter backed away toward the sliding glass door that led to the balcony. "They who? What the *hell* is going on here?"

"The men who stole my virus," she whispered, eyes huge and panicky. "We have to get out of here!"

There was a vicious kick, and the door shuddered in its frame. Whoever "they" were, they'd be in the room any minute now.

"Go," he said, opening the sliding door and shoving Doctor Lachaux out onto the balcony.

"What about you?" she asked, but he closed the door on her question.

The next thing he did was tip the heavy desk up on one end and shove it against the door. It wouldn't hold them for long, but long enough for him to retrieve the virus.

It still was hidden inside Tessa's sparkly purple vibrator. He'd stashed it in the bedside drawer and was about to grab it when the lock on the door broke loose under the assault. Because of the desk, however, the door still wouldn't open more than a few inches. Whoever was on the other side was shoving at it, slowly pushing the barrier out of the way.

Then a gloved hand holding a gun slipped through the crack, squeezing off a single shot. The bullet hit the bargain-basement abstract art print hanging over the bed, peppering Peter's arm and cheek with flying glass. He pulled open the drawer, grabbed the vibrator, and ran for the sliding glass doors.

Once he was out on the balcony, he slid the door shut and wedged one of the two rickety patio chairs into the track, to prevent it from opening. Doctor Lachaux looked at him, glanced down, and burst out laughing.

"What?" he asked, touching a fingertip to a warm trickle of blood running down the left side of his neck.

"Nothing," she said with a stifled snort. "I mean, I admire your priorities, but..." She tipped her chin at the sex toy in his hand, and failed to suppress another giggle.

He looked down at the purple vibrator and smiled.

"You can laugh later," he said. "But first, we better get the hell out of here. Is that Plexiglas cylinder—the one that contains the virus—waterproof?"

"Of course," she said. "It's airtight. It has to be."

Peter nodded.

"Okay," he said. "Then jump."

"What?" She frowned and peered over the edge.

Three stories below, the water in the pool was green and cloudy, with a scrim of leaves around the edge. But there was a gate at the far end that led out into the rear parking lot. On the other side, just to the left of that gate stood Peter's rental car.

He always had an exit strategy. This one was far from ideal, but it just might be workable.

He looked down from the balcony. There was a small

lip of concrete directly below them, but hitting it from this height would be dangerous. The pool itself was the only real option.

She opened her mouth to say something.

"Don't talk," he said. "Jump!"

"Well," she said. "It's just..." She blushed a little, looking away. "I'm not wearing a bra."

Before he could stop himself, Peter glanced down at her chest. She had what looked to be a perky, larger than average bust beneath a loose-fitting, white button-up blouse. That blouse itself was relatively unremarkable while dry, but it was easy to imagine what it would look like when it was wet. Never mind what was underneath.

Then he mentally kicked himself for wasting the time.

All thoughts along those lines evaporated when the men in the room started yanking on the sliding glass door, slamming it over and over into the flimsy chair. The aluminum frame wasn't going to hold for much longer.

One of them raised a gun to smash the glass.

"Go!" he said, giving her a shove toward the railing.

Once she committed herself, she was surprisingly graceful. She climbed over the rail and then launched herself at the rippling water, moving like a high-diver.

Peter was less graceful, but just as committed. He flopped over the railing, nearly falling, and then jumped, feet first and arms flailing, into the pool.

The water was shockingly cold, short-circuiting his brain and forcing all the air out of him in a bubbly rush. His kicking feet scraped bottom as he awkwardly dog-paddled upward toward the surface. He got his head above water and found that he had somehow twisted around on the way up, and was facing back toward the balcony from which he'd just jumped.

It was occupied by three men in dark suits.

The biggest of the three was a ruddy-faced blond with a stubbly, steam-shovel jaw and a massive, barrel-chested gorilla's build that seemed to deeply resent being stuffed into his ill-fitting suit. A good three inches of thick, freckled forearm stuck out of the too-short sleeves. His pistol was dwarfed by huge, hairy fingers.

The other two were a hamburger-and-hotdog pair. One was tall, thin, and white, the other short, stocky and black. Different in every way, except they both wore the exact same cheap blue-and-gray striped tie, and the same practiced bad-guy scowls. If they had guns—which Peter didn't doubt for a second—they had yet to draw them.

Doctor Lachaux was climbing out of the other end of the pool, and so Peter started swimming toward her. He had to do it one-handed, the precious virus clutched against his chest in the other.

The blond gorilla fired at Peter, missing him by an inch and sending a tiny, needle fine spray of water up into his face. Peter swore and called out.

"The gate!" he cried. "Run for the gate!"

Doctor Lachaux looked back over her shoulder at him and made a nervous, rabbit-like lunge toward the gate, just as a glass-top patio table a few feet in front of her exploded into a thousand glittering shards. She cringed and spun toward the balcony, staring up at the shooter like a deer in the headlights.

Peter dragged himself up out of the pool and tackled her bare, wet legs, knocking her to the ground just in time for a bullet to pass through the air where her head had been.

A hotel security guard appeared on the other end of the pool and shouted, drawing fire from the men in the balcony. He pulled out his own pistol and fired off a shot.

"Go!" Peter cried, shoving Doctor Lachaux in the direction of the gate. But she wouldn't budge. She was turtled up on the concrete lip of the pool, arms over her face and shaking her head.

"Move, will you?" Peter looked back over his shoulder as the security guard cried out. He'd been hit in the belly, but was still firing. Judging from the amount of blood, it didn't look good for him. "Hurry," Peter added.

"I can't," she wailed, curling up tighter. "I don't want to die!"

Knowing that the security guard might have bought them their only opportunity to get away, he weighed his options.

He didn't know her.

He didn't owe her anything.

Clearly the thing to do was to leave her behind, and save his own ass.

But she owed him. If she were killed, there would be no payoff. No way to get Big Eddie off his back. And even though his tidy little deal was rapidly devolving into lethal chaos, he still had to pull this off.

So he grabbed Doctor Lachaux's arm, and hauled her to her knees, gripping her chin and tilting her face up toward his.

"Look at me," he said. "We need to get out of here, *right now*."

Her eyes flickered in the direction of the bleeding security guard. There was way too much white visible around her pale blue irises.

"Never mind him," he said, turning her face back to him. "Just look at me, okay? I'm gonna get you out of here."

She looked up at him, pulling in a deep, shaky breath.

"You ready?" he asked.

She swallowed hard and nodded.

"Then let's go," he said.

He tucked the sparkly purple vibrator into the

waistband of his pants like a weapon, slung a protective arm around Doctor Lachaux's shaking shoulders, and duck-walked her as fast as he could toward the gate, keeping her head low. He could hear footsteps behind them, pounding on the metal exterior stairs that led from the third floor breezeway.

But he couldn't risk a backward glance.

On the other side of the gate sat Peter's rental, a light-blue hatchback. He pulled Doctor Lachaux around to the driver's side, keeping the bulk of the car between them and the action in the pool area. Then he thrust his hand into his pocket.

The key wasn't there.

6

They were screwed.

"Where's your car?" Peter asked.

"I took a cab," she hissed. "I'm not allowed to drive—I'm epileptic!"

Peter swore and started randomly trying door after door of the cars, checking to see if any of them were unlocked.

No dice.

Finally, he came to the end of the row—and the end of his nerves. It was looking like they were just going to have to make a run for it on foot when the last car in the line proved to be unlocked.

That was the good news. The bad news was that it was a tiny, two-seat vintage Jaguar E-type coupe that was unlike anything else on the road. It would stand out like a sore thumb—and of a make and model that was notoriously finicky about starting.

Well, beggars can't be choosers…

He yanked open the door and checked around for hiding places. Under the visor. Under the seat. Glove box.

Nothing.

"Check the wheel well," he whispered.

Doctor Lachaux did what he asked, fumbling around inside the wheel well on the driver's side of the coupe. While she searched, Peter peered over the roof at the open pool gate.

"Found it!" she said. "Here..."

The big blond guy picked that moment to appear, scanning the lot, gun sweeping back and forth like a bloodhound's muzzle casting for a scent. Peter ducked down and pulled his companion into a crouch beside him.

Too late. The blond spotted them and fired. His bullet blew the rear tire of a neighboring car with a bang, and Doctor Lachaux let out a terrified yelp, dropping the car key from her shaking fingers. It bounced off the asphalt between her feet and slid under the car.

Shit.

Peter crouched down and felt around to grab the key.

"Sorry," she whispered. "Sorry... I just..."

"Got it," he said.

He looked up at her and saw that she was crying, her whole body tense and curled in on itself as if she was expecting to die at any moment. An option that was entirely too possible. He felt a twinge of guilt at having thrust her into the middle of all this.

He also saw how wet her blouse was—completely see-through, as he'd predicted. Once he noticed this fact, it was impossible to unnotice.

Another gunshot hit the side window of the car right next to them.

"I thought virologists had to have steady hands," he said, trying lamely to take her mind off the bullets. "You know, from mixing up all those Ebola daiquiris inside the hot box."

To his surprise, it worked. She unwound noticeably.

"I guess I'm a little off my game," she said, flashing

a shaky smile. "Nobody shoots anyone in the lab." She climbed into the car and slid across to the passenger side. Peter got in behind the wheel.

"Well, if you shoot the person holding a vial full of live Ebola," he replied, jamming the key into the ignition and cranking the engine to life, "They tend to drop it. Then everybody loses." He glanced back over his shoulder, slammed the little car into reverse, and floored it.

The blond guy was stalking down the row toward them, and had just raised his pistol to shoot again when the sudden appearance of the car forced him to dive out of the way.

There was a *thunk* as something hit the frame of the coupe somewhere on the left rear side—someone else, presumably one or both of the matching-tie thugs, must've squeezed off a couple of shots. But the bullet didn't appear to have hit anything critical, and Peter hurriedly shifted into first. He floored it and made a sudden squealing left through a one-way entrance, taking out the mechanical arm that was supposed to lift after a ticket was removed.

It didn't even occur to him that there might have been security spikes—not until he was already pulling a screeching left across the wide parkway.

Luck was with him. No blowouts—nothing to slow him down.

Unfortunately, their pursuers were also unimpeded when they came speeding out of the hotel parking lot right behind the coupe, driving a slick black sedan that might as well have had a vanity plate that read "THUGCAR."

When Peter hit the intersection, the light was red, so he went to the right and cut through a crowded gas station. He swerved and barely missed a teenage boy with an arm full of junk food, causing the startled kid to send his supersized blue raspberry Slurpee flying across the coupe's windshield.

Momentarily blinded while he fumbled for the wipers, Peter let up on the gas, but kept the front end pointed in the direction of the exit. Doctor Lachaux reached across the wheel to hit the wipers for him, just in time for Peter to avoid T-boning a white minivan. He still clipped the rear bumper on his way out, losing a side mirror.

The black sedan remained hot on their tail as he floored it again and went screaming down the otherwise quiet suburban streets, shooting past cookie-cutter mini-malls and smoothie shops and big box stores. There was something so wrong about conducting a breakneck car chase through the bland, forgettable 'burbs.

Not that Peter had been in any other car chases, but he'd seen plenty in the movies, and he was pretty sure no action hero had ever crashed his getaway car into a gourmet burrito franchise. He came close to being the first, though, and avoided it only by swerving at the last possible second, sending the little car up over a decorative flower bed and into a neighboring mall lot.

Casting a quick glance over into the passenger seat, he saw that Doctor Lachaux had jammed herself up against the door, one hand braced against the dash and the other gripping the headrest, her knuckles white. Her blue eyes were wide and wild, and her plump lower lip was caught between her teeth.

Before he could stop himself from checking, he confirmed that her blouse was still soaked. Which reminded him that his own clothes were also wet—clinging in a revealing and unforgiving way.

He really needed to concentrate on not killing anyone.

Or dying.

He managed to focus his attention back on the

parking lot in front of him, just seconds before he had to avoid taking out an oblivious blond woman in mom jeans and pink sneakers, wandering along the row pointing her key fob aimlessly in an attempt to locate her vehicle.

As he swerved and barreled past her, she shot him a dirty look.

Suddenly he slammed on the brakes, pushing himself back to avoid cracking his head on the steering wheel. Doctor Lachaux gasped.

In front of him an ancient, dandelion-haired senior citizen was tentatively trying to wedge an enormous mint-green seventies-era sedan into a narrow parking slot. He laid on the horn while the flustered old bird backed up, scooched forward, and then backed up again.

Glancing in the rearview mirror, he spotted mom-jeans, stalking toward the Jaguar like a huffy little denim tugboat. Infinitely worse, he saw the black car, careening over the beleaguered flower bed and rolling down the aisle of parked cars, blocking any escape in that direction.

It would arrive in a matter of moments.

"Come on, come on, *come on*," Peter muttered through gritted teeth as the old lady inched slowly forward. He was ready to punch the accelerator the second there was enough space behind the massive old car.

Suddenly there was a sharp rapping on the driver's side window. An instinctive jolt of fear shot through his entire body.

It was the mom-jeans lady, gesturing with her pudgy, pink, manicured hand, demanding that he roll down the window.

Peter complied.

"What the hell do you think you're—" she began.

"Look, lady," he said. "You need to get out of here. It's not safe…"

"You're damned *right* it isn't safe!" she snapped, crossing her arms. "Driving like a maniac—what's the matter with you? There are children around here!"

"Please," Peter said, hands up. "Please, just *go*. You're gonna get hurt!"

"Are you threatening me?" she asked, raising a pencil-thin eyebrow. "I ought to call the cops. I wrote down your license number, you know." She frowned, looking him up and down. "Why are you all wet?"

The flat crack of a gunshot echoed through the lot, and the mom jeans lady staggered against the car door clutching at the side of her neck, where a fountain of blood appeared. She turned to Peter with a baffled, almost offended look, as if she couldn't believe something like this was happening.

And then she dropped to the asphalt.

Doctor Lachaux let out a strangled cry, but Peter didn't have time even to look.

In front of them, the gunshot startled the old woman into gunning the giant whale of a car. The behemoth lurched forward with a throaty roar and plowed into a sub-compact, allowing Peter just enough space to squeeze the little coupe through the gap without losing too much paint. Not that he cared, since it wasn't his car. But it seemed a shame to mess up such a classic ride.

Behind him, the bad-guy car tried to follow and slammed into the old woman's boat. It was a little bit too big to fit through the gap, and lost a headlight. The thug was forced to reverse out of the aisle, giving Peter a narrow but precious lead as he floored the gas and sped toward the nearest exit.

As he hit the street, the area around the mall was so generic that he couldn't tell if it was one he'd been on before, or if it just *seemed* familiar because all the streets looked the same. He was hoping to find his way to the highway, or get lost in some residential side streets, but he couldn't seem to find a clear path. He took several turns at random, yet the black car picked up his trail again, pulling to within barely a half a block of them.

Glancing at the passenger seat, he saw that Doctor Lachaux had gone stiff and glassy-eyed, staring at nothing.

"Hey," he said softly, placing a hand on her shoulder as his glance flicked up to the thug car in the rearview mirror. "You okay?"

She didn't respond. He thought he noticed something strange, an inexplicable iridescence flickering in the air just outside her window, but his attention was abruptly diverted as her eyes rolled up and her body was wracked with a short burst of jerky, twitching movement.

A seizure of some sort.

"Aw, man," he said, looking back up at the pursuers. "No, not now!"

He had no idea what to do to help her, other than a vague notion that maybe he should put something in her mouth so she wouldn't swallow her tongue. But even if it was the right thing to do, it wasn't going to happen, given the circumstances.

He needed some kind of clever plan, and he needed it five minutes ago.

At the far end of the block he spotted the giant, anthropomorphic Boston terrier on the roof of a Butchie Burger franchise. Below that familiar black-and-white dog holding its gargantuan hamburger stood something else that was also black-and-white.

A police prowler, pulling into the drive-thru.

He almost missed it as it turned the corner, moving around to the other side of the building, disappearing from view. With any luck, the goons in the bad-guy car hadn't seen it at all.

Before it could sink in that this was a really terrible plan, Peter swerved into the restaurant parking lot, braking just enough to make sure the thugs were able to catch up.

Beside him, Doctor Lachaux straightened up in her seat, and started looking around like a kid who had fallen asleep on a long road trip.

"What… where are we…?" she started to ask, but the rest of her sentence was lost in a quick, breathless gasp as Peter punched the gas, causing the reluctant coupe to rocket forward into the drive-thru lane.

"You okay?" he asked.

"I'm fine," she gasped. "I'm used to it."

"Want anything?" Peter said as they squealed around the corner of the building. "Maybe a Butchie shake?"

"Are you *insane*?" she asked.

"Probably," he said, sailing past the intercom and flying up behind the prowler at the window. "Hold on."

To the right of the drive-thru lane was a narrow strip of dirt with some patchy grass, struggling flowers, and a few crumpled burger wrappers. Beyond that stood a cement-block wall. Peter eyeballed the width of the strip, and desperately hoped the little coupe would fit between the wall and the police cruiser.

Only one way to find out…

Scant seconds before rear-ending the police prowler, Peter wrenched the wheel to the right. The wheels rode up along the curb that separated the dirt from the pavement, and there was a terrible grinding sound as the right side of the car struck sparks against the cement-block wall.

Doctor Lachaux curled up in her seat with her arms over her head, as if she was expecting to crash and die at any moment. Peter probably would have been doing the same thing, if he weren't driving. He fought the urge as he barely squeaked past the prowler's right front corner, and bumped back into the drive-thru lane ahead of it.

An emo teen with too much eye makeup was handing the cop behind the wheel a black-and-white Butchie shake. The cop dropped it onto the pavement, sending it splashing everywhere, and goosed the siren. Lights pulsed to life across the roof.

The black sedan came screaming around the corner, way too fast. The thug behind the wheel stomped on the breaks, but it wasn't enough to prevent him from rear-ending the prowler with a loud *crunch.*

Officer Not-So-Friendly was out of his car in a heartbeat, with his gun drawn.

Peter grinned as he sped away, victorious. He hung a sharp right and slowed down to a reasonable speed, sliding into a residential area. He took a moment to catch his breath before he spoke.

"Okay," he said, causing Doctor Lachaux to jump nervously at the sound. "It's time to get a few things straight. You first. Who the hell *were* those guys?"

Doctor Lachaux slowly uncurled her trembling body, like a reluctant snail coming out of its shell, peering around to make sure the coast was clear. It was a long moment before she spoke.

"Well," she said. "It's kind of a long story. You see…"

There was a bang, and a nasty jolt through Peter's spine as they were rear-ended by a large black pickup truck.

7

Peter shot a look into the rearview mirror at the pursuing truck. Behind the wheel was the big blond from the hotel. In the crazy chaos of trying to get away from his two buddies, Peter had forgotten all about the guy. He had a smear of something on his forehead, a strange silver liquid that seemed oddly familiar, but he couldn't quite put his finger on why.

Then the pickup slammed them again from behind, shoving the little coupe forward and pushing all other thoughts out of Peter's head. It would be no problem for the larger, heavier vehicle to push them off the road, and even to crush the coupe like a tin can. But the driver looked as if he was having fun messing with them.

Peter's clever-plan reservoir was running on empty. He was tired of the breakneck madness that had taken over his life, turning it into one crazy chase scene after another. Suddenly he had the feeling he knew what an Antarctic explorer might experience, in the moments before he froze to death. The sense that it would be a good idea to lie down for a nap in a comfy snow bank.

How much easier it would be just to give up.

But he didn't have any such option—he wasn't alone in the car. In fact, he'd put himself in a situation he'd successfully avoided for years. Peter wasn't a hero by any stretch of the imagination, but he wasn't willing to let Doctor Lachaux die just because he was tired of running.

No, he needed to dig deep, and figure a way out.

To buy some time, he swerved into the parking lot of a supermarket. It wasn't large, and was less than half full. Thin cover again, among the scattered suburban vehicles.

The pickup stuck right behind them.

Up ahead, he saw a large delivery truck about to ease into a loading bay along one side of the building. It had a large cupcake painted on the side, with a bite out of it to show the creamy filling. The driver was being cautious in the narrow space between the building and an adjoining cinder-block wall.

Suddenly, he had a decision to make, and quickly.

Option A: he could cut left, try to make it to the far aisle, and back out the way they'd come in, all before the pickup could cut them off. Option B: he could gun it down the side of the building. If he was fast enough, he might make it past the truck, just in time for it to block their pursuer.

Maybe.

Or maybe not. No time to think. He had to commit.

He gunned it toward option B.

"What are you...?" Doctor Lachaux braced herself, eyes wide. "Oh, my God!"

Peter swerved at the last second, squeezing the little coupe through the swiftly closing gap between the loading bay and the rear of the snack cake truck. He was nearly through when the rear corner of the truck smacked into the right rear corner of the coupe, sending the lightweight car skewing off to the side, toward the wall.

The truck driver laid on the horn, waving an angry

fist, but Peter barely noticed. He managed to miss the wall by inches, but there was no time to celebrate before he was confronted with another one, directly in his path.

Crap...

It was a cul-de-sac.

A dead end.

Damn! He'd been sure that he'd seen a driveway on the far side of the supermarket, but somehow it had vanished. *Wishful thinking, or maybe just sheer stupidity.* It didn't matter now. He had been dead wrong—obviously, since they were now trapped. The only upside to the situation was that the blond thug wasn't able to get to them—not unless he decided to get out of his pickup and crawl under the delivery truck.

Peter wouldn't put it past him. So they couldn't just sit there—they had to keep moving.

Like it or not, they were going to have to ditch the coupe and continue on foot.

"Come on," Peter said, climbing out of the battered car and running around to open the passenger door. He offered his hand to Doctor Lachaux. *"Hurry."*

She seemed to steel herself, then grabbed his hand and pulled herself out.

"What are we going to do now?" she asked.

Before he had a chance to answer, a bullet ricocheted off the wall beside them, hitting the coupe's rear tire and puncturing it with a *bang*.

"Run!" Peter cried as another shot hit the wall, showering them with stinging debris. He shoved her toward the loading dock.

Spurred forward by bullets, they bolted.

The loading dock was about waist-high to Peter, and the steps were on the other side, blocked by the body of the truck. He could see the blond thug crouching there, gun hand extended beneath the chassis to take shots at their running legs. There was no time to lose.

"Sorry," Peter said.

"What…?"

He grabbed Doctor Lachaux's ass and awkwardly shoved her upward onto the dock. She made a funny little squawking sound, feet flying as she sprawled across the surface in a splayed and undignified position. He avoided looking up her skirt, instead concentrating on hauling his own body up and not getting shot.

By the time he was beside her, she was on her feet, hauling the twisted hem of the damp skirt down to cover her thighs. There was a befuddled stock boy standing in the open bay door, staring at the two of them as if they'd just stepped out of a UFO.

"Hey," the boy said. "You can't be up here."

"Sorry," Peter said again. It seemed like he'd been saying that a lot lately.

He grabbed Doctor Lachaux's hand and shoved her past the stock boy, then followed close behind, running into the back room of the supermarket.

Inside, it was a lot colder than it had been outside. Air-conditioned to keep the food fresh. Although Peter's clothes were no longer dripping, they were still far from dry, and he immediately started to shiver. It was hard to act like a tough-guy action-hero with his teeth chattering, but he did his best.

He sprinted toward the double doors that led into the market itself. When he and Doctor Lachaux burst through, he immediately slowed to what he hoped would seem like a swift but casual walk, just like any normal shopper in a hurry.

The shoppers and employees mostly ignored them, except for the ones who noticed the doctor's damp blouse.

Peter hoped they'd focus on speculating whether or not her perky breasts were natural, instead of wondering why two strangers had just appeared from the employees-only stock room. Or if the sounds they'd heard out back were firecrackers.

He looked around, half expecting someone to question them.

Nothing.

We might as well be invisible, he thought with a touch of indignation.

But he put it aside. Shivering and desperate to get away from the chill coming off of the refrigerated meat cases, Peter cut down through the produce section, heading for the automatic doors. They were briefly thwarted by a rail-thin woman with a shopping cart full of diet soda and hand sanitizer. She'd left her cart skewed and blocking the aisle, and was examining a head of organic lettuce as if she was a pawnbroker evaluating a questionable diamond.

"Excuse me," Peter said, hip-checking the cart to clear the way.

To his chagrin, he apparently pushed it way harder than he intended to, because it rolled across the aisle and crashed into a pyramid of grapefruit. The pile collapsed, and fruit went rolling in every direction.

"Hey!" the woman cried, clutching the lettuce to her bony chest and spinning to face him.

So much for not attracting any attention.

"Yeah, um..." Peter began, backing away with his hands up. "Really, I'm very—"

The thin woman grabbed Peter's wet sleeve.

"What's the matter with you?" she hissed. "Jerk!"

To his surprise, Doctor Lachaux spoke up. Her blue eyes were bright and mischievous, and any remaining sluggishness from her brief seizure seemed to have been burned away by adrenaline.

"Did you know," she said, leaning over Peter's shoulder and arching a brow at the woman's lettuce, "that you're more likely to contract the Norovirus through salad than any other food? That's because it doesn't get subjected to high-temperature cooking, which would disrupt the virus's fecal-oral transmission pathway."

The woman went pale, let go of Peter's sleeve, and dropped the lettuce as if it was radioactive. She pulled a bottle of hand sanitizer out of her purse and doused her shaking hands. The doctor smiled and took Peter's arm, leading him away from the scene of their fruit-disrupting crime.

"Is that true about salad?" he asked her as they made their way through the produce section, toward the door.

"Well," she said, "truthfully, you're more likely to get it through consuming raw oysters, because of all the sewage being pumped into the ocean. But salad is a close second."

"Remind me never to invite you out to dinner," Peter replied.

"Occupational hazard," she said with a little Mona Lisa smile. "That's why I never get a date. I start talking about my doctoral thesis, and guys run for the door."

"I probably shouldn't ask," he said.

"Herpes," she replied. "Really it's such an elegant, sophisticated, and genetically fascinating virus. Anyway, that was before I got into smallpox."

The two of them exchanged a look and burst out laughing. It was a tremendous rush of relief after the tension of the chase—a chase that was still far from over. But that small moment of humor and humanity seemed to tighten down everything that felt like it had jangled loose inside.

Suddenly Peter felt focused and steady. Ready for whatever was next.

There was a female security guard standing by the door, texting on her phone. She appeared completely uninterested in the recent grapefruit fiasco, and didn't even bother to look up as Peter and Doctor Lachaux speed-walked past her.

Out in the parking lot there was no sign of the blond thug or his black pickup truck. Yet.

They needed wheels, and quickly.

Peter cast an opportunistic gaze around the lot, weighing their options. A young man loading several cases of beer into a crummy little hatchback caught his eye.

As the fellow moved to return the cart to its proper corral at the head of the row, Peter spotted the keys dangling in the lock of the still-open hatch. He debated for a moment whether or not to take a chance.

Then the decision was made for him.

The blond thug came barreling around the side of the supermarket building. He spotted them, lifted his gun, and opened fire.

Peter grabbed the scientist and ran for the hatchback, while its owner dove for cover, cowering in fear behind the row of carts. Shoving Doctor Lachaux into the open hatch so that she fell awkwardly over the cases of beer and into the back seat, Peter slammed it shut, grabbed the dangling keys, and made a mad dash for the driver's-side door.

It wasn't locked, so he was able to jump in, start the car and peel out of the lot in a matter of seconds.

As soon as he got out of the lot he swung a hard left, then a right, then another left. Even if the blond thug could run back to his truck to try to follow them, he'd be too slow to see which way they had gone.

They were safe.

For the moment.

8

Doctor Lachaux righted herself in the back seat and leaned forward between the two front seats.

Peter forced himself not to look. Almost.

"Now what?" she asked.

"You tell me," Peter said taking another random turn. "Who *are* those guys anyway?"

"God, I don't even know where to start."

"How about the beginning?"

She was quiet for a moment, and Peter didn't say anything more. He just drove.

"Okay," she said. "So remember, I mentioned smallpox?"

"Right," Peter said. "Back in the grocery store. And…?"

"Well, I don't know how much you know about smallpox," she said, "But it's essentially been eliminated in the wild, through the widespread use of vaccines. There are only a handful of scabs left in the world from which live virus can be extracted, and it's been becoming increasingly difficult to acquire samples for research purposes. Nearly impossible, really. In fact, the World Health Organization has been agitating for the sterilization of all of the remaining scabs."

"What does that have to do with the guys who are trying to kill us?"

"To put it in layman's terms, my retrovirus uses smallpox as the chassis. Not unlike a custom car. The thing about smallpox is that it's physically massive—comparatively speaking, of course—and built like a tank. It's perfect for my work.

"Anyway," she continued, "I burn through a lot of virus during the testing process, and there's a five-year waiting list for fresh samples. My research was at a standstill without the raw material I needed. Then I met this Englishman.

"He said he had 'accidentally' acquired a smallpox scab in Bangladesh, as part of a mixed lot of antiques and medical specimens in the estate of a turn-of-the-century English doctor. He told me he'd be willing to donate some live virus for me to use in my epilepsy research. You know, 'to help the kids.'"

She paused for a moment, causing Peter to glance briefly back at her. She was looking away, her face bright red.

"How could I have been so stupid?" she said, her voice thick with anger.

"Okay, so you got duped," Peter said. "It happens to the best of us." He frowned, remembering his own experience in Edinburgh. "But why would the Englishman want a cure for epilepsy, anyway?"

"This newest strain of my virus has the potential to cure it, but there needs to be a lot more testing before it can be made available to patients. You see, the epileptic brain has a unique chemistry that works in harmony with the retrovirus, to suppress seizure activity in the subject and the more, well... *problematic* side effects.

"In a non-epileptic subject, the retrovirus can be

deadly," she said. "It has the potential to overwrite DNA, and cause catastrophic mutation. If released into the general population..."

She didn't finish her sentence, but she didn't have to.

Peter understood, and he was appalled.

I thought I got away from shit like this, he thought, but he didn't say it. *It's just what I need—another mad scientist in my life.*

"So you're basically saying that this Englishman gave you the raw materials to make him a... I don't know... a *people* bomb?"

"A biological bomb, yes." she said. "Which his thugs then stole from my lab, and which you, in turn, stole from him."

"I didn't steal it," Peter said. "I just got lucky. Or maybe not so lucky, considering what's happened since it dropped into my lap."

"However you got it," she said, "those men aren't going to give up until they get it back."

Peter frowned, eyes on the road.

"Jesus," he said. "This virus is way too dangerous—to us and to the world. If it ever gets used as a biological weapon... I don't care what your research is for, the risks far outweigh the benefits." He paused, frowning. "I can't believe I'm saying this about something that could be making me a shitload of money, but... we have to destroy it."

"I can't do that," she said. "It's my life's work."

"Sure it is," Peter began. "But that doesn't..."

"You don't know what it's *like,*" she said, her voice rising. "Living with the seizures. They dominate you, and control your life. I'm one of the fortunate ones—my own seizures are generally preceded by a distinct aura, so I'm able to recognize the early symptoms, safely put away whatever I'm doing, and lie down before the convulsions start. But many of my patients at the institute aren't so lucky.

"They suffer from terrible injuries," she continued. "Burns, broken limbs. Not to mention the shame and public humiliation." She stopped, and her breathing was coming in small gasps.

"Look," Peter said, somewhat mollified by her intensity. "I feel for you, honestly I do, but this is a clear case of the 'needs of the many' outweighing 'the needs of the few.' And trust me, I know what I'm talking about. I mean, we're looking at a potential outbreak of uncontrollable, contagious mutation. That seems like way too high a price to pay just so that some kid doesn't have to be embarrassed because he pitched a fit and wet his pants in gym class."

Nothing.

There was nothing but silence from the back seat. He wondered what she was thinking. If she was even listening to what he said. After all, she had no reason to trust him. And why should she?

"I killed my baby sister," she said. Her voice was low, and he had trouble hearing her.

Peter's eyes went wide. His gaze flicked up to the rearview mirror, but Doctor Lachaux's face was down, matted hair hiding her expression.

"I was ten," she continued, voice still small and nearly lost beneath the sound of the car engine. "I was visiting my mom and the new baby in the hospital. It had been a rough delivery, and my mom was pretty out of it. The nurse had come to take the baby away after feeding.

"Mom had fallen asleep, and my aunt Josie was in the bathroom or something. The nurse asked me if I wanted to hold the baby for a minute. I had that funny electric taste in my mouth and everything seemed too sharp and crisp, but I didn't say anything. I felt so proud and excited to be allowed to hold my little sister, almost like a grown-up.

"It wasn't the nurse's fault. She didn't know about me."

Peter had no idea how to respond to this sudden terrible confession, so he just kept driving.

"When I came to," she continued. "I had three broken fingers, and the baby was gone. My shirt was covered in blood, but it wasn't mine. They said I fell on her. Snapped her neck. I found out later that it took three orderlies to get her little body out of my grip. That's how my fingers got broken." She paused, looked away out the window.

"Her name was Jessica. She was only one day old."

"I'm so sorry," Peter said softly. "Jesus."

An uncomfortable silence settled in around them like a bad smell. She broke it first.

"Do you ever fantasize about rewriting history?" she asked. "Like, maybe there could be another world where certain things never happened? Or happened differently?"

Peter glanced up again at the rearview mirror. She was looking right at him now, but her eyes seemed far away. He would never in a million years admit how close to home she'd hit. That he'd had that exact daydream, countless times during his troubled childhood.

Still did, to be honest.

"Sure I have," Peter said, trying for a light-hearted tone, and almost succeeding. "I can't tell you the number of times I woke up with a 3 a.m. mistake lying in the bed next to me, and wished she'd never happened."

"Yeah," she said, her tone more melancholy than amused. "It's just like that." She went quiet again.

"Of course, it's not possible," she continued. Her voice cleared, and she spoke with conviction. "But if I can't change my own past, I'd like to think I can change the future. Can't you see why this retrovirus is so important to me? If only I could continue with the clinical trials. I *know* I can engineer a more stable strain—one that wouldn't pose a threat to anyone, epileptic or otherwise.

"I just need a little bit more time."

Peter didn't respond. And then it struck him.

In the space of less than an hour, he'd gone from wanting to swindle this woman out of her money, to wanting to save her life—wanting her to destroy the very thing he'd planned to use in the swindle. He didn't know if there was such a thing as moral whiplash, but if there was, it was hitting him now.

It was his turn to break the silence.

"Well, we can't just keep driving around," he said, mostly because he couldn't think of anything else to say. "We've got to find someplace to stop, and decide what our next move will be."

"You're right," she agreed. "But we can't go back to my place. They probably know where I live."

"We could try to find another hotel," Peter suggested.

"Wait," she said, and her eyes went wide. "I know just the place, and it's not far from here." She gave him a series of directions, for the most part avoiding the busier byways. After about ten minutes of weaving through the maze of streets, she said, "This is it—this is the neighborhood. Turn right here, at this light."

He did as she requested, turning onto a quiet, residential side street.

"Just down this way—there's someplace they won't know about." She pointed at a tidy moss-green house on the left. "Ted Westerson. Best teacher I ever had. One of the best in the entire field of virology. Anyway, he's in Costa Rica right now, and he gave me his keys so I could water his orchids. No one will think to look for us there. We can get some dry clothes and figure out what to do next."

Peter continued in the direction she was pointing, heading for the cottage-style house. He was cold and exhausted, and worn down to nothing.

What he *really* wanted to do was kick this woman and her apocalyptic chaos to the curb, and then run for his life. Yet he couldn't. If he refused to help her, and some crazy bastard got his hands on the vial, there wouldn't be anywhere left to run.

Besides, she was shivering, and it looked way better on her than it did on him. It wouldn't hurt to go in and get some dry clothes.

Just for a minute.

9

Inside, the green house was pin neat and sparsely furnished with older but well-maintained furniture.

On the far side of the long, narrow living room was a large glassed-in porch populated by orchids. Peter went over to examine them, while Doctor Lachaux excused herself to change out of her still-damp clothes, which looked pretty nasty.

"I'll see if I can find something big enough for you to wear, too," she said.

Peter frowned as she left the room, wondering just *how* familiar the good doctor was with the house… and its occupant. *Not that it's any of my business,* he mused. Yet as he stood there in the fading evening light, the feeling of unease wouldn't let go.

When she came back into the living room she was holding a large towel. She wore a bathrobe that didn't even come down to her knees, and was much too short in the sleeves. She tossed the towel to Peter.

"I knew Ted was a smaller guy," she said. "But I had no idea how small until I tried on his clothes." She smiled and held up her arms, twisting her exposed wrists. The bottom of the robe rose hazardously, as well. "If his stuff is too small for me, there's no way anything will fit you."

Peter used the towel to dry his hair.

"That's okay," he said, plucking at the damp shirt. It was stained with grit and other souvenirs of their activities. "I'll dry out eventually."

"Come on," she said, shooting him a look. "Don't just sit there all damp and miserable. Wrap that towel around yourself and give me your clothes. I'll put them in the drier with mine." She turned away from him. "I won't look."

He just stood there for a moment, watching her not watching him and feeling weirdly self-conscious. Finally, he gave in, and started unbuttoning his shirt.

"I suppose it would be ironic to catch cold, what with the deadly mutagenic retrovirus and all," he said, pulling the vibrator out of his waistband and setting it on a small Asian end table before unbuckling his belt. "There's got to be some kind of quota. You know, one disease per customer?"

"You aren't any more likely to contract acute viral nasopharyngitis if you're cold and wet than you would be if you were warm and dry," she replied. "Either a viable, contagious strain of rhinovirus is already present in the environment, or it isn't."

"You're killing my 'A' material, you know," he said, toeing off his soggy shoes. "You know that, right?" As he peeled off his socks, he was pretty sure they were beginning to grow mold.

She let out a little, stifled half laugh and shook her head.

"Sorry," she said. "But if you're going to crack virology jokes in this crowd, your science has to be solid. We're a discriminating audience."

He laughed too, and stripped the clinging pants and damp shorts off his sticky legs and kicked them away, wrapping the towel around his waist. Even shirtless, it was amazing how good it felt finally to be rid of the clothes and relatively dry. As opposed to being wet and dead. Which, up until about twenty minutes ago, had seemed a great deal more likely.

"You can turn around now if you want," he said, gathering his things into a bundle. "Where's that dryer?"

She turned to face him, gaze involuntarily dropping to take in his towel-clad body. She blushed and looked away again.

"Right," she said. "Um… this way."

He followed her down the hallway to a narrow laundry room off the kitchen. It was barely big enough for the two of them, standing side by side. There were a small utility sink, a washer, and a dryer—which was already running.

"Give me your clothes," she said, holding out her hand.

He handed over the wet bundle and she pulled open the dryer door, interrupting the cycle. She popped his clothes in with her own, closing the door and hitting the button to restart.

"Thanks," he said, feeling awkward again, and unsure of what to do next. He was intensely aware of her closeness in the tight space as she turned toward him, looking up, then twisting shyly away. He could smell her, her damp red hair and warm body. No flowery perfume, just a subtle hint of something like tart, green apples and warm grass and her own clean-skin scent.

He really wished he were wearing something more substantial than a towel.

"Thank you," she said, not meeting his gaze. "For saving me, I mean. You didn't have to."

"Yeah," he said. "I did, actually."

She looked up at him again, and there was something in her eyes, a kind of guileless vulnerability.

This is probably a really bad idea…

Julia extracted herself from the tangled bedclothes and Peter's lazy, satisfied embrace. He made a little non-verbal sound of protest, reaching out to caress her naked back. She smiled and tipped her chin toward the bathroom.

"I'll be right back," she said.

He nodded and returned her smile, eyes at half-mast.

Inside the bathroom, she closed and locked the door, then turned on the shower. While the water ran, she opened the cabinet beneath the sink and pulled out a forensic rape kit.

Ignoring the comb used to extract hair and fibers, and the nail pick for matter that was embedded beneath the fingernails, she used the sterile swabs to meticulously collect Peter's DNA. Once all the swab-tips were broken off and safely sealed inside sterile containers, she went ahead and got into the shower.

Moments later, scrubbed clean and feeling buoyant with success, she gathered her sterile containers, slipped them into a zippered pocket in her purse, and made her way back to the bed where she stood silently looking down at the now sleeping Peter. It was amazing to her that he had no idea who he was, or what had been done to him.

Or how long she'd been waiting for a chance to see him again.

She grabbed the purple vibrator off the table where he had carelessly left it before being so easily distracted. She paused in the kitchen to open the battery compartment and remove the cylinder. Turning it over in her hand for a moment, she smiled to herself, then cracked it open and poured the colored liquid down the garbage disposal.

It would have been far too dangerous to allow Peter to handle live virus, she mused, especially since they couldn't be certain that he would do exactly what she wanted. Fortunately for her, he couldn't have behaved more predictably if he'd been following a script.

She pulled her phone from her purse and sent a text.

Everything is according to plan.

Then she put the phone away and headed down into the basement lab, where she had prepared everything in advance.

PART THREE

1

CAMBRIDGE, MASSACHUSETTS
1991

Peter Bishop shuffled his boots through the damp autumn leaves scattered across the walkways between the bus stop and the building that housed his father's lab.

In his hands he held a chemistry test that had been folded and unfolded way too many times since his science teacher, Ms. Chiang, had handed it to him that morning with a broad, encouraging smile. At the top there was—in bright red pen—a circled "A+" with the word "EXCELLENT!" written in small, neat capital letters below.

It was cold and blustery, but he barely felt it, as excited as he was to show the test to his father. He felt sure that scoring an A+ in his father's favorite subject would finally be enough to pull the old man's head out of his experiments, and get him to take notice of his newly minted teenage son.

Their relationship had always been complex, and somewhat rocky. When he was little, he'd actually been afraid of his father, and did everything he could to avoid being noticed. To be noticed was to be criticized… and found wanting. He could never seem to do anything right in his father's eyes. He could never be smart enough, or work hard enough to please the elder Bishop.

Walter had been a cold, hard bastard up until Peter was nine. Then the boy had gotten so sick he nearly died. His memories surrounding that time were kind of mixed up and confusing, probably because of the fevers and the medication he'd been on. But the effect of his illness on his father was unquestionable. Seemingly overnight, his father went from an uncaring hard-ass to being almost *too* nice. As if he were overcompensating in some way, trying to make up for all the years he'd been so cold.

But inevitably, the new caring, attentive dad started getting wrapped up in his work again. He never went back to being as cruel and critical as he had been before Peter got sick—he just got distracted. More and more often, he would spend all night working at the lab, finally staggering in and collapsing on the couch minutes before Peter left for school in the morning. Even when he was in the room with Peter, his eyes were far away, as if lost in some theoretical contemplation. There seemed to be less and less space left over in that big brain for his son.

As a result, Peter had thrown himself with determined fervor into his schoolwork, particularly science and math. He figured if he could just learn enough to understand the experiments his father was working on, they might have a chance of connecting on some level.

Until then, Peter at least hoped his dad would be proud of the "A+" on his chemistry test.

He walked into the lab building, greeting the friendly and familiar security guard, a paunchy older man with bushy eyebrows named Norman something.

"Hey, Peter," Norman said as Peter passed. "How's the junior mad scientist today?"

"Great," Peter said, grinning and holding up the test. "Got an A-plus!"

"Good job, Junior," Norman said. He nodded to one side. "Go on in."

Peter followed the long hallway to his father's lab. When he pushed the door open, the first thing he saw was his father's pretty assistant, Carla, on whom he'd always had a ferocious secret crush. She was lying on a low table right in the middle of the room. There were all sorts of wires stuck to her head, avoiding her blond hair, and a weird rubber blindfold sort of thing covering her blue eyes. She was turned in his direction, and as he walked toward the table, he couldn't help but noticing that he could sort of see down the front of her lab coat.

In fact, he was pretty sure that the tiny sliver of pale purple lace he could see on the left side was part of her bra. Which made him feel hot and a little dizzy.

His father was wearing a lab coat too, and was hunched over some kind of console that looked as if it had been Frankensteined together from a hundred other dead machines.

"How about now, Carla?" he was asking.

"Nothing," she replied.

"*Dammit*," his father said. "I was sure I'd adequately compensated for the second reconfiguration."

"Hey, Dad," Peter said. "What are you working on?"

"Huh?" His father looked up, startled. "Oh, hello Peter." He picked up a hemostat and started using it to strip the rubber coating off a stray wire without responding to his son's question.

"Is that you, Peter?" Carla asked, tilting her blindfolded head toward his voice.

"Hi, Carla," he replied shyly, feeling himself blushing.

He was unable to resist looking down the front of her lab coat again. Once he did, though, he realized that, since her eyes were covered, she couldn't tell where he was looking. Which made him feel weird—but not so weird that he didn't keep looking, anyway. She shifted slightly then, and that little purple sliver of fabric that may or may not have been her bra disappeared from sight.

"How about now?" his father asked her.

"I'm sorry, Walter," she replied, shaking her wire-crowned head.

"What's wrong with it?" Peter asked, peering over his father's shoulder at the console.

His father turned back to him as if he was just as surprised to see him there as he had been when Peter had first greeted him. He frowned slightly, though, pushing his fingers through his wild hair.

"Listen, Peter," his father said. "I'm sorry, but we're right in the middle of something here. Don't you have some studying or homework or something? Just give me a minute..."

His father trailed off, focusing in again on the dysfunctional equipment, and totally dismissing him as if he didn't even exist. Peter knew all too well that it wouldn't be a minute.

It was never just a minute.

"Walter!" Carla cried, and he thought she might stick up for him. "I'm starting to get the faintest hint of color," she continued, "a deep fluctuating indigo. Whatever you're doing, it's working!"

For a moment, Peter had hoped maybe she would tell his father not to blow him off like that, but no such luck. It seemed like nobody cared about him, one way or the other. And it wasn't like there was any point going back home, where his mom would already be well on her way to her daily drunk, lost in her own silent melancholy.

No, Peter had been alienated from everyone around him, ever since his miraculous recovery, and it seemed to get worse all the time. Now that he was thirteen, the gulf between him and the rest of the world was growing and deepening, and leaving him more and more disconnected. Every time he tried to reach out, he was harshly reminded that there just wasn't any point.

Ah, what the hell…

As he walked dejectedly over to an unused table in the far corner of the lab, he looked down at the folded test in his hand and realized he'd never even had a chance to show the A+ to his father. He felt the sting of angry tears gathering in his eyes, but he didn't want to cry like a baby—not in front of Carla, even if she was blindfolded.

"Hey," a female voice said. "What do you have there?"

When he turned, he saw one of his father's students. A girl, about five years older than him. He'd met her before, there in the lab, and thought maybe her name was Julie or something like that. She was tall and skinny as a rail with absolutely nothing going on under her lab coat in the way of a chest. Her hair was mousy brown and she wore large round plastic glasses. It was kind of hard to notice her with the beautiful Carla in the room, but she'd always been nice enough.

"Chemistry test," he told her. "I got an A-plus."

"Awesome," she replied. "I love chemistry."

"Me, too," Peter said. "Especially organic chemistry."

"I started out studying organic chemistry," she told him. "But my real passion is virology."

"Really?" Peter said. "That's pretty cool."

Her eyes sparkled behind her glasses.

"You want to help me with a little experiment?" she asked.

"Sure," he replied, and then he frowned. "You're not gonna make me sick or anything, are you?"

"Of course not," she said with an impish grin. "I'm

not allowed to handle *live* viruses—not in this lab. I'm just working as a lab assistant to offset my tuition. I'm hoping to score an internship in the virology lab next semester."

"Okay, then," Peter said. "What do you need me to do?"

She led him over to a table where she had some equipment set up, and a stack of photocopied papers that were crammed with what looked like his father's handwriting. When he stepped up to her work area, she slid the papers underneath a textbook, almost like she didn't want him to read them.

He frowned, but decided it was nothing.

"Open your mouth," she said, taking a long swab out of a sterile packet.

"What are you gonna do?" he asked, flinching away from the swab.

"I'm just going to practice sequencing DNA," she said. "I did your dad already, and it would be fun to compare two people who are related. Don't worry. It won't hurt."

"Okay," he said doubtfully.

"Open," she said.

He did as she requested, and she stuck the swab into the side of his cheek, rubbing it up and down. It felt a little weird, and he almost gagged, but it didn't hurt—just like she promised.

"Your father can be a dick sometimes," she said, her voice almost a whisper. She glanced in his dad's direction. "But he doesn't mean it. He really loves you. Well, he tries to, anyway."

"Well," his father said, appearing suddenly behind him and clapping his hands. "That wasn't entirely successful, but I feel as if we've compiled some useful new data. Who's up for root-beer floats?"

Peter turned back to face his father, who seemed like a totally different person. He was beaming and happy, with a big childlike grin. Peter had to stop himself from looking over his own shoulder, to see if there was someone else behind him that his father was inviting to go get ice cream.

No, he realized, *he means me!*

"Um, okay," he said.

"How about you, Julia?"

"I'm going to work late again tonight, Doctor Bishop," she replied. "If you don't mind."

"Fine, fine," his father said, putting a hand on his son's shoulder. "Let's go."

2

It felt as if it had taken forever to get rid of the Bishops, but once she was alone in the lab, Julia immediately began to scrutinize her results.

She had been *right*.

There it was, just like Walter's diary said it would be. That thin, nearly undetectable protein coating, clinging to the extracted strands of the boy's DNA. The same coating that had been present on his father's DNA.

But this anomaly wasn't hereditary. Walter's diary had revealed as much—that he wasn't Peter's real father. It had seemed like the ravings of a madman when she first read it, but curiosity had compelled her to investigate. And now, extremely subtle variations in his DNA left no room for doubt, though if Julia hadn't known to look for differences, she might not have spotted them.

No, this abnormal coating was a defensive reaction to an unknown radiation, the unfathomable effects of passing between universes. On its own, it didn't have any measurable impact whatsoever on the organism in question, any more than the calluses had on a guitar player's fingers.

Nevertheless, Julia felt as if she had hit the jackpot.

Walter's secret diaries had been extremely confusing, and frequently difficult to decipher. Some pages seemed to have been penned by a completely different person, right down to some subtle changes in the wild, scrawling handwriting. He would often switch topics in mid-sentence, and had a rambling, often poetic, but ultimately baffling writing style. Yet Julia had studied the diary in minute detail for more than three months, carefully copying all the relevant passages and returning the document to its cubbyhole under the lab floor, where she'd originally found it.

Walter had only hinted—in an erratic, elliptical way—at the idea that had possessed Julia since the day she had discovered this unique protein coating. The idea itself was like being in love. It consumed every moment of her waking, and haunted her dreams. And it was tied directly into her two deepest passions.

Virology, and epilepsy.

The first part of her theory was both exciting and terrifying, and full of potential to revolutionize the world. It involved taking this seemingly harmless build-up, and using it to replace the normal protective protein coat around a genetically modified virus. Theoretically, that modification would give a virus a kind of chemical skeleton key that would allow it to unlock, penetrate, and actually *rewrite* the host's DNA.

It was genetic sculpture at its most sublime, and could be employed on a living subject. Of course, if such a virus were allowed to reproduce unchecked, and infect free-roaming host organisms outside of a sterile lab environment, it might lead to an epidemic of horrific mutation.

But, there was another, even more exciting implication—something that Walter had never considered. Because he had no reason to think of it. His life hadn't been torn apart by the terrible consequences of epilepsy.

Like Julia, Walter had been desperate to find a way to undo a traumatic loss in his life. He was endlessly trying to access a gateway, via the chemical crutch of LSD, Cortexiphan, and other artificial, mind-altering substances. But what he didn't have was the naturally chaotic brain chemistry that allowed Julia to achieve altered mental states—always in the form of her seizures. Seizures during which she occasionally caught teasing glimpses of the same kind of organic gateways that Walter had sketched and documented in his journal.

Julia's plan—which she knew would take years and years to bring to fruition—was to find a way to create a genetically engineered viral key that would unlock her own psychic potential. To saddle and *break* her epileptic power like a skittish wild horse, so that she could ride it through the membrane separating her from an alternate universe.

One in which her little sister might still be alive.

There was precedent, after all. Peter was living proof of it. And if it could be done once, it could be replicated.

Only, her version was infinitely more subtle. Rather than snatching her living sister, and bringing her back to the universe in which she had been killed as an infant, Julia planned to stalk and eliminate the other-universe version of herself—the one who had never murdered her little sister.

And then she would take her place. To seamlessly slide into her fantasy of a fresh start, with a family that would love and embrace her without the toxic grief, blame, and utter loathing that had poisoned any hope she had ever had of a relationship in this universe.

Yet she couldn't get too far ahead of herself. She had to take it one step at a time. Check and recheck her work. Confirm her results. Be meticulous, and careful not to let her emotions get in the way of her goal.

With the lab to herself, Julia took the opportunity to pull Walter's journal out of its hiding place again, and double-check to make sure there weren't any other critical passages that she might need later, even if they didn't seem particularly relevant right now.

The book was filled with scrawled schematics for wacky inventions and irrelevant mechanisms, but there were also a hundred little cryptic notes and asides scribbled in the margins. Individually, they didn't seem to mean anything, but when considered in the broader context, they took on profound and ominous significance.

She was sitting on a tall stool with the small leather-bound book open in her lap, thumbing through the most recent entries.

"Hello, Julia."

She almost jumped out of her own skin. It was that smug bitch, Carla Warren, popping up like a judgmental fairy godmother.

Julia had always disliked the pretty, perfect blonde, for a million reasons. She hated Carla for the way men fell all over themselves to give her everything she wanted. How all she had to do was bat her big blue eyes and flash her kittenish smile, and everything was handed to her on a silver platter.

But, as much as Julia resented the way men reacted to Carla, she found herself studying her nemesis, filing away all of her subtle moves and gestures for future use. Because Julia had already saved up more than half of the money she would need for cosmetic surgery. Eventually, she would become the kind of woman for whom men wanted to do things.

Things that would further her long-term plans.

Still, the trait Julia really hated in Carla wasn't her looks. It was the fact that she wasn't any kind of *real* scientist. She called herself a "theoretical physicist," which—as far as Julia was concerned—meant bullshit artist. A sanctimonious, stuck-up windbag who sat around all day talking about a bunch of imaginary ideas, rather than getting her hands dirty with the real-world, meat-and-potatoes kind of science that really mattered.

Even worse, Carla was *religious*. She was always going on and on about spirituality, and irrefutable morality, and other made-up black-and-white fairy tales that had no place in a scientific laboratory. She was the diametric *opposite* of a scientist, in Julia's eyes. Nothing but an ethical hall monitor. A tiresome, pretentious Goody Two-Shoes who thought scientific inquiry should be restricted by her arbitrary rules, just because she said so.

And now, here she was. The hall monitor, come to stick her pretty little nose into Julia's business.

"What are you doing?" Carla asked, glancing down at the book in Julia's lap before she was able to close it. "Isn't that Walter's handwriting? What is that? Where did you get it?"

There was no time to think. She had to come up with a plan to spin this unfortunate intrusion in her favor, and fast.

Then it came to her, in a perfect moment of awe-inspiring clarity. The way to get rid of Carla once and for all—and Walter, too, while she was at it. That way, no one alive would possess the knowledge that she had.

It was almost too perfect.

"Carla," Julia said, making her voice all quivery and sincere. "I'm so glad you're here. I need to talk to you. It's about Doctor Bishop."

Carla's perfect, unblemished forehead creased with worry.

"What is it?" she asked, taking a seat on a stool and putting a gentle, motherly hand on Julia's arm. It took effort not to flinch at her intrusive touch. Julia's heart was pounding so hard, she felt as if it was going to leap out of her chest.

She had never been so excited and nervous. One wrong word, and she would blow it.

She forced herself to take a deep slow breath, hoping her hesitation translated into something that read like genuine concern.

"You've been working with him for years," Julia said. "So you know that he's, well, eccentric. But..." Julia paused dramatically, allowing a little quiver to start up in her lower lip as she placed her flat hand on the cover of the diary. "Oh, Carla, it's so much worse than I thought. He's a very sick man. A dangerous man, I think."

"Listen," Carla said. "I know Walter. Better than anyone, I think. Even Elizabeth."

Julia looked up sharply, narrowing her eyes.

She'd always wondered if Carla was having an affair with Walter, but had never seen any real evidence to back up her suspicions. Now, she suddenly found herself wondering again. It didn't make sense that a beautiful woman, who could pretty much have any man on campus, would go for an odd duck like Walter. But stranger things had happened.

Julia herself never really understood the point of sexual relationships, anyway, unless they could be used to achieve a productive goal. What goal might Carla be striving to achieve by sleeping with Walter? "Bumping uglies," she had heard it called colloquially. Assuming, of course, that those uptight religious beliefs even allowed for such behavior.

"I know he's got a lot of complex issues," Carla added. "But I honestly believe that the good side of him is still there. Still worth fighting for."

"That's what I thought, too," Julia said. "Until I read this diary. Now I'm afraid of what he may do. Afraid that he's planning something terrible. Something that could have catastrophic consequences. He..." She paused again, this time to try and stifle helpless giggles that she struggled to disguise as sobs. "I think he's going to... tamper in God's domain and try to create his own universe!"

Julia looked up at Carla, wondering if maybe she'd pushed it just a little bit too far with the "God's domain" thing. But Carla looked serious—and concerned. She was taking the bait.

It's working!

She felt the same kind of cold, ecstatic rush that she always got when a tricky and complicated experiment went exactly the way she had planned. She handed the little book over with what she hoped was a solemn, serious look on her face. Now all she had to do was let Carla read through Walter's madness, and then carefully plant a little seed about how best to deal with it.

When Carla had finished reading through Walter's journal, she paused for a moment with a deeply pained expression that made Julia want to jump up and cheer. But she didn't. She stayed seated and quiet, arranging her own face into an exact mirror image of the one worn by the other woman.

"You're so right," Carla said. "It is worse than I thought." She frowned, gesturing toward Julia's little experiment with Peter's DNA. "What are you doing here? Surely you're not attempting to implement this madness?"

"Listen," Julia said, spreading protective fingers over her results. "It's just that... well, I thought maybe he was just crazy. I had to confirm his theory about the unusual residue that forms around the DNA of an organism that passes between the universes, and see for myself. He was right, and *here* is the proof." Julia could see the pieces of her plan sliding smoothly into place. "This discovery, if it fell into the wrong hands, could be incredibly dangerous."

She gave Carla a moment to look over the notes that contained her results, feeling a little bit sick with anxious adrenaline. This was where things could go very wrong.

"You're right," Carla said again. "This is far too dangerous. It has to be destroyed. All of this."

Together they dumped all of the samples out into the steel sink, then tossed Julia's notes in after them and turned on the hot water. Watching the ink run as the wet pages softened and turned to useless mush made Julia feel sick to her stomach, but it was the perfect gesture to prime Carla for what needed to happen next.

It was a small sacrifice to make for the greater goal. She didn't doubt for a second that she'd be able to extract another sample from Peter, later on, once she was closer to the completion of her plan.

Eye on the prize...

"Yes," Julia said. "We have no choice." She paused for effect, then added, "The journal must also be destroyed." She chose her words very carefully. "But if we just throw it away, it's not going to mean anything to Walter. He'll be angry, but he won't understand why."

"I agree," Carla said. "He needs to address it himself as a symbolic gesture. That's the only hope I... *we* have of reaching the old Walter. The *good* Walter."

Julia had absolutely no idea what Carla was rattling on about. She'd only known Walter for a short time and, while he was obviously eccentric, she hadn't noticed anything particularly bad about him at all.

Of course, he was adamant in his refusal to subjugate scientific curiosity to the dubious authority of Carla's fairy-tale God. Maybe that was what she thought was the "bad" part of Walter. Yet in Julia's book, this was a good thing.

It didn't matter, though. What mattered was that Carla walked away from their conversation thinking it was all her idea. Particularly one aspect of it.

"*He* should burn it," Julia said. "The diary."

Carla nodded. Her eyes were far away, as if contemplating her options, or whatever occupied her pretty little blond brain when it wasn't getting all up in other people's business.

"He's coming back in at eight o'clock, isn't he?" Julia continued. "To work on that mental generator he's been tinkering with in his spare time. Why don't you come back then, and have a talk with him. It'll be more private. I'll be long gone, and you'll pretty much have the whole building to yourselves."

"Good idea," Carla said. "But what about you?" Again, the hand on her arm and the sweet, simpering, oh-so-concerned look. "Are you going to be okay? If you need to talk, I'm always here."

"Thank you," Julia replied, struggling not to roll her eyes. "I'll be okay. I think I'm going to apply for a transfer to another department. I just want to forget all this madness. Start fresh."

"I think that's probably best," Carla said. "But don't be a stranger, Julia. Any time you need to talk... I mean it."

Julia would have rather eaten broken glass, but still she made herself reach out and hug Carla, exactly as she'd seen other students do in the past.

"I will," she said. Then she glanced around. "I'm just going to clean up here, and head back to the dorm."

Carla nodded and turned to go, taking Walter's journal with her.

As soon as her nemesis was out of sight, Julia took her hidden copies of the relevant pages and tucked them carefully away in her backpack. Once everything was clean and straightened up, all she had to do was wait for Walter to return.

3

Walter arrived a few minutes early, carrying a number of large, awkward packages and nearly tripping over his own feet as he entered. Julia ran to his side and helped steady him, taking one of the packages from his arms.

"Here," she said. "Let me help you, Doctor Bishop."

"Thank you, Astrid," Walter replied, seeming distracted—as if he was already thinking about something else.

"Astrid?" Julia frowned. "My name is Julia."

"Oh, of course it is," Walter replied, tipping his head to the left and muttering to no one. "Why did you say her name was Astrid?"

Julia frowned at him. His eyes were glazed and pupils dilated.

He's on something, she thought, and she felt like cheering. This was too perfect.

"Did you drop acid again, Doctor Bishop?" she asked.

"What?" He turned to his left again, making it look as if he was listening to someone or something other than her. "I suppose you're right," he said to thin air, "but I don't see how that's *relevant*."

"Will you be working on your generator again tonight?" Julia asked, already knowing the answer, but wanting to confirm it.

"It's a new blend," Walter replied, answering her first question and ignoring the second. "Seems to have a strange effect on my sense of separation between the past and the future. But I believe it will also boost the electrical output that I'm able to channel through my generator."

"Well, you'd better be careful—remember the last time? When you blew the circuit and set the phonebook on fire?" Julia set Walter's package on his workstation. "Here, let me check all the burners, and make sure the gas is turned off."

Walter ignored her completely, focusing on whatever was going on inside his head. Julia smiled and walked over to the closest burner, gripping the knob so hard that its cold metal edge dug deeply into her fingers. She paused, her heart slam-dancing in her chest, feeling light-headed and sweaty. It was one thing to plan something like this, but another thing to actually do it.

It was just the smallest movement of her wrist. Just the slightest turn to the left. Just enough to allow a slow, undetectable leak. So that when Carla tried to make Walter burn the journal…

It doesn't matter. They *don't matter. I've got what I want. Just do it.*

She turned the knob, and quickly backed away.

"They're all off," she called over her shoulder. "It's safe now." She picked up her own backpack, and headed for the door. "Have a good night, Doctor Bishop."

She could hear him muttering to himself as he hunched over his packages. He probably didn't even know she was still there.

On her way out, she took the small fire extinguisher off the wall and slid it into her bag.

Walter thought he heard a female voice coming from behind the centrifuge, but it sounded strange—distorted and foreign, as if it were a weak pirate-radio broadcast, perhaps from another country. The only words he could make out were, "*Doctor Bishop*." And even though it was his own name, something in the vowels seemed sinister, unrealistic. The sibilant *sh* sound lasted far too long, resonating snakelike inside his left ear.

He turned back toward the green fairy with whom he'd been conversing, and found that she was gone. In her place was a younger version of himself. Twenty-two and utterly guileless in that ratty old Norfolk jacket he'd worn every day until it disintegrated into rags sometime in the mid-seventies.

This younger Walter was staring at him with a worried frown.

"I think we might be in trouble," Younger Walter said.

"Trouble?" Walter frowned. "What kind of trouble."

For a moment, Younger Walter didn't speak. He looked emotional and unsure, as if struggling with a difficult task, like the decision to euthanize a suffering pet. When he opened his mouth again to speak, the voice that came out was a woman's voice. A soft, familiar voice, speaking words that he would never forget.

"Walter," this impossible voice said. "There has to be a line somewhere."

Then another voice spoke, coming from behind him and to his right.

A male voice.

His own voice.

"There's only one God in this lab."

Walter spun to face the source, and saw yet *another* version of himself. This one was older than the first, but still a few years younger than he was now. His eyes were cold and hard, like iron. As if they belonged to someone else.

"Walter?" The woman's voice again.

When he turned to face the speaker, the twenty-two-year-old version of himself was gone. In his place was Carla Warren, looking both tired and worried.

"Walter," she said, her voice imploring. "We need to talk."

In her pale, slender hands, she held his journal.

"How dare you?" the Hard Walter demanded, stepping forward. "That's private."

Walter peered at him, and noticed Hard Walter was now wearing his familiar stained lab coat. When he looked down at his own chest and arms, he discovered that he was now wearing the long-gone Norfolk jacket he'd loved so much in his twenties. And his hands—his hands were youthful, smooth, and unscarred.

Had he somehow become his younger self, while that chilly doppelganger had taken over his modern self?

It was all so confusing.

"Please," Carla was saying. "Look at me, Walter."

He looked up from his tattered tweed sleeves, and saw that she wasn't facing him. She was talking to the Hard Walter. He also noticed that she had sprouted flaming wings so large they swept the ceiling. Like an angel, but not a cute greeting-card cupid. A fierce, Old Testament angel, both beautiful and terrible to behold. Then, in a flash, the flaming wings fluttered and disintegrated into black ash, swirling around them both like the glitter inside a snow globe.

"Carla?" Walter said, taking a step closer to her.

She ignored him completely, as if he were invisible. She remained focused on the Hard Walter, and looked exceptionally beautiful.

Beautiful and sad.

"You need a reality check," she was saying. "You've lost sight of the things that really matter. Like Peter. Why did you bother to bring the boy here in the first place, if you're just going to ignore him? Can't you see he's dying for your attention?"

Her curly blond hair pulsed with a strange internal glow, as if each individual strand had been replaced with a delicate optical fiber. The brilliant tips swayed around her small, anxious face, stirred by a nonexistent current.

"The families of great men have to accept the fact that they will always come second to the work," Hard Walter said with a dismissive shrug.

"The work?" Carla replied with a frown. "The *work*?"

"*My* work," Hard Walter repeated. "It is the only thing that matters. Everything else is just window dressing."

"But what is the point of *any* work if it drives away the people who care about you? Peter. Elizabeth." She paused, biting her lower lip. "Me, Walter. I care about you, and that's why I can't let you continue down this path. I know you."

"You don't know anything about me," Hard Walter said. "If you did, you would never be so impudent as to question my priorities."

"I know the good Walter," she said. "The Walter I care about is still there, inside you. He knows that what you're doing is wrong, just as well as I do." Her voice softened. "Don't you?"

"I..." Walter started to say, but Hard Walter turned to him and hissed a wordless warning, cold eyes flashing like sparks struck from iron. Then he turned back to face Carla.

"This conversation is asinine and irrelevant," he said. "Now, if you'll excuse me, I have work to do. You can put that journal back where you found it."

"Please, Walter," Carla said, gripping Hard Walter's forearm and looking up into his hard eyes. "Don't shut me out."

Walter shivered, feeling the ghostly brush of her fingers against his own arm, burning through the rough fabric of his old jacket. When he looked down at his sleeve, he saw that there were smeary red fingerprints, as if he'd just been touched by a bloody hand. He was hit with a sudden crushing vertigo, forcing him to cling to the edge of a nearby worktable.

He wanted to say something, to cry out or make any kind of noise at all, but his mouth was filled with tangled organic fibers that strangled any sound before it could escape.

When he tried to move toward Carla, desperate to signal to her in some way, it felt as if he were struggling against a vicious riptide. Meanwhile, she was leaning in toward Hard Walter, whispering. The glow that infused her golden hair was spreading beneath her skin, making her pulse with strange light that seemed to emanate from the center of her chest, as if her heart had been replaced with a miniature supernova.

Walter tried to breathe slowly and evenly, clinging to his rational, scientific objectivity as tightly as he clung to the edge of the table. This was just a particularly vivid and intense hallucination, that's all. For all he knew, Carla wasn't even there in the lab.

He forced himself to focus, to think.

This new blend of acid he had dropped was supposed

to be quite mild, and intended simply to enhance his more esoteric brain functions without impeding his thought processes or distorting his perception too strongly. In previous tests, it had produced a sense of sharpness, even focus—accompanied by some minor visual hallucinations that were limited to subtle changes in the color, texture, or shape of existing objects or individuals.

But nothing like this.

So what, exactly, was happening to him?

Was it hallucinogen-persisting perception disorder? Certainly, he'd ingested enough mind-altering chemicals over the years that a flashback remained a distinct possibility. But he'd never suffered from anything like this in the past.

Then again, many of the people who knew him might argue that his perceptions hadn't been normal to start with.

Suddenly, an even more disturbing thought struck him.

Could it be some kind of genuine psychotic break? He'd been troubled by a persistent sense of disassociation lately, and suffered from several small blackouts. When they ended, he found himself in the midst of a task he didn't remember starting, or saying goodbye to someone over the phone—even though he had no idea who was on the other end of the line.

More and more it seemed as if his work was the only thing that made any kind of sense. His only anchor in a world where day-to-day events seemed like complex puzzles that refused to be solved. The only time he felt completely at ease was when he was here, in the lab. Only here did he feel sure of himself, and the world around him.

And now, he was being forced to doubt even that reality.

Because the last and most awful possibility was that this terrifying, inexplicable series of events was real. That there really *was* another him—a terrible, cold, alien version of him who had been slowly, stealthily taking control while Walter wasn't paying attention, and now had broken free.

But *why*?

Before he could answer any of these questions, Carla reached up and touched the other Walter's cheek.

And everything changed.

The strange, invisible riptide against which he'd been fighting suddenly reversed and he was swept off his feet, hurtling headlong through the air and crashing into Hard Walter with such force that it stunned him, knocking the breath out of him.

When he twisted around and peered at his own body, he saw that he hadn't just bumped into the other Walter—he'd melded into him, leaving a crooked, multi-limbed monstrosity, like conjoined twins, that never could have survived outside of the womb.

He glanced at Carla. To his surprise, she didn't seem to notice anything unusual about him. She was looking up into his face with her sad blue eyes.

"Science is a tool," she was saying. "Like a wrench or a shovel. Or a gun. You choose what you want to do with that tool. What you want to build, and what you want to destroy.

"*You* choose, Walter."

And then, the floor beneath his sneakers cracked and opened up, and before he could react, he was plunged into the icy water beneath.

4

For a terrifying moment, the shock of it—the vicious toothy cold so intense it felt like burning—completely overwhelmed his senses.

He flailed, and thrashed in the water, consumed by a blind panic, his eyes clenched tightly shut. But when he opened them, he found that he could see perfectly, as if he were wearing goggles in a clear, clean pool. There were throbbing red shapes dancing around the edges of his vision, and he could see that he wasn't alone.

A small child was floating, just out of reach, asleep or unconscious. Head tucked down, dark hair drifting around a pale face. Walter stretched his arm out, fingers brushing against the child's sleeve. The contact seemed to jolt the child back to terrified consciousness, body jerking and face turning, eyes wide and unseeing.

Peter.

Now that he was turned toward Walter, he seemed to age. It was clear that this was Peter today, thirteen years old and dressed in the same black sweatshirt and jeans he'd been wearing when he came to the lab earlier.

Peter…

Was this a hallucination, or a memory? Had this already happened? It seemed so vivid and real at its core, as solid and unquestionably true as any other memory. But it couldn't be. It was impossible.

He and Peter were *alive.*

Or were they?

Walter tried to say his son's name, but all that came out of his mouth was a rush of silver bubbles. Peter reached out his hand, eyes desperate and pleading as he began to sink into the inky darkness below.

His lungs ached for air. Close to blacking out from lack of oxygen, Walter flailed with all his remaining strength, paddling toward the receding form. Reaching out, he gripped the boy's hand. It felt ice cold and rigid—like the hand of a corpse.

He pulled his son into his arms, not sure what he actually planned to do, but not willing to let him go down alone. Above them was an unbroken bluish-white ceiling of ice. They were trapped.

Darkness began to eclipse his vision, the unforgiving cold swiftly shutting his body down and making his thoughts sluggish and murky. Just before he blacked out completely, he looked down at Peter and was shocked to see a totally different child, looking back up at him. A strange, frail child with a smooth, bald head like that of a chemotherapy patient, and big dark eyes that seemed to look right through him.

Then he felt a dozen hands gripping him, all at once, grabbing his arms and twisted fistfuls of his shirt and hauling him rapidly upward until he slammed violently against the ice. Only now it wasn't a ceiling above him anymore, it was a wall. An opaque smooth wall, like frosted glass. And he himself was no longer underwater.

He was standing upright in the middle of his safe familiar lab.

The strange child that used to be Peter was gone.

He took a moment to collect himself, to breathe deeply and try to stabilize his thoughts. This was just a bad trip. A particularly vivid, frightening trip, but nothing Walter couldn't handle. The key was to remain calm, rational, and objective. Observe the unusual effects of this new blend and accurately remember them in detail, so that he would be able to use this data when the time came to reformulate.

Yet he still felt scattered and breathless, heart skittish and desperate like a trapped rat in his chest. He remained pressed against the inexplicable glass wall that trapped him in the middle of the lab, unable to move. Nothing seemed certain. Even the simplest, most fundamental things seemed ephemeral.

Who was he, really?

And who was that other me?

As if summoned by his question, the other Walter—the hard one—appeared on the other side of the frosted glass, facing away. Indistinct and blurred at first, just a sinister shadow, then becoming clearer as the glass became clear around him, the way a warm hand melts the frost on a winter window.

Walter touched the glass and found it soft and yielding, like living skin.

By peering over Hard Walter's shoulder, he could see Carla standing there, still glowing as if lit from within.

"You need to burn it," Carla was saying, holding up the journal. "It's the only way."

"Don't be ridiculous," Hard Walter replied. "Why should I do that?"

"No," Walter whispered. "It's my... my life's work..."

"This isn't your life's work," Carla said, her hand on the cover of the journal. "*You* are your life's work. You choose who you want to be. But you need to make the right choice.

"Burn the journal," she insisted. She walked over to one of the worktables and placed the journal in a steel basin. Then she reached into the pocket of her lab coat and pulled out a heavy silver cigarette lighter.

"You wouldn't dare," Hard Walter said.

"Carla... please," Walter said.

"No, I wouldn't," she agreed. "*You* need to do it." She held out the lighter and thumbed back the cover.

"You need to do it," she repeated, and she struck the flint.

A burst of roiling blue flame engulfed her. Instantly her curly blond hair was on fire, her mouth wide open in a silent scream. Then she flailed her burning arms, knocking the steel basin and several glass beakers from the table. The beakers shattered on the floor. The journal slid across it toward the open cubbyhole where Julia had found it, stopping just inches short.

As the glass shattered, the flammable liquid caught fire, too, releasing a toxic cloud of choking smoke and sending burning tendrils flowing toward the diary.

Walter was still trapped behind the soft glass, pounding his fists against it and screaming Carla's name, but time seemed to have slowed to a crawl in the lab. On the other side of the barrier, the graceful serpentine flames were almost beautiful. Carla looked beautiful, too, as if she were dancing a dreamy, slow motion ballet. He could see the other Walter, standing between the burning angel that Carla had become and the threatened diary. Hard Walter was equidistant between them, and Walter could see that he was torn, deciding who—or what—he should save.

There was a large, ratty blanket stuffed into one of

the lower cupboards, put there the last time Walter had slept in the lab. The other Walter could grab it and throw it over Carla to smother the flames and save her life. But if he did, the flaming liquid would reach the journal.

On the other hand, he could save the journal, dive across the floor and push it back into its hiding place, replacing the fireproof tile that had protected it all these years. But by the time he did that, it might be too late to save Carla.

It was no choice at all.

So why was the other Walter hesitating?

"Go!" Walter implored. "Save her."

He pressed his hands against the soft glass, desperately searching for any breach or weakness where he might be able to break through. It was a solid membrane that would bend, but not break. More than that, it was all around him now, on all sides and above in an unbroken ovoid shell that gave him little more than the space taken up by his outstretched arms.

"Save her!" he cried again, banging on the glass to try to get the other Walter's attention. "Don't just stand there, save her! *Carla!*"

But then, to his horror, the Hard Walter dove for the journal.

Walter felt the impact of that decision as if it was a kick to the stomach. He cried out in wordless anguish, turning to see Carla collapse to the floor, her angelic flames lost in the sea of fire that was swiftly engulfing that entire side of the room.

When he shifted to see what the other Walter was doing, he found himself on the other side of the lab, crouching over the cubbyhole in the floor, pressing the fireproof tile back into place.

There was no glass membrane.

No other him.

He had chosen to save the journal, instead of rescuing Carla.

And with that awful revelation came a deep, rumbling crack down the center of his psyche, splitting him open from inside and sending him spinning into a bottomless abyss of madness.

5

Peter sat on the sofa, a book open in his lap, but not reading.

He was staring resentfully at his mother, who was "napping" on the other couch in front of some vapid television program. She was always napping these days, an empty glass never far away.

She had been napping when he got home from school and decided to go over to his father's lab, and was napping again when he returned from the strange, cheerfully manic trip to the ice-cream parlor for root-beer floats. Which Peter didn't even like all that much, but he was so happy to have his father paying attention to him again that he sucked one down without protest. His father had even looked at his chemistry test, and said that he was proud of Peter. He still had a warm, happy, birthday kind of feeling in his belly when he got home, but that feeling quickly drained away to a dull depression.

She had changed clothes since the last nap, and now had an empty rocks glass instead of an empty wine glass. Other than that, nothing had changed.

Probably never would.

The more isolated Peter became, the more disconnected from his family, the more convinced he became that he didn't fit in anywhere. And any time he would experience a moment of shared intimacy or a feeling of belonging, it would be quickly eclipsed by moments like this. Moments where he felt alone again, even with someone else in the room.

He'd made a concerted effort to find friends, carefully studying other guys who were popular and adopting their mannerisms and tastes. He found that he was extremely good at mimicry and manipulation, but although he was able to charm people into thinking they liked him, those other kids didn't really know him. They knew the easygoing, friendly, wisecracking mask Peter presented for their benefit.

But under that mask, he still felt like an outsider. And he secretly resented them for befriending him only after he'd made the effort to pretend he was the kind of person they liked.

Then he started pulling little scams in the lunchroom, tricking other kids out of their coveted snack items. It wasn't that he actually *wanted* the candy—he could just have bought whatever he wanted from the vending machines. His mom gave him plenty of money.

It was her morning ritual, a bleary, red-eyed routine. She fished the money out of her purse and pressed it into his hand like some kind of payoff. Maybe it made her feel better for checking out on him every night.

No, he perpetrated these minor swindles because he could. And because it was fun. He'd even thought about trying something involving real money, but that was probably a bad idea. Because no matter how disconnected he felt from his family, he couldn't stand the thought of his father finding out about something like that.

The phone rang, causing him to jump.

Peter's mother rolled over, but didn't wake up.

He sighed and got up. It took him a minute to figure out where his mother had left the cordless handset, but he followed the electronic chirping sound and eventually found it under the dining-room table.

"Hello," he said into the phone.

There was a clipped, official-sounding voice on the other end. Male, and no-nonsense.

"May I please speak to Elizabeth Bishop?"

"She's sleeping," Peter said. "This is her son."

"It's an emergency," the voice replied. "You need to wake her up."

Peter felt a cold twist in his belly.

"Is it my father?" he asked. "Did something happen to my dad?"

"Please, son," the voice said, a little less officious now. "Go get your mother."

Peter held the handset away from his ear and eyed it warily, as if it might bite him. Then he turned and ran into the living room.

"Mom!" he said, shaking her by the shoulder. "Mom, wake up!"

"What's your problem?" Her voice was thick and slurred, and she swatted at his fingers as if they were flies. "God! Can't you see I'm resting?"

"Mom, it's an emergency," he said, holding out the phone. "Something's happened to Dad!"

She opened her bleary, bloodshot eyes and frowned at him as if he wasn't speaking English, then looked down at the phone as if she had no idea what it was for.

"What?" she said.

Aching with frustration, he grabbed her hand and put the phone into it.

"Phone!" he said. "Emergency!"

She ran her fingers through her tangled hair, and then slowly raised the handset to her ear.

"Yes," she said. "Yes, this is she." She paused, eyes squinting down to narrow slits. "What kind of accident? Fatality? What's that supposed to mean?"

Peter's heart was racing. He wanted to rip the phone out of his mother's grip and demand answers for himself. She was in no shape to handle anything right now, and he was deeply ashamed by the thought that whoever was on the other end would realize she was drunk.

"I see," she said, and then she hit the "off" button.

The handset chirped.

For a second she just sat there. Her face was blotchy and red, and tears were gathering in her bloodshot eyes.

"Mom," Peter said. "What the hell is going on?"

She let out a little noise that was maybe supposed to be a laugh, but sounded more like the hissing of an angry cat.

"Well, your father finally had his nervous breakdown," she said. "There was a fire in the lab, and some woman died. Now I've gotta go sign him into the loony bin or something, I don't know."

"Some woman?" Peter grabbed her arm. "A student? Was it Carla?"

"How should I know?" she asked. "He doesn't tell me anything anymore."

She shook off his grip, lurched up off the couch, and started searching for her purse. She stumbled and swore and finally Peter just went to the table by the door and got the purse, handing it to her.

She opened it and started pawing through the contents until she found a pack of cigarettes. Peter frowned as she took one out and lit it.

"I thought you quit smoking," he said.

"You know," she said, taking a deep drag of the cigarette and pointing at him with the glowing end, "I wish I could have a nervous breakdown. But no. I have to deal with everything, all by myself. I have to *do everything*!"

That was more than he could handle.

"You don't handle anything!" Peter snapped. "All you do is drink and sleep."

She paused, cigarette halfway to her mouth, and looked at him. The expression on her face was stricken, as if he'd slapped her. Then she burst into tears.

"I never wanted this," she said, dropping her face into her shaking hands. "I told him it was wrong to take you, but he wouldn't listen."

"Mom, you're not making any sense," he said, turning away and shutting her out the way he always did when she was like this.

"Fine," she said, storming off toward the door and jerking it open. "Fine I'll just *handle it*!" She stumbled out, slamming it behind her, and moments later Peter heard the car start in the driveway. He knew she shouldn't be driving in her condition, and he suddenly had an awful vision of her crashing her car and killing herself. If his father was in a psych ward, and his mother was dead, what would happen to him?

So he ran to the door and flung it open, just in time to see her peel out of the driveway and take off down the street, away from the house.

Leaving Peter alone.

He paused for a moment, there in the doorway, pressing the back of his hand to his lips. She'd left him. His father had left him, gone crazy or worse for who knew how long. The fear and anger over this latest in a long string of abandonments flared up bright inside him.

And then faded.

Because wasn't he alone anyway? Hadn't he *always* been alone?

He closed the door and went back into the house.

PART FOUR

1

NEAR HARTFORD, CT 2008

It had been touch and go for a while there.

For one thing, she was working in a small, stripped-down lab without some of the heavier, more expensive equipment she normally relied upon. For another, the mysterious protein coating surrounding Peter's DNA was much thinner, more delicate than it had been the last time she'd examined a sample of it.

That degradation was probably due to the passage of time. Most likely, if a person regularly traveled back and forth between the parallel universes, exposing themselves to whatever unknowable forces existed within the wormhole through which they passed, then the residue would remain thick and easy to collect.

But, like the fingers of a guitar player who is out of practice, which will soften and lose their calluses, the DNA of a person who hadn't been through a wormhole in many years would no longer need that protective coating. From what she could see, it would become thin and patchy and start to slough away. That looked to be what had happened with Peter.

She was infinitely grateful that she'd thought ahead,

and managed to bring her designer virus to the point where it was ready to be fused with his DNA. And that she had located him before any more time had passed. Because in just another year or two, the organic coating she needed might have degraded to the point of being useless.

She supposed she owed a debt of gratitude to the Englishman, as well, since she couldn't have made this happen without his help.

Too bad for him.

Collecting everything she needed for her transition and pulling some directions out of the printer, she carefully slipped the newly enhanced virus into a padded inner pocket inside her purse, and crept up the stairs.

Outside, dawn was breaking and casting a pale watery-blue light through the eastern windows. When she peered in at Peter, she saw that he was still asleep on his back with one arm thrown wide across the bed. Clearly, the action opera she'd composed for him had worn him out. She felt a kind of strange fondness toward him in that moment, knowing that she couldn't have accomplished any of this without him.

Then she turned on her heel and headed away from the house.

Out in the driveway, she was about to get into their stolen car when she heard a distinctive, sardonic voice, bearing an all-too-familiar accent.

"Clever girl," McCoy said.

She spun to face him, tightly gripping her purse.

He was wearing a brand new plaid shirt and a broke-brim trucker hat over his thinning salt-and-pepper hair in a laughably unsuccessful attempt to look more American. At his elbow stood the blond thug who'd participated in the previous day's orchestrated chase scene. He'd been following orders then, to make sure that she wasn't really hurt during the charade, but he didn't look as if he had any such instructions this morning.

"Planning a little trip, are we?" the Englishman asked, snatching the printed directions out of her hand. "Reiden Lake? You have good taste, my dear. I hear it's lovely this time of year." He crumpled the printout and dropped it at her feet, glancing toward the thug. "Get the purse."

"No!" she cried, clutching it to her chest as the thug's big hairy fist came down on her like a cartoon anvil.

When Peter woke up, he thought he heard voices out in the driveway, but he felt too lazy to go investigate. Then he heard Julia's distressed voice yell out, and he scrambled to his feet.

It took him precious seconds to remember first what had happened to his clothes, and then where the dryer was in this unfamiliar house. Once he remembered, he had to extract his pants from the tangle of other clothes and put them on while half running, half hopping toward the front door.

When he flung it open, he saw Julia lying in the driveway, groaning softly and struggling to roll onto her side. She was hurt, but not unconscious. Her spilled purse lay about six feet away, its contents scattered down the drive. The car door was open, and by the front left tire was a crumpled piece of paper.

He ran to her side.

"Julia?" he said. "Julia, what happened?"

"Peter?" She looked up at him, eyes swollen and wet with tears. "Peter, they got the virus!"

2

McCoy's phone buzzed in his pocket. He let it ring a few times before thumbing the button on his Bluetooth headset to answer the call. He might be a marionette, but he was damned if he was going to accept being on short strings.

"You have it?" Jones said on the other end of the phone.

"You know I do," McCoy replied. He and the blond thug had parted ways, and McCoy was just now getting to his rented SUV. He had set up a Wi-Fi camera across the street so that Jones could see their little drama play out with Julia. He'd been tempted to flash the camera the finger, but knew that there was no point in antagonizing the man.

Normally he wouldn't care. This wasn't just his job, after all—it was his purpose. This was the sort of thing he was designed for. Not for the first time he wondered if he was beginning to pick up the habits of the people whose forms he had taken. It was an absurd thought, but there it was. He hoped not, though.

It would be damn inconvenient.

"And Doctor Lachaux's lab?"

"Prepped and waiting for her. It's a shambles, but we left her notes and enough equipment intact for her to get the job done. Provided she does what you think she'll do."

"She will," Jones said. "She's rather predictable that way."

"May I ask a question?" McCoy said. Something had been bothering him since he'd left Bangkok.

"You're wondering why we had her get the DNA from Peter rather than doing it ourselves," Jones said.

"I... Yes." The man was infuriating—he'd hate to play chess against him. Jones always seemed to be three steps ahead of everyone else. Annoyed, McCoy trudged on anyway.

"Wouldn't it have been easier to grab one of his Thai bargirls in Bangkok? His DNA would have been all over her."

"Wheels within wheels. On the one hand, it's akin to eagles stealing fish from falcons after all the work's been done for them. But more importantly, we need skills only Doctor Lachaux possesses—need her to do certain things in a certain order. Using her to get the DNA from Peter steers her in the proper direction—she's even more invested now. She'll go where we need her to go, when we need her to go there.

"She's dancing to our tune, and when the time is right, she'll be our big finale."

"Understood," McCoy said, though he didn't really believe it. There were games going on here to which he wasn't privy, and much as it irked him, it was probably best he not know. "Where am I off to now?"

"New York," Jones said. "There are some people I need you to make contact with."

⅄

Peter hurried Julia inside, eased her to the couch, and then went to the window to scan the street. Whoever had attacked her was gone. He didn't think they'd be back, either. What was there left for them to take? So he turned back toward Julia.

"How are you feeling?"

"I'm okay," she said. "A little dizzy." She touched one finger to a lump forming on her head and winced. "And sore."

"I'll get you some ice," he said, and he stepped toward the kitchen. He called back over his shoulder. "What happened? You were leaving, weren't you?"

"No, I was… Dammit. Yes, I was leaving."

"Why?" he said from the kitchen. He smoothed out the piece of paper he had found by the car's tire when he grabbed the contents of her purse. It was a map, printed out, showing the route to a place called Reiden Lake. It took him a second to dredge the name up out of his memory before he had it. His family had a cabin there when he was a kid. He had a flash of memory of the lake, of cold, of his father.

He pushed it aside. Grabbing a dishtowel, he then went to the freezer and scooped out some ice. He dropped it onto the towel, folding it into an impromptu ice pack.

Peter could feel this score starting to slip out of his grip. He still needed the money to pay Big Eddie, and he was damned if he was going to see it disappear. He needed to pull things back on track. The best route was honesty. Or at least the appearance of it.

He returned to the living room, and she looked up.

"Peter, I like you," she said. "Obviously. But…"

"But you don't entirely trust me." He placed the ice on the goose egg forming on her scalp. "Hold this here."

"Thanks," she said. She put her hand on his to hold the

ice in place. He let it linger there a little too long. "This isn't just my life's work, Peter. It's my cure. It's important that this goes to the people who are afflicted, but I've got a personal stake in this, too. These seizures, they take everything from a person. You don't know what that's like."

"No, I don't know what that's like," he responded. "But I *do* understand you not trusting me."

"You do?"

"Of course I do," he said. "I come out of nowhere, your stolen work in my hands, and offer to sell it to you. For all you know, I could have been the one who stole it. Last night's fiasco could have been an elaborate ruse."

"No," she said, turning away from him. "That's ridiculous."

"I've seen stranger cons."

"Well, if it helps," she said, turning back, "I trust you now. Whoever stole it before has it again. And I'm afraid of what they're going to do with it."

"Can you describe the people who took it?"

"I think one of them was a driver from last night—the blond man. And the other one..." She paused. "It was the Englishman. The one who supplied me with the smallpox samples."

A thought occurred to Peter. Considering how much traveling he did, seeing an Englishman abroad was hardly surprising. Still, an Englishman in Bangkok? The one with the vial? It couldn't be the same guy, of course. The man in Bangkok was dead. Had to be. But there was a connection between the two.

"What if we tackle this from a different direction?" he suggested. "This is an epilepsy drug, right? Experimental. Chances are he's going to want to sell it. It's bound to be worth a lot of money to the right people."

"What are you suggesting?" she asked.

"I know a guy who knows a guy..." he began.

"And what if the Englishman's not selling it?" she said, cutting him off. "What if he's going to use it to hurt people?"

"This guy I know, he might still be able to help. He's got his ear to the ground for all sorts of things."

She looked at him, silently, and he wondered what she was thinking.

"I can't think of a better idea," Julia said finally. "Okay, what do you need from me?"

Peter looked over the email to make sure it had all of the details it needed. He didn't want to put too much into it, but it needed to include enough to be useful.

Once he was satisfied with it, he ran it through an encryption algorithm and sent it to the digital equivalent of a dead drop. It was encrypted with a public key system that only the recipient—Bernard Stokes—would be able to read. And if by chance anyone was able to crack the encryption, all they would find was a recipe for apple pie, and not a very good apple pie at that. The real message was encoded through a null cipher he and Bernard had agreed upon years ago, where every fifth letter in the email was a letter from the real message.

Bernard Stokes was a good man to know if you were very wealthy, and very sick. He dealt in gray-market drugs. Nothing so prosaic as opium or cocaine. Need an experimental drug for your stage IV pancreatic cancer? Trying to stave off HIV and your cocktail's gone bad? Then Stokes was your man.

Peter had long ago stopped trying to justify Stokes's occupation. At one point he had rationalized that the man was doing a service, getting medications to people who needed them. But the more he dealt with Stokes, the more it became apparent that he specialized in the diseases of the rich.

"Well, that's that," Peter said. "Now we wait."

"You can't just call him?" Julia said.

"He's not like your average street dealer. The mail I sent will go to a secure server somewhere, and let him know it's there. If we're lucky, he reads it. If we're luckier, he answers me."

"All that security, and he's just going to call you?"

Peter laughed. "No. I told him we're somewhere near Hartford. He'll encode the address of a nearby phone booth into his response, and a number to call him. He'll have taken steps to secure both lines."

"Do you really think someone will be listening in?"

Peter shrugged. "I don't, but he does. He's not doing all this for our benefit. He's got a lot to lose if he gets caught. This may take some time. But if he does have any information for us, we might have to move fast. You said that if this thing gets into someone without epilepsy, it's bad. Is there a vaccine for it? Or an antiviral if someone gets infected?"

"I've been working on that," she said, "but it hasn't been my highest priority. I've got some inactivated samples of the virus to work with, back at the lab, and I've had some computer models running. The virus has a regulatory protein and there's some indication that introducing a new amino acid might fold that protein into..." She stopped, and studied his face. "I'm sorry, am I getting too technical? I do that sometimes."

"No, that's fine. I'm following. Mostly. Proteins are developed from chains of amino acids into 3D forms, right? And the form it takes changes its function?"

"Right," she said. "Different acids lead to different structures. Folded one way, the protein does its job. Folded another, it can have disastrous effects on an organism, like causing cystic fibrosis, or creating amyloid plaques in the brain leading to Creutzfeldt–Jakob disease."

"Mad cow disease."

"Right. Some viruses have proteins that make up a protective coating."

"That's the capsid, right?" Peter said, dredging up long-forgotten biology lessons. He was a little surprised that he could remember it. He hadn't had to think about any of this stuff for years.

"Yes," she replied, "But this one also has a protein it uses to regulate function. The last models I ran suggested that introducing a new amino acid into the mix would cause a mis-fold of the protein, essentially rendering the virus inert and unable to function properly. Introduced into an infected host, the virus with the mis-fold should transfer the new protein to the rest, and halt the process."

Peter thought about that for a second.

"Infect the infection."

"Basically, yes."

"How far did you get?"

"I left a model running on the computers in the lab before I came to meet you." She looked at her watch. "It takes a long time for the calculations to run as it goes through different fold permutations, but if it's not finished now, it should be soon."

Peter checked his email.

"Nothing from Stokes yet. Not surprising. It could be hours before he gets back to us." *If he gets back to us at all.* "Why don't we check on the progress of the model? You said it's in your lab?"

"Yes," Julia said, her face creasing into a frown. "But what if the Englishman's there?"

"I don't think he will be. They had a chance to grab

you earlier, and they didn't take it. You don't have any live virus at the lab, right? Just dead samples? I think they probably have what they wanted. Still, I can go in on my own and check it out. You can stay here."

"No," she said. "You won't know what you're looking for. We'll go together." She took Peter's hands in her own. They were cold, shaking.

"We'll be okay," he said. "I promise."

3

"That's it?" Peter said, parking the car.

The Center for Seizure Disorder Research looked a lot more impressive on its website. Forced perspective in the marketing photos had taken a small, generic office building in an industrial park in Hartford, with its stucco walls and dark glass front door and windows, and made it look as though it were part of something larger. Instead of the sprawling complex the photos implied, it was a single-story building that couldn't hold more than a few offices and a moderately sized lab.

His sense of anticlimax must have come across in his tone. He caught Julia frowning at him.

"It may not look like much, "she said, "but there's more science going on in that building than in most universities in the country."

"Not saying there isn't," he said. "Better than a lot of places I've seen." Better than Walter's lab, that was for sure. All he had was a dingy set of rooms at Harvard. At least this place wasn't stuck in a basement.

"You've seen a lot of labs?"

"Enough," he said, getting out of the car and heading

toward the building. "Come on. Let's see what we can—"

Peter paused near the front door, putting a hand out to stop Julia from going further. She had her keys in her hand and froze when she saw it.

The glass door had been shattered.

Only a handful of cars were scattered through the lot, and theirs was the only one parked near the building. Peter didn't think anyone was still here, but he couldn't rule it out.

He wished he had a gun. He'd searched through Westerson's house, looking for something that might come in handy, but all he could find was a small can of pepper spray. It wasn't much, but it was something. He pulled it out of his pocket and edged slowly toward the door.

"This the alarm panel?" Peter asked, pointing to a small metal box. The front of it was torn off and the wires had been stripped, alligator-clipped together to short it out. Julia nodded, eyes wide with fear. She held her keys in a tight fist, Peter noted, making an impromptu weapon.

He edged the door open with his foot. Shattered glass lay strewn across the floor of the small lobby.

"Where's the lab?" he said. "Is anyone normally here at this time?"

"Not on a Saturday, no," she said, stepping over the shards. "Lab's in the back. God, if they've destroyed my research..."

She pushed past Peter and headed toward a set of double metal doors at the end of a small hallway. The keypad next to these doors was just as damaged as the one in the front.

The room they entered was split by two thick, Plexiglas partitions, which created an airlock between the two that that held a few hazmat suits, and a decontamination shower. Their side of the room held computers and desks, the other side held centrifuges, refrigerators, microscopes, and other lab equipment. The whole place had been tossed. Computers lay on the floor, chairs overturned. In the clean room all of the refrigerators were open and broken glass containers were strewn across the floor.

He tried not to think what might have been in them.

Vials of slide stains, used for enhancing the visibility of bacteria and cells under a microscope, lay broken on the floor, leaving dark patches of red and blue that someone had walked through, resulting in a track from one room to the other.

Peter bent down and studied a footprint. It was dry.

"This is hours old," he said, sliding the pepper spray back into his pocket. "Whoever did this is gone now."

"Damn," Julia said. "This is worse than when they stole the virus the first time."

"Is anything missing?"

"I can't tell." She bent down to one of the laptops on the floor. Though the screen was cracked, it was still on, and it sprang to life when she tapped a key. "At least we have some good news."

"Oh?"

"They didn't destroy the computers. The folding program has been running since I started it." She tapped a few keys, pulled up a chart on the screen. "This is promising. There are a few candidates here for the folding sequence we need."

"That is good news," he agreed. "What now?"

"Without a live sample of the virus, all I can do is run more computer models," Julia said. She tapped some more keys. "But this is a good start. There's one in particular that looks like it might do the trick. I'll get started."

"Will it work?" he said.

"I can't say for certain," she said. "Normally we'd

need a live sample, infected subjects, and thorough testing. Barring those, we won't know until we try it."

"Hopefully we won't have to use it at all," Peter said. "Anything I can do?"

She smiled at him.

"Sit there and look pretty?"

"I don't know if I can do pretty. How about ruggedly handsome?"

"That works," she said. "Oh, and if they haven't destroyed the coffee maker, maybe make us a pot? This could take a while."

Peter sipped the coffee and checked his email for the third time in an hour. He hated waiting, and he was getting restless.

Though the lab had been trashed, several of the room's computers were still intact. After finding a laptop that worked, then getting it up and running, he was able to get online while Julia tweaked her program and ran her models. There wasn't much he could contribute on that front. He understood the concepts, had enough of a grounding in biology that he could follow along, but the data was so dense it would take him three times as long to interpret information that Julia already knew by heart.

So he contented himself with drinking his coffee and waiting for Stokes's email to appear.

"You're doing it again," Julia said.

"What?"

"Drumming on the table." She looked up from a spreadsheet of data and rubbed her eyes. "I know this is boring, but I'm trying to concentrate."

"Sorry," he said. "How about I go and get us sandwiches, or something. Stretch my legs a bit."

The computer chimed, drawing his attention back to his screen. In his email was a message from Bernard Stokes.

"Is that your friend?" Julia asked eagerly.

"Friend might be stretching the definition a bit, but yes."

If the message really was from Stokes, then he would have encrypted it with one-half of an encryption key for which only Peter had the match, just as Peter had done when he sent the original message. Peter ran the decryption software, and a minute later he had a long poem of gibberish on the screen.

"Do you have a pen?" he asked. He found a business card on the floor from an up-ended wastebasket, while Julia searched for a pen, finding one under a drawer that had been yanked out of one of the desks.

Stokes's security measures were a pain in the ass, but Peter understood the need to be careful. Peter had to worry about local cops and people like Big Eddie. But Stokes operated at a level where one wrong move could mean a visit from the feds, or a highly paid assassin. Such was the life when you dealt with the very rich.

He counted every fifth letter in the message until he had an address on Capitol Avenue in Hartford. There weren't as many payphones as there used to be, so it was probably a public place like a gas station or a diner.

He checked the address online and laughed.

"What's so funny?" Julia said.

"An old joke," he said, and stood up. "I'm going to check this out."

"Do you want me to come with you?"

"No, I got this." Peter grabbed his jacket. "Besides, we need to get that antiviral figured out as soon as possible."

"Okay. Where exactly is it you're going?"

"To find religion."

4

BOSTON, MA 2005

A cold, rainswept, December day. Peter was acting as a go-between for a socialite whose daughter was fighting a particularly nasty form of leukemia. Stokes had the product, an experimental cancer drug that had been mysteriously "liberated" from a lab in New York, while the socialite had the money.

Peter didn't know the particulars, didn't even know the socialite's name. He'd gotten the job through a friend, Nathan Wallace, who owed him a favor, and Peter wanted to stay as much in the dark as possible. What he did know was that the girl was in bad shape, and the woman would do anything in her power to save her child. So for a cut off the top, Peter was going to play drug mule.

"You're Peter Bishop," Stokes said by way of greeting. "Wallace vouches for you." They stood in the nave of the St. Joseph Catholic Church. He was a short, wiry man in his fifties, with skin that was tight on his face and gray hair that stuck up, giving him the appearance of a bristle-brush.

"You're Bernard Stokes," Peter replied. "He vouches for you, too." He looked around. "Where's the product?"

"Where's the money?"

Peter hefted a metal briefcase in his hand.

"Presumably here."

"Presumably?"

"I'm just the errand boy. I haven't looked, haven't counted it. I don't even have the combination. Could be a stack of dead fish, as far as I know."

"Well, let's hope not." Stokes reached out. "Give it here."

Peter handed the briefcase over. Stokes put it on top of one of the church pews and spun the combination lock. It snapped open, and Stokes looked at the stacks of hundred-dollar bills inside, all neatly wrapped in their mustard-colored currency straps. He closed the case and nodded at a nearby statue.

"You'll find what you're looking for behind the Blessed Virgin."

"Much obliged," Peter said. He walked over, and found a similar briefcase behind the statue. He didn't bother looking inside. He wouldn't know what he was looking at, but from its heft and the way it shifted in his hand, he guessed it was full of plastic IV bags.

He was about to leave when a gunshot echoed through the church. The bullet hit the far side of the wall, sending shards of stone flying. He and Stokes dropped to the floor.

"Something I should know about?" Peter muttered, trying to keep his voice from echoing all through the church. He looked under the pews, and saw the feet of three men wearing dress slacks and long, black coats. They were entering the church, and bickering. Seemed the one who had fired had gotten ahead of himself, and the other two were chewing him out over it.

"I was going to ask you the same thing," Stokes said.

"Like I said, I'm just the errand boy."

"Dammit," Stokes said. "Probably the girl's father. Horrible man. Been involved in an ugly custody battle with his wife. Now that the poor thing's got cancer, it seems he wants to use her medication as leverage against his wife. One of those, 'if he can't have her, no one will' sorts of things. Man's a psychopath."

"That's messed up. How do you know all that?"

"I do thorough research regarding every business transaction," Stokes said. Then he looked around. "How the hell do we get out of here? I've never been in a church before."

So much for thorough research, Peter thought.

"Not getting shot would be a good start."

Stokes just looked at him as if he was an idiot. Peter scanned the room from his lowered vantage point, and saw a doorway on the side of the nave two rows up from their position. He pulled a pen from his pocket.

"I don't think they know exactly where we are," he said. "So when I throw this, crawl as quickly and quietly as you can to that door." He gestured to indicate where he should go.

Peter tossed the pen under the pews. It skittered across the floor, the sound echoing loudly in the empty church. He watched the men rush to the other side of the room, and then quickly followed Stokes to the door.

It didn't take long for their pursuers to figure out they'd been had. Stokes and Peter had just made it to the parking lot when more shots rang out, barely missing Stokes and blowing out a tire instead.

"This way!" Peter yelled, grabbing a clearly panicked Stokes and shoving him toward his own car.

"Hooligans!" someone yelled. Peter looked behind him to see an old priest running out of the church brandishing an umbrella. The three men, surprised by the screaming priest, panicked and ran, giving Peter and Stokes just enough time to get into the car.

Moments later, they were peeling out of the parking lot. Stokes shook from the adrenaline, and crossed himself—awkwardly and incorrectly.

"Wrong order."

"What?"

"It's left, then right," Peter said. "Not the other way around. Did you just find religion?"

"There are no atheists in foxholes," Stokes replied.

"Bullshit," Peter said, but he laughed. "Where am I dropping you off?"

"Anywhere with alcohol," Stokes said.

NEAR HARTFORD, CT 2008

The Sacred Heart Catholic Church on Capitol Avenue in Hartford was an imposing, red-brick structure with two wide towers flanking an entrance with large, arched stained-glass windows running along the sides. Peter stood on the steps and wondered if Stokes realized just how closely this place resembled St. Joseph's in Boston, where the two of them had met.

The man has a healthy sense of irony, he mused.

Peter walked into the church and looked for the payphone. It didn't take him long to find it next to the restrooms near the side entrance. Stokes wasn't one to sit by a phone, waiting for a call. Whatever number he had given Peter was undoubtedly a burner. The man probably had dozens of them.

He punched in a code Stokes had sent him and waited for the dial tone to shift before punching the phone number in. He let it ring three times and hung up.

A few seconds later the payphone rang.

"Did you just find religion?" Stokes said the moment Peter picked up.

"There are no atheists in foxholes," Peter said.

"Bullshit," Stokes said. "What can I do for you, Peter? Your message said something about an epilepsy drug."

"What do you know about the Center for Seizure Disorder Research?"

"Julia Lachaux," Stokes said immediately. "Thought that might be her work you were describing. Some fascinating experiments using viruses, of all things, though there appears to be some controversy over the direction her treatment is taking. Rumors abound that it could overwrite a person's DNA, though how exactly isn't entirely clear.

"She's published very little about it, and most of the news out of her lab is vague at best. One particularly juicy tidbit is that the virus was stolen from her lab a short while ago."

"It was," Peter said.

"Oh, that could be bad," Stokes said. "Especially if some of the other rumors are true. Particularly the one that says it's based on smallpox."

"That one's true, too," Peter said. Stokes said nothing for a long time. "You there?"

"I'm digesting all this," Stokes said. "All right, boy, out with it. I think you need to tell me everything."

Peter looked around. There was no one in the church that he could see, and from a sign on the front door it looked as if afternoon Mass wouldn't be starting for another few hours.

"Well," Peter said, "let's start with Bangkok."

Peter had been talking for the better part of an hour, and he was starting to get a sore neck from being on the phone so long. Every now and then a member of the church personnel passed by, tossing him a curious look. He just grinned, pointed to the earpiece, and mouthed, *my mother*.

That seemed to satisfy them.

"An Englishman," Stokes said.

"Yeah," Peter replied. "I'm thinking there might be a connection between Julia's guy, and the one I saw in Bangkok."

"First-name basis already?" Stokes paused. "You slept with her, didn't you?"

"Focus, Stokes. The Englishman."

"Right. Interesting. Have you ever heard of a man named Richard McCoy?"

"Doesn't ring a bell. Should it?"

"Not unless you're a fan of Royal Shakespeare washouts, London dinner theater, or early nineties British horror films, no. He's an actor, if you can call it that, who had some minor fame in the late eighties until he drank it away." Peter could hear the tapping of a keyboard and wondered what sorts of databases Stokes could access.

"He's been doing bit parts since then," Stokes continued. "Barely staying one step ahead of the bill collectors. He disappeared about three months ago, and his name's been bouncing around the sorts of message boards the authorities would sell their grandmothers to get access to. Talking about wanting to move some merchandise. Somebody's taken him up on it, too. Though his messages are rather cryptic, epilepsy figures prominently in them."

"What the hell would a has-been actor be doing with an epilepsy cure?"

"No idea. Might not even be him. Identity theft is big business, as you well know. That's not the strange thing, though. I've moved medications like this before, and there's a particular pattern these sorts of deals take. A particular way the language is used."

Peter was beginning to get a sinking feeling.

"It's not a drug deal, is it?"

"No, I don't think so. Particularly because it looks like they'll be moving the merchandise at"—Stokes paused as he typed some more—"the Ambassador Hotel in Manhattan, the day after tomorrow."

"Why would that be unusual?" Given the types of people Stokes dealt with, he saw no reason why McCoy and his people wouldn't stay at a high-end hotel like the Ambassador.

"Because the hotel's going to be crawling with police and federal agents," Stokes said. "There's a fund-raising dinner that night for the black guy who's running for president. If that's not a place for a terrorist bio-weapon, I don't know what is."

PART FIVE

1

The Ambassador Hotel, tucked away in the theater district in midtown Manhattan, was famous for political and presidential goings-on. It was a venerable old building, full of history and secrets. Its turn-of-the-century splendor had been lovingly maintained through the decades and it had recently been granted historic landmark status, assuring that it would remain pristine and unaltered well into the future.

With the security surrounding the presidential candidate and his party, Peter and Julia weren't going to be able to get anywhere near the place without Curt.

Curt Caldwell, like many chefs, had a checkered past.

He had long since gone straight, and worked his ass off, scrubbing pots and deveining mountains of shrimp in a dozen New York kitchens. He'd risen through the ranks, made his bones, and finally scored a plum gig as executive chef in the Ambassador's massive kitchen. It was a pretty stodgy, old school steak-and-chocolate kind of operation, all Waldorf salads and Beef Wellington with no room for culinary creativity, but Curt was glad to be there.

Especially considering the alternative.

Peter figured his best bet would be to give Curt a little reminder of that alternative, and the person who'd helped him avoid it. It was time to cash in a favor.

He and Julia sat in the Stage Deli, a touristy restaurant on Seventh Avenue just north of Times Square. It had been decorated with a ham-fisted New York theme, but just as easily could have been in Los Angeles, Las Vegas, or Atlantic City.

Julia was picking apart a dry, crumbling black-and-white cookie without eating it, while he forced down a culinary abomination that had billed itself as a "Pastrami Burrito."

"I don't know how you can eat at a time like this," she said, shoving away her plateful of crumbs and downing the dregs of her third black coffee.

"Gotta feed the machine," Peter replied, shrugging. "That's biology 101, isn't it?" She just grimaced.

"Are you sure this friend of yours can be trusted?" she asked for the umpteenth time.

"Positive," he replied. "Given everything I know about Curt Caldwell's less-than-kosher past, it'll be in his best interests to keep me happy."

As if on cue, a tall man in his mid-forties walked into the restaurant, scanning the tables. He was thick through the middle, with a pale, nocturnal complexion and full sleeves of ink on both arms. Dark, messy hair and blood-shot blue eyes, dressed in civvies—jeans and sneakers with a vintage rock-and-roll T-shirt under a battered leather jacket. But his relaxed clothing clashed with the tense, tightly wound body language beneath. He had a black canvas duffle bag slung over one shoulder.

Peter held up his hand and Curt spotted him, heading over to their table.

"This is a really bad idea," Curt said, not bothering with a greeting. He stared straight at Peter, and if he even noticed Julia, he gave no hint of it.

"Duly noted," Peter said. He gestured to the bag. "That the stuff?"

Curt nodded, setting the duffle on the booth seat next to him.

"Uniforms, IDs, everything you need to get into the kitchen," he said. "After that, you're on your own."

"Curt, you're a lifesaver," Peter said. "You have no idea."

"I don't *want* an idea," he replied. "I don't want to know nothing. All I want to know is, are we square?"

Peter nodded.

"Square," he said. "More than square—I owe you one."

"No," Curt replied, eyes narrow and face gone hard. "You don't owe me a damn thing, kid. We're square. That's it."

He turned and walked away without another word.

"Nice meeting you, too," Julia said to his retreating back, her eyebrow arched.

"Forget it," Peter said. "That's the best you'll get out of him on a good day." He unzipped the bag. "Let's see what we've got here."

Inside he found two chef jackets with the Ambassador Hotel logo on one breast and last names embroidered on the other. The larger jacket said Wheatley, while the smaller was labeled Cooper. Also included were two pairs of checked pants, two pairs of sturdy clogs, and two laminated IDs, complete with photos so badly blurred that they were rendered useless.

Peter handed Julia the ID with the name "Lucy Cooper."

"We don't have time to go back to our hotel. Hit the restroom and get changed," he said. "We need to hurry."

They walked briskly up 5th Avenue toward the Ambassador, just a couple of harried line cooks, running late for a shift. The streets were closed for several blocks in every direction around the hotel.

Peter whistled inwardly at the security, which was tighter than he'd ever seen it. Not really surprising, though, what with the combination of post-9/11 paranoia and the fact that an African-American was running for president—and looked like he might actually have a shot at winning. Not that Peter paid any real attention to politics, unless there was a way he could turn them to his advantage.

On this particular day, the politics presented a serious *disadvantage*. And while the security was crazy over-the-top, they were right to be paranoid, for once. Someone really did want to kill the candidate, and all his supporters. Even crazier was the fact that if all that security succeeded, and managed to keep Peter and Julia out, the real terrorists would succeed.

They'd infect the entire city, regardless of political affiliation. The virus was naturally bipartisan.

First Peter and Julia needed to get past the street cops. Several heavy wooden barriers had been placed to block off the street, while knots of police in full SWAT armor patrolled the sidewalks. There were pretty big crowds milling around the edges of the secure area. Curious natives and confused tourists mingled with a smattering of nut jobs carrying handwritten signs. As Peter led Julia through the onlookers toward the checkpoint, he gripped her elbow and spoke in a low voice.

"Act bored," he said. "Like this is just a minor annoyance, and all you want is to get to work without being hassled. Let me do the talking."

"Right," she said.

He started shouldering his way through the crowd with Julia in tow, allowing his expression to go soft and neutral with just the slightest hint of mild annoyance in the brow. When he reached the barrier, he was stopped by a handsome Puerto Rican cop with a clean-cut, central-casting kind of face.

"Street's closed," the officer said to Peter with the air of a man who had said the exact same words so many times that they had lost all their meaning. He might as well have been a tape recording.

"We're line cooks at the Ambassador," Peter said, holding out the ID Curt had provided. "And we're already late for the banquet prep."

The cop took his ID and scowled at it, then did the same with Julia. Peter glanced over at her, and saw that she was giving an Oscar-winning performance of bored New York indifference. Impressive—better than his, even. She continued to surprise him with her hidden talents.

"Okay," the cop said, handing back the IDs. "Go on through." He turned and called over his shoulder. "Shulberg, you wanna escort these two around to the service entrance."

Another cop, presumably Shulberg, came over to the barrier and moved it aside just enough for Peter and Julia to squeeze through. He was tall and lean, like an upright greyhound, even with the added bulk of the body armor filling out his long narrow torso. His eyes were cold and blue, all business.

"This way," he said, and nothing more.

He led the two of them around a variety of large,

bulky vehicles that looked more military than police, and down a gauntlet of armed and surly men who all glowered at Peter as they passed. He didn't let it rattle him.

The service entrance was around the corner from the showy main doors, almost hidden between a large parked van and a locked dumpster. Standing by the dented metal door was a fed wearing a rumpled suit and a grim, humorless expression. His body language was all stress and anxiety, shoulders pinched and hands fisted, and a tic at the hinge of his jaw. But he was fighting not to let it creep into his eyes.

Peter could relate.

"Cooks," the cop named Shulberg told him, presenting Peter and Julia like a hunting dog dropping a dead duck at his master's feet.

The fed nodded and sized them up.

"IDs," he said.

They presented the IDs again, and this time, the fed pulled out a little hand-held device to scan the barcode under each of their fake names. Peter had to force himself to breathe, calm and slow. Beside him, Julia was a brick wall. Unflappable.

The device pinged its approval, and Peter fought a smile.

Mr. Caldwell, you are a miracle worker.

"Go on in," the fed told him, pushing the door open.

On the other side was a short hallway containing two other feds, one black and male, the other white and female. The male agent was a stocky little bantam rooster type, shorter than his red-headed female partner, and he didn't look very happy about the fact. The way he held his shoulders and chin, Peter would have bet money that he felt threatened by her.

The woman, on the other hand, was calm and

confident, her body loose and relaxed, but far from lazy. If things went bad, she was going to be the one Peter would have to worry about. She had it under control, and that made her the most dangerous person in the room.

The fed from outside nodded, silently indicating that Peter and Julia had been cleared. It was like a worker ant passing signals to its sisters. The two partners nodded back, and motioned for them to step forward.

The man took Peter by the arm, while the woman took Julia, placing her purse and shoulder bag on a table. Electronic wands were passed up and down their bodies, and then they were patted down thoroughly by hand.

At least buy a guy dinner first, Peter thought.

"What's this?" the female agent asked Julia.

Peter craned his head to see what she was talking about, and then he fought to keep his expression neutral.

The female agent was holding up the unzipped case that held the antidote and a syringe.

"It's my insulin," Julia said. "I'm diabetic. See?"

To Peter's amazement, she pulled a blood glucose monitoring kit from her purse. He was impressed, and let himself start breathing again.

"Fine," the female agent said, zipping the case again. "Go ahead in."

"Now what?" Julia said as they rounded a corner. "We're not going to the kitchens, are we?" Now that they were out of sight of the feds, her hands began to shake. She closed her eyes and steadied herself.

Peter had kept most of the plan to himself—partly because he wasn't sure how much it would freak her out, but also because he was making a lot of it up as he went along. He probably should have given her more credit;

but she had been ready to bolt once before. While it was one thing to be chased by crazy thugs with guns, it was another to actively go looking for them. She'd gotten this far, but how much further would she go?

"No," he replied. "Me cooking would be a bad idea. We're here to prevent a terrorist action, not create one." He hoped the joke would get her to crack a smile, but her face remained stone-cold serious. "Now that we're in, we should be able to move around without anyone questioning us, but we're going to need to steal another ID."

"Why?" she asked, a puzzled look on her face. "Can't we get around like this?"

"Yeah, but we don't know where we're going. We need to access the hotel's reservation system, and see if we can find out where these people are. Most of it's online, but to find out who's actually here at any given moment, we need to get into the records of who they've scanned using the ID cards. A line cook isn't going to have access.

"If you have the right card," he continued, "The system knows who you are and logs you in the moment you swipe it at one of the terminals."

"Where do we get one of those?"

"We're going to start with the staff locker room. If we don't find one there, we'll see if we can lift one from someone on the desk staff."

"Lift?" she said. "Like, steal?"

"Don't tell me you have a problem with that."

"No," she said. "I've just never done it before."

"If it comes to that, I'll handle it. I've got enough experience for the both of us."

The Ambassador's service corridors were like every other hotel all over the world—drab, utilitarian passageways with scratched and scraped white walls, allowing the staff to scurry through its innards like rats in a maze, invisible to the guests until they were needed. Peter found the employee locker room by watching people in their civvies passing through the corridors, and tracing them back. He needn't have bothered, though. It was exactly where he thought it would be.

He had seen this kind of layout in every hotel he'd ever been in. He found himself flashing back to the hallways of the Infinity Towers in Bangkok, where this all had started. It was almost identical, save for the language most of the signs were in.

"Okay, the locker room's going to be split between a men's and a women's section," Peter said quietly as they approached. "We'll split up. You're looking for anyone in a blazer, or an open locker with one hanging in it. Those people are going to be with guest services, and probably have access to the front desk for reservations, concierge, that sort of thing. One of those ID cards should get us what we need. You see one of those, you poke your head into the men's section and grab me."

Julia nodded, and Peter slipped away from her, speeding up to make it appear as if they weren't together when they got to the locker-room doors.

Inside, Peter found row upon row of orange lockers with worn, wooden benches sitting between them. A few men were changing into their uniforms—cook's whites, every one of them.

He walked the aisles looking for an open locker, or an unattended pocket he could pilfer. He found a blazer hanging over a hook next to the bathroom and quickly checked the pockets. Nothing. But it wasn't a total loss. Some hotel staff members were less visible than others, so he switched his cook's jacket for the blazer.

He had timed their arrival in the hope that they would catch a shift break, giving them a greater opportunity to find a card, but though the corridors all looked the same, different hotels adhered to different schedules. It didn't look as if there was a changing of the guard happening at the moment.

Suddenly, Peter heard a loud banging coming from the women's locker room, then unintelligible yelling. Somebody was having a fight. A sinking feeling crawled through his stomach and he ran over to the other side, doing his best to look like a concerned employee.

What he saw was pretty much what he'd expected. Julia had tried to lift somebody's ID card and gotten caught. A short Latina woman in a rust-colored blazer, whose ID card was clipped to her left breast pocket, was yelling at her, accusing Julia of theft. To her credit, Julia was throwing accusations right back at her.

A few other people were gathered around them, but as soon as he appeared they scattered, and did their best to act as if nothing had happened.

"Everybody all right in here?" he said.

"No, everything is *not* all right," the Latina said. "She was trying to steal my wallet."

"I was not stealing your wallet," Julia protested. "I said I lost mine, and that the one on the bench looked like it. God, you are such a bitch."

Yikes!

"Whoa, hang on," Peter said, shoving himself between them and putting his hands out to separate them. "I'm sure we can work this out. That is your wallet, right Miss—" He looked at the name on the woman's uniform. "—Marquez?"

"I wasn't trying to steal anything," Julia said.

"I'm going to lodge a complaint," the Latina replied. She squinted at Julia's ID badge. "Lucy Cooper? I am *so* going to get you goddamn fired." Marquez grabbed her wallet from the bench, and stormed out of the locker room.

"Okay, let's go," Peter said. "Before anybody starts wondering what a guy is doing in the women's locker room."

"But what about the badge?"

"I have it," Peter said, clipping Marquez's ID card to his blazer pocket. "I had mine palmed when I walked in here, and switched it with hers when I got between the two of you. She probably won't notice that it's the wrong one until she doesn't have access to something she needs to do."

"Slick," Julia said.

"I do have my moments."

From there it didn't take long for them to find a terminal. Besides the front desk, there was one near the kitchen where the orders for room service were verified against room reservations. A quick scan of his card and the terminal logged him in under the name Leanna Marquez.

"What are we looking for?"

"I honestly don't know," Peter admitted, bringing up a list of all of the hotel's current guests. "Anything that seems, well, *wrong*. I don't know how to describe it—it's sort of a sixth sense you develop.

"Something that sounds English, maybe?" he said. "It's hard to hide an accent, so he'd want to have something that explains it. I doubt he'd use the McCoy name, though. That would just be stu—"

He stopped, staring at the screen.

"Well, what do you know," he said. "Richard McCoy. Room 803." He looked at her, a smile on his face. "Let's go stop a terrorist."

2

"We have to hurry," Peter said. "If they've already left the room, we don't stand a chance."

When they reached 803, Peter took what appeared to be a common cell phone out of his pocket and removed a cover from the back. He pulled out a flat, square plate and inserted it into the lock, then turned over the "phone" and activated the tiny screen. Green numerals spun while the little machine chatted up the lock and found out what it wanted to hear.

There was a soft *click*, and the light on the lock flashed green.

Peter and Julia exchanged a look, then he pushed the door open.

In the room was an attractive couple in their early thirties. He was dirty blond with a soft, thoughtful face and spidery glasses. She was lighter blond and petite with a boyish build and freckles. They were both in their underwear—he in boxers and she in a thin camisole and lacy boy-shorts.

But when Peter and Julia entered, the woman was injecting a familiar liquid into a vein in the crook of the man's arm. There was another empty syringe sitting on the bedside table, and a revolver sitting on the top of a low wooden dresser.

They both looked up, startled.

"Who the hell are you?" the woman asked, withdrawing the now empty syringe from the man's arm.

Julia stepped forward.

"I'm a doctor," she said. "I'm here to help you."

"Help us?" The man frowned and stood. "Help us how?"

"You have no idea what you're dealing with," Julia said. "Whatever you were told that liquid will do, it was a lie. It's a virus, and when it matures inside of you, it will put you through the most excruciating agony you can imagine. It could take as long as twelve hours for your heart to finally stop beating and you will be conscious and aware the entire time.

"I have an antidote," she continued. "Please, let me help you."

"You don't know what you're talking about," the woman replied, anger beginning to play across her features. "The Englishman said..."

"He lied to me, too," Julia said, "don't you see? I *invented* the virus. I know better than anyone what it's capable of doing."

While this little chat was going on, Peter was edging slowly toward the revolver on the dresser. He couldn't tell if it was loaded, but it might give them an edge—or at least a bargaining chip. So he continued to inch closer and closer, willing himself to be invisible, eyes fixed on the angry woman.

Then he stopped.

Something was happening to her.

It was subtle, just a little bit of swelling under the

hinges of her jaw, and a rosy flush creeping up her cheeks. But then lumps appeared in her neck, and as he watched they grew so fast that they went from peas to goose eggs in a matter of seconds. Around the edges of the lumps, clusters of tiny, red-and-white pustules appeared like a crop of glistening fairy-tale mushrooms.

The woman's breathing was becoming rapid and irregular.

Peter didn't have any idea if this virus was airborne or not, but the room suddenly felt stagnant, thick, almost claustrophobic. It was as if he could *feel* the infection floating in the air like ash. His skin went tight all over, and he had to fight the urge to cut and run.

He started to move again, careful not to attract her attention.

Just focus on the gun.

"You're already showing symptoms of infection," Julia said, her voice as steady and calm as ever. The man was staring now, too. "Different metabolisms circulate the viral load through the bloodstream at differing speeds, but I wouldn't be surprised if you begin to experience seizure activity within the next..."

She glanced at her watch, but before she could finish her sentence, the blond woman let out a strangled gasp, went rigid, and dropped as if she'd been hit with a cattle prod. The man backed away from her, eyes saucer wide as bloody pink foam started to ooze from between the woman's tightly clenched teeth.

"Well, about now," Julia said, pulling the antidote from her purse and filling the syringe. "You'd better step back. She may become violent."

As she moved toward the prone figure, the man lunged forward to block her. Stretching to the side, he reached into the pocket of a jacket that had been slung over the back of a chair, and pulled out a .45 automat

With shaking hands, he drew a bead between Julia's eyes.

"Stay away from her," he rasped.

The woman on the floor began to writhe, mewling sounds coming from between her lips. The man glanced down in terror.

Peter saw his chance and lunged for the gun on the dresser. Grabbing it, he swung it up in a smooth arc.

"Drop it," he said, pointing the weapon at the terrified man. For a moment, everyone was frozen in place. Everyone except for the woman, who was flopping around on the carpet like a gaffed bass. The flesh of her throat continued mutating, delicate red fans of flesh like gills multiplying beneath her chin as her neck became grotesquely elongated. The egg-sized lumps grew stalks, stretching away from her body like a snail's eyes.

Suddenly the air on the other side of the bed rippled like water, and for a fraction of a second, Peter glimpsed a choppy, almost lenticular image of a *different room*, as if he was viewing it through thick, old-fashioned horizontal blinds. The other room was identical in layout, but shabby and sad, with peeling wallpaper and stained plaster. The dim, dingy light sifting through those impossible slashes in the air was the color of nicotine-stained teeth, and the atmosphere was suddenly thick with a distinct new odor.

Roach spray and cheap paint, mixed with sour sweat and urine.

Julia saw it, too, and stared.

Before Peter could reconcile what he was seeing, the woman on the floor let out a shriek like a pig in a slaughterhouse, and arched her back so high off the carpet that Peter thought her spine was about to snap in two. He watched in amazement and horror as her ribs started elongating and punching through her skin like ivory knives. As if an angry velociraptor was trapped inside her chest, and was trying to claw its way out.

That was too much for the man—with a gargled cry, he bolted for the door. Caught entirely flat-footed, Peter just watched as his intended target slipped out of sight.

"*Dammit,*" Julia said, glancing over her shoulder at the closing door, and then back at the woman on the floor. "Hold her."

Peter took a step back.

"Are you crazy?" he asked. "I'm not touching her."

"Don't be childish," Julia snapped. "She's not infectious... not yet. See those nodes?" She used her foot to pin down the flailing woman's chest and gestured to the egg-sized ovoids dangling from her rapidly mutating neck. "When they reach the size of my fist, they'll burst, and that's when the virus will go airborne. At that point, there will be nothing we can do to stop it."

He looked down at the woman, unconsciously rubbing the hand that wasn't holding the gun against his pant leg, feeling like it was dirty.

"Can't we just shoot her?" he asked. As soon as he said it, it sounded wrong, but he continued. "There's no way she can survive this. It would put her out of her misery, and might—"

"It would be a spectacularly bad idea," Julia replied. "If the host dies, the virus will go into emergency survival mode and eject itself forcibly through every orifice of the body, in a desperate bid to find a new host. That would be us."

"But what about the guy?" he asked, looking back at the door. "We have to stop him before he gets anywhere near the banquet."

"He won't get far in his condition," she said. "But our

first priority has to be to inject this one with the antidote. So do you want to talk about it some more, or do you want to do it?"

Peter took a cautious step toward the woman, sticking the gun into his belt.

Without warning, she curled all of her limbs into a tight ball, and then lurched to a shuddering crouch.

He put both hands out, palms forward. Half placating, and half ready to grab her.

"Okay, now," he said. "Let's just take it easy."

The blond woman's eyes rolled and widened, blood leaking from the corners like gory tears. Her eyeballs seemed to pulse, swelling and shrinking like beating hearts. He had no idea if she could even see him.

Julia began to approach from Peter's right, holding the loaded syringe at the ready.

The woman's body started to tic, and then spasm on the left side, so Peter shifted his weight to his left foot, ready to shoot in and grab her if she made a break in that direction. To his shock and surprise, her head whipped around toward Julia. She shrieked, her lower jaw splitting open in the center like that of a feeding snake.

She lunged, faster than he thought she could.

Julia flinched and stumbled backward, catching herself against the desk and throwing her free arm up in front of her face. She dropped the syringe, and it bounced off the carpet and rolled away.

Peter grabbed the back of the woman's half-shredded camisole and tried to haul her toward him, but he could feel the fabric stretching and tearing and threatening to give out completely as she twisted and flailed.

"Get the syringe, dammit!" Peter hissed between gritted teeth.

Julia ducked down, reaching for the antidote, and

the infected woman suddenly seemed to realize that Peter was behind her. She tried to twist her body backward to grab at him, crooked jaw scissoring and snapping, but he shoved her away as hard as he could. She slammed into the wall, and before she could rebound, Peter grabbed a chair and used it to keep her at bay.

He felt like some kind of demented lion tamer, but it worked, holding her off until Julia was able to grab the syringe.

"Pin her against the wall," she said. "Use the legs."

He did what she suggested, using the legs of the chair to trap the infected woman in place with her arms at her sides as he leaned into it with his full weight. Being so close to her, he could smell a strange, sharp ammonia-like odor wafting out of her howling maw. The swollen nodes dangling from the chaotic mess that used to be her throat were getting bigger with every adrenaline-fueled heartbeat.

"Hurry," Peter said. "I think she's getting ready to pop here."

"I need a vein," she said. "Sub-q won't work fast enough. Grab her hair and pull her head away from me."

He grabbed a handful of her short blond hair and it came out in his fingers with a small wet rag of scalp attached. In place of the patch of hair, a dozen tiny red cilia sprouted from her exposed skull, each moving independently, like the tentacles of a curious mollusk.

It was all he could do not to vomit. But he kept the chair in place.

"My God," Julia said. "This new strain is even more potent than my most optimistic projections." She sounded more impressed than horrified.

Peter shoved the heel of his hand into the infected woman's slippery cheek, cranking her head to one side and exposing the throbbing carotid artery beneath her ear.

"We're gonna find out just how potent any minute now," he said. "Stick her, willya?"

Peter didn't have to tell her twice. Julia nodded, pulled the cap off of the syringe with her teeth, and slid it expertly into the woman's vein. As soon as she depressed the plunger, the woman let out one last spasm, then sagged against the wall, tense and twitching muscles going soft and loose.

"That was fast," Peter said, cautiously taking his weight off the chair. As soon as it ceased holding her up, she sagged to the floor and curled on her side.

"I included 20 milligrams of diazepam in addition to the antiviral agent, to quell seizure activity in the brain and decrease violent agitation."

"Good thinking," Peter said. He looked down at the shivering, bloody mess—all that was left of the woman. "Is she going to be okay?"

Julia frowned at Peter as if he'd lost his mind.

"It's not like you're some kind of patriot," Julia said, "but she's a crazy terrorist who was planning to assassinate a presidential candidate, and take God knows how many innocent bystanders with him. What do you care if she's going to be okay?" Then she paused, and seemed to calm down. "It's not out of the question that she might survive, but I think the world will be a better place if she doesn't."

"Right," he said, trying not to look back at the crumpled woman. He glanced at the doorway. "We'd better go find the other guy."

3

Out in the narrow hotel hallway, Peter started to ask Julia which way she thought the other terrorist might have gone—but he stopped even before he began.

It couldn't have been clearer if their quarry had left a trail of breadcrumbs.

To the right, the hallway was normal, its plush carpet, gold-framed mirrors, and fancy crown molding exactly the way they had been when they entered the hotel room. But to the left was a distorted fun-house nightmare that looked as if rags of flickering shadow and light had been sewn together into a crazy quilt of conflicting and unstable realities. Shapes shifted and jumped so that nothing—not the furniture, not even the walls, floor, and ceiling—seemed able to hold a consistent shape.

"What *is* this?" Peter asked, clutching the doorjamb as a sudden wave of vertigo washed over him.

"There's no time to explain," Julia said, recapping the used syringe and slipping it into her pocket, along with the vial of antidote. "Come on."

She strode purposefully down the fluctuating hallway as if to her it was all perfectly normal, and Peter had no choice but to follow. As he moved down the hall toward the fire stairs at the far end, he realized that what his eye had first interpreted as light and shadows were actually fragments—the same kind of grungy, variant version of the hotel that had appeared inside the room.

One moment the wall was clean and covered in creamy, gilded wallpaper, then, only a few feet further along, it was water damaged and grimy, patched and marked with graffiti. The floor beneath his feet would be luxuriously carpeted for one step, and cigarette-burned linoleum the next.

He was so mesmerized by this curious anomaly that he walked right into a man he could have sworn wasn't there, just a moment earlier.

Peter jumped back, a ripple of fear running through him. But it wasn't the infected terrorist—it was a man in his sixties with long, lank white hair and a dirty beard. It was a toss-up as to whether he had more teeth than he'd had recent showers, but it was clear to Peter that he didn't have many of either.

His breath was 150 proof.

"What the hell's the matter with the wall?" the man asked, rheumy eyes fixed on Peter. He lunged forward, gripping the front of Peter's shirt. "What's the matter with *everything*?"

"I..." Peter began, but before he could finish, the man grabbed the pistol that was tucked in Peter's waistband.

He lurched backward.

"Stay back!" the man said, pointing the gun at Peter. "I don't know you!"

Peter racked his brain for some smooth, clever response that would cool the old drunk and diffuse this inexplicable situation. Then there was a strange flicker in the air between them, like smoke in the beam of a movie projector, and the man was gone just as suddenly as he'd appeared.

Mostly gone.

There was a wet thump as the gun, the man's hand, and about six inches of his skinny forearm dropped to the carpet at Peter's feet. The pristine, expensive, normal and familiar carpet. Then, as he watched, the carpet shifted to linoleum and back again beneath the twitching hand.

He nudged the hand with the tip of his shoe, then pulled his foot back.

Nothing happened.

He looked down to the far end of the hall, where Julia was staring out a window, then turned and looked the other way, where everything was normal. There were no other people anywhere to be seen.

He reached slowly toward the gun, mentally preparing himself for the unpleasant task of prying the vanished man's dead fingers off of the grip.

Again, that smoky shimmer in the air and this time, Peter flinched away from it, snatching his fingers back. He felt something like a thousand needle-sharp cat claws raking the skin on his hand as he pulled it out of the shimmer. When he looked down at it, he saw that the skin was beaded with tiny crimson droplets. But thankfully it was still attached to his arm.

The severed hand and the gun were gone, though, although the bloodstain on the carpet remained as a grim reminder that everything he had seen was real.

At least I hope it was, he mused. *I think…*

He looked back at Julia and realized that both the cracked and dirty window and the little patch of worn linoleum under her feet were starting to shimmer just a little around the edges. Without conscious thought, he sprinted down the hallway at top speed and tackled her with his full weight, shoving her away from the shimmering window and knocking her to the floor. One of her chef's clogs went flying.

It happened so fast that he didn't have time to pay much attention to the view outside, but just for a second, he could have sworn that he saw a glimpse of the Twin Towers, looming between two office buildings.

"What's the matter with you?" Julia demanded, squirming away from him.

"Look!" he said, pointing to her fallen shoe, lying on the carpet beneath the now clean and undamaged window.

The shoe had been raggedly cut, not exactly in half, but more like two-thirds of the way back. The rest was missing.

"Whatever this is," Peter said, "It's dangerous. Stay away from anything that shimmers."

Julia got cautiously to her feet, kicking off her other clog. Her brows creased, and she spoke softly, almost as if to herself.

"Clearly the rifts are unstable here," she muttered. "That, combined with the diffuse brain chemistry of the non-epileptic host..." She trailed off, walking over to the window and putting her palm against the flawless glass. Peter stepped up behind her and glanced out over her shoulder. The view was of the normal, familiar New York City skyline.

No Twin Towers. Of *course* they weren't there.

They'd been gone for five years.

"Come on," he said, gesturing toward the stairway door that was half clean and solid, and half dented and boarded up, covered with several scabby, peeling layers of cheap paint in a grim rainbow of drab, depressing shades. "He went thataway."

Julia nodded and walked over to the stairway door.

When she gripped the knob and pushed, only half of it opened, while the grungy half remained solidly in place. She turned her body sideways to squeeze through the open half.

Peter was taking a last, uncertain glance out of the window when she called for him to follow her. He did, and ran right into the fully closed door.

Rebounding and shaking his head, he realized that the entire thing had been replaced. The doorknob had been removed, and the hole that it left behind was plugged with a crumpled twist of newspaper.

He looked back down the hallway and saw that it was almost all back to its glossy, upscale normal. All except for about a six-foot radius around the door.

"Julia?" He rapped his knuckles on the barrier, then pressed his ear to it. "Julia can you hear me?"

Nothing.

If she could, he certainly couldn't hear her. He couldn't hear anything but the faint sound of city traffic.

He frowned and pulled the wadded-up newspaper out of the hole where the doorknob should have been. The traffic sounds became louder, and a light breeze fluttered through the hole.

He knelt down to peer through.

Instead of a view of the staircase that should have been on the other side of the door, Peter could see all the way outside. Buildings, fire escapes, and the faint yellow glow from streetlights below. The pulsing orange flash cast by a utility vehicle.

No stairs.

And there, on the very far right of his tiny, circular view of the city skyline, was what certainly looked very much like the World Trade Center.

That strange shimmer caught the corner of his eye

again, causing him to leap back in alarm. The last thing he wanted was for his face to follow the example of the bum's arm and Julia's shoe. As he watched in awe, the shimmer increased, and the battered old door was swallowed up, shifting back to its smooth, normal form.

With hesitant fingers, Peter reached for the knob and pushed the door fully open, slipping through quickly before it had time to change again. Stepping onto the landing and listening to the heavy door swing automatically closed behind him, he froze.

No Julia, but without a doubt, their quarry had come this way. The stairs were partially there, but partially not. In the missing sections of staircase, there was nothing but eight stories of empty air above a crowded parking lot.

Yet there was no parking lot next to the Ambassador Hotel. In fact, there were no open-air parking lots at all in this pricy neighborhood—only underground garages.

It looked as if a large chunk of the stately old hotel had been demolished, exposing the building's weathered brick hide in the place where the staircase should have been. But the brick was sooty and aged, as if it had been exposed to the elements for years—perhaps decades. Even assuming that the stairway had somehow partially collapsed, the brick that would have been revealed wouldn't have deteriorated that way.

Something drifted overhead, casting a large shadow. It looked like the Goodyear blimp, but not quite. Then he noticed another one, smaller and further in the distance.

There were so many things wrong with this that Peter's brain could hardly process them all. But a moment later he spotted Julia—she seemed to be stranded on the switchback landing below, which was suspended in mid-air halfway down to the next floor. She was frozen with an expression of dreamy, mesmerized terror.

That was the moment the landing under his feet chose to begin to shimmer at the edges.

Almost in a panic, he leapt over a large, irregular gap in the steps, clinging to a chunk of floating railing, toes on a small chunk of fire escape. To his surprise, the railing was solid and steady, even though it didn't seem to be attached to anything. When he looked back up at the landing he'd just left, it was gone—nothing left but the outside of the rusty and battered door.

No way to go but down.

"Julia," he called. "Stay right where you are."

She didn't seem to hear him.

He told himself not to look down, but that just seemed to draw his attention to the yawning gaps in the stairs and the empty air below. He forced himself to hopscotch two steps, then three. Arms wheeling for balance, he steadied himself and then looked down at Julia. He was only three more stairs away from her.

There should have been five.

She was kneeling on her hands and knees, clinging to the edge of her floating landing and staring down at the bustling street below like a suicide trying to work up the nerve. The step on which he was precariously balanced began to shimmer and shift around the edges. He swore and leapt for the landing.

He made it, but there was barely enough room for the two of them together and he wound up having to stand straddling her waist as if he were about to ride on her back like a kid playing horsey.

"I have to get down," she was saying over and over, so softly that Peter could barely hear her over the rush of the wind and the hum of city traffic. They had to get to safety, somehow, and he glanced around, finally spotting something that might do the trick.

"I have to get down," she said again.

"I know," Peter said, reaching down to touch her shoulder. "Come on, we can make it."

She flinched away from his touch, grip tightening on the edge of the landing.

"You don't understand," she said. "I have to get down *there...*"

"Julia." He gripped her arm. "Julia, look at me. We *are* going to get down. But unless you plan on jumping to your death, the only other option is there."

She looked up at him, eyes wild and way too wide. He pointed to a door in the side of the hotel building about a dozen steps below them. Give or take a missing step or two. Or ten. The stairs kept shifting, winking in and out of existence with no recognizable rhythm.

Peter was trying to come up with a way to get her moving, when their landing began to shimmer around the edges.

That'll do it, he thought.

Julia yanked her hands away from the edge as if it was on fire, and sprang to her feet as if she'd been hit with a riding crop, almost knocking him from their perch. She leapt for the next solid step down. When she landed, her adrenaline-fueled forward momentum made her half fall and half jump to the next step, and then the one after. She clung to a small chunk of floating railing the size of a baseball bat, and craned her neck to look back at him.

The solid section of landing beneath Peter's feet had shrunken down to the size of a seat cushion, and the deadly shimmering fault lines were creeping inexorably closer to his toes. He had no choice but to jump.

The awkward, desperate leap propelled him forward and down with way too much momentum. Before he could stop himself, he slammed into Julia from behind, knocking the two of them down to the lower landing and into the door. It flew open under their combined weight, and they spilled together into the hallway, landing in a sprawling pile on the carpeted floor.

He groaned, and untangled himself from her.

"You okay?" Peter asked, rolling off Julia and pulling himself up on his elbows.

"I think so," she said.

The scary, unfathomable intensity he'd seen in her eyes, out on the impossible staircase, seemed to have dissipated. She still looked frightened, but sane. He hoped the madness hadn't just ducked under the surface.

When Peter looked around, he realized they were on the spa level. Fortunately for them, it was deserted—most likely because anyone who might have been using the spa was downstairs at the Democrats banquet. The lighting in this part of the hotel was low and indirect, mostly hidden behind extravagant arrangements of orchids and tropical foliage. The color palate that had been chosen for the walls and carpet was soothing and muted. There was a subtle aroma of lavender and chlorine in the warm air.

Once again, however, he could tell where their mutating quarry had to have gone—there was a clear trail of fluctuating, lenticular weirdness that led down the hall to the pool door. There were also several long, uneven smears along the walls and carpet that couldn't be anything but blood.

4

"How much time do we have before that guy and his fist-sized zits go kablooey?" Peter asked, scrambling to his feet and offering his hand to help Julia.

"As I said earlier," she replied, taking his hand, "Different people, different metabolisms. However, I've found that female subjects consistently reach the critical stage much faster than males."

"Well, that's a refreshing change," he said. "I just hope you're right. Come on."

Peter took the lead, following the trail and avoiding the shimmers until he reached the heavy door that led to the pool area. When he pushed it open, a warm blast of chlorinated air wafted out, reminding him of childhood swimming lessons.

The area was decorated with extravagant art deco tile work, blue and white with gold accents. All around the pool itself were large, vertically striped columns with gilded tops and inlaid images of stylized sea creatures. There was a design of some kind on the bottom of the pool, as well, glittering abstract swirls intersecting beneath the clear still water.

The shimmering of the water was made more disconcerting by the shimmering of reality around it. The motion was so disorienting that he found himself becoming queasy with motion sickness.

Here and there tiles were missing, cracked, or shattered, leaving random piles of rubble. One of the columns was held up by two-by-fours, and along the far side of the pool was a row of wooden lounge chairs, some ornately carved, others ruined and falling apart. Beyond them were three doors labeled "Ladies," "Gentlemen," and "Steam Room" respectively.

One of the lounge chairs had been knocked over, and crouching behind it was the man from room 803. The mutations that wracked his pale and sweating flesh were totally different from those endured by his female companion. He had the same egg-like swollen nodes under his jaw, but the majority of the changes seemed hard and bony, instead of soft and fleshy.

His shoulders and elbows had sprouted miniature mountain ranges of jagged bone that pushed up through the skin like teeth. The contours of his skull were shifting, elongating and fanning out, until the result resembled the collar of a triceratops. The tortured skin of his scalp was stretched and splitting, blood oozing down between his wild eyes and along his nose.

He was swaying back and forth.

In addition to the changes to his flesh, there was a halo of shimmering corruption all around him. The tile beneath his feet was cracked and stained. The ceiling above him was full of holes, decorated only with overlapping colonies of different colored mildew. Most disturbingly, the section of the pool closest to him was empty, almost as if a slice of the water had been removed, like a cake with a piece cut out.

"Take it easy," Peter said softly, hands out toward the swiftly mutating man. "We're here to help you." He tipped his chin to the right, indicating that Julia should go that way while he started moving slowly in the other direction. He kept his body and attention turned toward the man, but still had to watch out for shimmering rifts in the tile beneath his feet.

He tracked Julia's progress out of the corner of his eye. She was keeping pace with him, coming around the far end of the pool and reaching the other side. As she walked, she was filling the syringe.

The terrorist began whipping his increasingly unstable head back and forth from Peter to Julia, gripping the edge of the lounge chair so hard it was starting to crack. The bony collar added weight, and made the movement even more grotesque.

"It's okay," Peter continued, trying to draw the man's focus away from Julia. "It's okay. Let us help you. You don't want this, do you? Of course not. Please, let us help you."

The man seemed to hesitate for a moment, then let out a high-pitched shriek and lurched upward, flinging the lounge chair.

Peter threw himself to the left and managed to avoid taking the brunt of the attack, but the chair still glanced painfully off the side of his body before clattering into the wall and shattering into pieces. In the time it took him to recover and refocus, the man had scuttled backward and ducked through the door marked "Steam Room."

"Damn," Julia said, running up to the door. "This is bad. That kind of moist heat will speed up the reproduction of the virus."

"Okay, then," Peter replied, selecting a sturdy, foot-long chunk of wood from the wreckage and testing its heft. "We'd better go in after him." He hoped he sounded more confident about it than he felt.

Julia nodded her agreement.

"Ready?" she asked, hand on the doorknob.

Peter nodded, switching his grip on the wooden club and pressing his back against the wall beside the door.

She nodded and pushed the door slowly open, keeping her body pressed against the wall on the opposite side. Once the door was open, all that was revealed was thick, swirling steam, obscuring everything.

The two of them waited for a few seconds that felt like hours. Waiting to see if the terrorist would come lunging out, or if they were going to have to go in after him.

As time ticked by, it became clear that the guy wasn't coming out.

Peter exchanged a look with Julia, and cautiously stepped into the doorway.

Once inside, he saw that the space was larger than he had expected, and realized that the steam wasn't as solid as he thought. It was like everything around the sick terrorist—flawed with inexplicable *otherness*. There and not there, in a pattern almost like ephemeral tiger stripes hanging in mid-air. The areas that weren't entirely obscured by the steam looked more like an old forgotten storage room, complete with jagged, shifting chunks of decayed furniture and wooden crates.

There was a sound like voodoo drumming coming from the far end of the long, narrow space—a rapid series of hollow, rhythmic thumps.

"Sounds like a seizure," Julia said, slipping in behind Peter. "Where is he? Can you see him? We should try to grab him and inject him now, while he's unable to resist."

Peter didn't reply, but held up a hand, indicating that she should be quiet.

The steam was messing with the acoustics, but he

was pretty sure that the sound was centered inside a thick cloud clinging to a corner of the back wall. He edged slowly along the wall to the right, keeping his eyes on the far corner, but he kept on bumping into things that were there and then not. He barked his shin on a length of rusty metal tubing that might or might not be the leg of a damaged card table, and then half tripped over a mildewy heap of damp cardboard.

Yet by the time he regained his footing, whatever it was that had been in his way was gone.

Muttering a curse under his breath, he continued making his way toward the sound.

When he got closer to the far end of the room, a dark shape became visible within the steam, but it didn't seem even remotely human. What he saw looked more like the spasms of a dying cockroach.

He reached out to poke at the thing with the piece of wood, like a little kid who'd been dared by his friends to touch some road kill. Nothing happened. The convulsions continued unabated, and the writhing steam alternately hid and revealed the terrible new shape, parting like a stripper's veils.

"What are you waiting for?" Julia hissed, lifting the syringe. "*Grab him.*"

Peter reached into the steam, blindly hunting for something he could grab onto in the twitching chaos. But nothing his fingers encountered felt anything like a normal human limb. More like storm-tossed tree branches, rough and abrasive, with sharp points and edges.

"I can't..." Peter began, but whatever he was about to say was eclipsed by a roughly swallowed gasp when something shot out from within the steam, and grabbed his arm.

It felt like a long, thin crab claw and as it clamped

down and twisted, he shouted out before he could stop himself. With his other hand, he tried to grab whatever had a hold of him, to pry its grip loose. Suddenly a second and then a third claw shot out and grabbed his free arm.

He swore and kicked out blindly at the thing, feeling the skin of his wrist and arm tearing and bleeding as he wrenched free first one hand, and then the other.

"We've got to get him out of here," Julia said, picking up a fragment of what looked like wrought iron. "Back toward the door." She put one flat hand in the center of Peter's chest and started backing up, using the other hand to bang loudly against the wall with the piece of iron. "Come on!" she shouted, and the sound echoed. "*Come get us!*"

The shadowy shape seemed to hunch and twist, not so much standing up as reconfiguring itself into something more vertical. It let out a weird, breathlessly warbling cry like a frightened screech owl, and launched itself at them.

Peter shoved Julia out of the way just as the heavy, chaotic mass of the terrorist's impossibly mutated body slammed into him, sending him reeling back out though the door and into the pool.

The water was warm and highly chlorinated, burning as it flooded up his nose. The wounds on his arms hurt like a bitch. He flailed out with both hands, but lost any sense of where his attacker was. His lungs began aching for oxygen as he gathered himself and kicked upward toward the distant, shimmering surface.

When he reached it, he sucked in a massive gasp of air and frantically looked around for the mutant. He couldn't see anything that lay beneath the churning surface, and was suddenly excruciatingly aware of his legs, dangling beneath him. It was like floating in a murky shark tank, knowing that terrible things lurked somewhere below.

He had to get out of the water.

He cast an eye around the perimeter of the pool, and spotted Julia standing by the ladder on the right side, waving him over. That ladder was much closer than the steps leading out of the shallow end, so he started paddling in her direction.

He was nearly halfway there when Julia's face went tight and grim.

"Hurry, Peter," she called. She didn't have to say it twice.

5

He risked a look back and saw the dark irregular shape of the creature rising up toward him, reaching with way too many long, thin limbs.

He started swimming hard, making a beeline for the ladder, when the water he was swimming through suddenly disappeared, dropping him ten feet to the cracked cement at the bottom of the pool. He let out a grunt of dismay, but couldn't bring himself to be surprised. So many impossible things had happened, in so short an amount of time, that he was beginning to suffer from surprise fatigue.

He cracked his chin on the cement, tasting blood in his mouth. The impact left him breathless and gasping as he struggled up on his bruised knees, and looked around. He was trapped at the bottom of a triangular well, with walls made of water. Curious, he reached out to touch the water, but a shimmer flickering along the impossible surface made him yank his hand away, letting out a cry of alarm.

Then, just as suddenly as they had appeared, the walls were gone.

It wasn't like having a ton of water dropped on him. It was just *there*, all around him, as if it had been there all along. Only now he was on the bottom of the deep end, with ten feet of water above his head. Worse, he had just exhaled, so his lungs were completely empty.

With a spurt of adrenaline he kicked off the bottom and started swimming for the surface. The water was so strongly chlorinated that it hurt to open his eyes, and even when he did, his vision was too blurry to see around him. His heart was pounding, his empty airless chest starting to burn, and he was about to break the surface when the water disappeared again.

The sound that was wrenched out from between his clenched teeth as he tumbled back to the bottom was more frustration than fear. He scrambled to get his feet under him, shook off the impact, and looked up. He could hear Julia calling out to him, but he couldn't see her. The shifting channel of water made her voice seem distant and echoey.

Then she stepped into his view, looking like a mourner standing over an open grave and giving him the impression that he was about to be buried alive. But she was pointing behind him and yelling.

When he turned around, he spotted what used to be the terrorist at the other end of the empty channel, twitching and squirming half in and half out of the liquid wall. Whatever human form remained was hidden beneath what looked like a dense layer of the kind of junk that gets stuck in a storm drain after a heavy rain. Twiggy appendages, flapping rags of skin and irregular, jagged lumps, all various sickly shades of ashy gray and cyanotic blue. Every one of the dozens of quivering, disorganized limbs ended in something different—crablike claws and bony hooks and abnormally jointed fingers tipped with what looked more like teeth than nails.

The only thing that made the head distinguishable from the rest of the mess was a cavernous mouth full of slick, bloody tusks. They were growing so fast Peter could see them curling and twisting like eager bean sprouts, making a hideous creaking sound as they did. He could also see the now familiar swelling egg-like nodes on their ropy stalks beneath what should have been the man's chin.

They were growing, too.

Time was running out.

The creature seemed to spot him suddenly, though Peter couldn't imagine how—his eyes, ears, and nose were completely obscured by mutated flesh. His top-heavy, irregular form hunched and flexed, claws clicking and reaching. Then somehow he broke free of the wall between the realities, and charged like an angry bull.

Peter backed against the pool wall, fists up and as ready as he could be, but then the water was there again, blinding him and causing him to bounce off the wall and drift weightlessly upward.

He felt something clutching at the leg of his pants and kicked out against it in reflexive fear and revulsion.

But then the water was gone and he fell awkwardly on one leg, twisting his ankle and sending a shooting pain up his calf. Before he could right himself, the water stuttered in and out several times, disorienting him completely. He heard a buzzing shriek, and in a moment of gasping for precious air he looked over at the terrorist. A twisting shimmer in the nearby water had sheared a large chunk of rag-like flesh away from the lower part of his body. The blood pouring from the wound was bright red, surprisingly normal.

Peter scrabbled away from the spreading crimson stain that came creeping across the dry pool bottom.

He had to figure out how to get away from the bleeding monstrosity, and get his ass the hell out of this pool.

The walls of water on either side of him were pulsing with deadly shimmers, but the one on the left less so than the right. If he timed it right, he figured he should be able to push through the impossible vertical surface and into the water, so he could swim up and out of this hellish trap.

He took a step to the left, and immediately regretted it. His ankle was badly twisted, and let him know it the second he tried to put any weight on it at all. Pain caused his vision to go white for a moment. He swore under his breath and did a little limping shuffle to shift his weight to the other leg.

"Peter?" Julia called from the deck above. "Peter, are you all right?"

"Never better," Peter replied through gritted teeth, mostly to himself.

He concentrated on watching the shimmers, timing their pulsing patterns until there was a miraculous lull, leaving a section of clear, safe water about the size of a surfboard. He sucked in a deep breath and dove through the vertical surface, pushing off with his good leg. There was some resistance, but not enough to stop him.

Once underwater, he made for the surface like a torpedo. No thought of the terrorist or the shimmers or anything other than getting up and out.

He breached the surface with a huge gasp and grasped the edge of the pool. He felt something grip the back of his wet shirt and started to fight instinctively against it until he realized it was Julia, trying to help him. She hauled him upward, nearly pulling his shirt up over his head.

He was half out of the pool with his chest pressed against the tile between Julia's bare feet when the water disappeared, leaving his legs dangling in the air. If it had happened just seconds earlier, he would have fallen again and taken Julia down with him. But, thankfully, he was able to swing his good leg, then the other, up onto the pool deck.

6

For a moment, all he could do was lie there on the tiles, suck in oxygen, and be happy to be alive and out of the treacherous water.

He turned to Julia to thank her, but she was gone. He pushed himself up on an elbow and spotted her at the far end of the pool, wrestling a large, old-fashioned blue-and-white-striped life preserver off the wall.

"What...?" he started to ask, but she was ignoring him completely, her attention completely fixed on the terrorist still flailing at the bottom of the pool.

"Help me," she said, unwinding the white plastic rope attached to the life preserver. "We need to get him out of there. *Hurry.*"

Peter quickly realized what she was thinking. They needed to get him out of there so that she could inject him before the nodes on his neck burst and released their deadly airborne payload.

Airborne...

"Julia," Peter asked, frowning. "What would happen if the nodes burst underwater?"

Julia stopped, then squinted at him, head cocked and thoughtful.

"Well," she said. "Theoretically, the chlorine would kill the virus. However, I can't say with one hundred percent certainty, since the theory hasn't been tested in a controlled laboratory environment."

"What if we held him under, instead of pulling him out?"

"It might work," Julia said. "In fact, there's a good chance that it would. Except..."

"It's wrong, isn't it?" Peter said, picking up on her train of thought. "Drowning the poor bastard. I mean, he didn't know what he was getting into. It's one thing, not being able to save him, but cold-blooded—"

"Don't be stupid," Julia hissed. "It's not that. It's the fact that the rifts are causing the water to fluctuate in an erratic manner. If it were to disappear at the moment when the nodes burst, well..." She didn't finish her sentence, but she didn't have to.

Peter nodded, the weight of the decision heavy on his shoulders.

"The mutation is progressing at an accelerated rate in this subject," she continued. "Surface changes are so profound that finding an accessible vein to inject the antidote may be near impossible at this late stage." She tossed the life preserver away and picked up a long wooden pole with a hook at the end. "Your option makes more sense. We have to take a chance at trying to force him into the water and hold him there until the danger of infection has passed."

"Until the danger of infection has passed." Peter thought. *"Not until he's dead."*

He had to look away from Julia for a moment, genuinely disturbed by her icy, ruthless determination.

Peter had done some, well, bad things in his life—things he regretted or wished he'd done differently, but he'd never actually killed anyone. He'd been caught up in scenarios in which people had been killed. He'd participated in scams and con games that went wrong and resulted in people getting killed. And maybe those people would still be alive today, if they'd never had anything to do with him.

But he had never actually taken a life with his own two hands.

Not that the terrorist at the bottom of the pool would have hesitated to end Peter's life, given the chance. But it would be a stretch to call it "self-defense" when his victim was trapped like the proverbial fish in a barrel.

Julia took his hand. Her voice was low and soothing.

"Whatever is left of that man's consciousness is experiencing unbearable pain right now." She pulled a hook-tipped rescue pole off of a wall rack, and pressed it into Peter's hand. "It would be a mercy killing. Like putting a dying animal out of its misery.

"Besides, it's our only option," she added.

Peter nodded and took the pole. Julia set her mouth into a tight, determined line and grabbed the pole's twin off the wall for herself.

"Ready?" she asked.

"Let's do it," Peter said.

Bracing himself to avoid putting weight on his ankle, he reached the pole experimentally down toward the terrorist, who was in an empty portion of the pool. The pole was about twelve inches shy of long enough to reach.

"Damn," he said. "Now what?"

Julia didn't answer, and climbed down the ladder and into the pool in a section that currently had water in it, but was close to the empty area. Keeping her head above the surface, she reached down through the water with the pole, pushed through the anomalous surface, and managed to hook the writhing mass of the terrorist's body. His convulsions changed with the introduction of this new enemy, but she managed to anchor her grip, pinning him to the pool bottom. There was a slick beneath him, a little water, but mostly a disgusting mixture of blood and other unidentifiable fluids. It was pooling, leaving a slippery surface.

"Come on," she said, leaning over and still clinging to the ladder with one hand, motioning with her head for him to get in beside her.

He did as she asked, easing himself back into the water, climbing down with one hand, anchoring himself on his good foot, and reaching out with the pole. After some brief fumbling, he was able to hook part of the terrorist.

Realizing in some animalistic, hindbrain way that he was under attack, the terrorist started to flail and squirm more violently than ever, but he couldn't gain sufficient balance. He was unable to get free.

"Pull him toward us," Julia said. "Into the water. On three."

Peter tightened his grip on the pole, and nodded.

"One... two..." She arched a brow at him.

"Three!"

Peter struggled for leverage, dragging the bleeding mess headfirst into the water. The mysterious shimmers sliced and needled the flailing bulk of the misshapen body, releasing swirling clouds of blood into the water like chum. The wall of liquid began to shift, the empty area changing with it and then winking out of existence as if it had never been.

Seconds later, the empty space reappeared around the terrorist. Without the buoyant water to hold him up, his full struggling weight nearly yanked the pole out of Peter's hands. Julia teetered and almost slipped completely under the surface, but the hook on the end of her pole came free and abruptly released her from the battle.

With all the weight on the end of Peter's pole, he needed to better anchor himself. He hooked his elbow around one of the rungs on the ladder, and his open wounds sent fiery pain up his arm. He hung on for a moment, but whatever the hook had been attached to came loose in a bloody clump, and the creature flopped back down to the bottom.

"I can't reach him there!" Julia said, extending the pole to the limit of her reach. "My arm's not long enough."

Peter was taller, with longer limbs, but he still had to go down two more rungs of the ladder to reach the terrorist, leaving him submerged up to his neck. He had to tip his chin upward to keep his nose and mouth out of the water, which made it difficult to see what he was doing down below.

God, I hope none of that shit's in the water around me, he thought. Then he pushed aside the idea, and focused. He managed to hook a twitching appendage, and started battling to move the terrorist back into the water.

"Hurry!" Julia said. "Those nodes are going to rupture any second now. Just try to get the head into the water!"

Easier said than done, Peter thought, but he didn't waste the effort needed to speak. Instead, he gritted his teeth against the pain in his arms and ankle.

The thrashing increased. It was hard to tell if the terrorist was suffering from another seizure, or just fighting like a panicked, dying animal, but the result was the same.

"I can't see a damned thing," Peter said. "Which end is the head?"

"The end that's closest to you," Julia replied. "Pull it toward you."

The water shifted, and shifted again, but Peter kept on pulling him closer to the wall. Once he had the terrorist pinned to the bottom directly below them, he leaned his full weight on the pole, riding out the bucking and thrashing until it started to slow.

Then, suddenly, the water Peter was in was gone, and both he and the terrorist were in a narrow tunnel of air.

No longer buoyant, Peter clung tight to the ladder and looked down. Below him, the terrorist's whole deformed body had gone a deep, dusky blue—except for the quivering nodes, which were pearly white and glistening. They had swollen to the size of mangoes.

"Oh, my God," Julia said, flinching with her knuckles pressed to her lips. "They're going to rupture!"

Adrenaline pumped into him, and Peter gave the pole a desperate shove, pushing what was left of the terrorist's head into the shimmering water just as the nodes burst, releasing a thick, milky fluid into the water. Julia let out a sharp sound that sounded like a cross between a gasp and a laugh, but Peter was in no mood for it. He just held on, grimly keeping the terrorist pinned against the bottom of the pool until he stopped moving.

It only took about a minute, but it felt like the longest minute of Peter's life.

When it was finally over, the shimmering tunnel of air—and all the other anomalies—just vanished, leaving the pool and its surrounding area looking normal. Gone were the piles of trash and broken tiles. The only evidence that anything unusual had occurred was the broken lounge chair. That and the body, floating in a spreading, milky cloud.

Seeing that cloud, Peter scrambled to get out of the

pool before it could reach him. Julia followed, and as they stood there, dripping, he looked down at the pole he was holding. A tool designed to save lives.

The irony wasn't lost on him.

"Should we… fish him out?"

She shook her head.

"Leave him," she said. "Let the chlorine finish its job."

7

"Now what?" Peter asked, doing his best to wring the water out of his clothes and trying not to look at the body.

"We should go back to the room," Julia said. "Get some dry clothes and safely dispose of any bio-hazardous material left behind by these idiots."

The sodden trudge back up to room 803 was silent and uncomfortable. Peter had to lean on Julia's arm, limping heavily on his twisted ankle, but they didn't speak.

They'd stopped a dangerous plague from being unleashed on the city, and he knew that he had done the right thing, but he still felt strange, even hollow inside. He also felt wary of Julia. Killing seemed way too easy for her. He also wasn't sure if he should be impressed by or suspicious of her new tough, take-charge attitude. She'd certainly come a long way from the cowering, fearful girl he'd rescued from the hotel.

As Julia had predicted, the blond woman had in fact succumbed to her injuries and lay dead, just where they'd left her. The whole room stank of ammonia, making it slightly difficult to breathe.

"Here," Julia said, tossing the dead man's tuxedo

onto the bed. "Put this on. It may not be a perfect fit, but people will just assume it's rented."

Without further comment, she began to strip out of her wet chef's clothes. Peter should have felt something at the sight of her damp, goose-bumped flesh, but he didn't. Certainly not arousal—there was a grotesque corpse in the room, and it wasn't exactly an aphrodisiac.

He pulled the cover off the bed, and used it to cover the dead body.

"Great," Julia said, and he glanced in her direction. She was struggling to fit her surgically enhanced breasts into a shimmery silver gown that had clearly been made for a much more modest bust. "Of all the terrorists in the world, why do I have to end up with a member of the Itty-Bitty-Titty Committee? I'm going be falling out of this dress like a porn star." She slipped her bare feet into a pair of strappy metallic sandals. "At least we wear roughly the same size shoes."

She smiled and looked up at him, then arched a brow when she noticed that he wasn't smiling, too. But she didn't say anything. She just pulled a pair of bright purple disposable gloves out of her purse, and put them on.

"That's a good look for you," Peter said, hoping a bit of wisecracking would help him relax, and reignite what he'd felt before. "Nothing like a nice pop of color for evening."

Julia smiled and made quick jazz-hands in the air before collecting the two used syringes and placing them carefully into a red plastic bag marked "biohazard." Then she found the empty vial where it had fallen near the covered corpse, and held it up to the light.

"Looks like the Englishman only gave them enough virus for this one attack," she said. "He has much more than this in his possession."

"What do you think that means?" Peter asked. "That he's breaking it up into dime bags, and selling it all over town?"

"If so," she said, slipping the empty vial into the bag, "we'd better find him and stop him."

Peter stripped off his sopping wet clothes, wondering how many more times he was going to have to get into a pool fully dressed. He considered the tuxedo, but knew it was going to be a tight fit and figured he should dry off a little more before trying to squeeze into those pants. So he limped into the bathroom and reached for a towel.

Then he stopped dead.

"Julia?" he called over his shoulder.

"What?"

"How many syringes did you find?"

"Both of them," she said, stepping into the doorway with the biohazard bag in one gloved hand. "Why?"

Peter cocked his chin.

Sitting there on the edge of the sink, left as casually as a toothbrush or a razor, was a third syringe.

"Three?" Julia said, stepping up to the sink and picking up the syringe. "There's *three* of them? So..."

She turned to Peter with wide, disbelieving eyes as he finished the sentence for her.

"Where's the third terrorist?" he asked.

"This isn't good," she said, stashing the extra syringe in the bag with the other two. "This isn't good at all."

"We have to find him," Peter said.

"Or her." Julia took out a container of anti-viral wipes and started wiping down every hard surface in the room. "We need to get down to that banquet right away. That's got to be where whoever used this syringe will be headed."

"But if that person shot up and left before we got here," Peter asked, "aren't we already too late?"

"We might be," Julia said. "Or we might not be. I told you, the speed with which the virus takes hold varies from subject to subject. Considering the fact that the hotel doesn't appear to have descended into apocalyptic mayhem,"—she gestured at the open window, inviting Peter to look outside—"I think it's safe to say that we're in luck.

"For now, anyway," she added.

Peter peered out the window. Everything looked normal. Normal flow of traffic, yellow with taxis. Normal flow of pedestrians, busy, bustling people on their way to important places. No one seemed sick, mutated, or overtly homicidal.

"Still," Julia said, casting an eye up and down Peter's wet body, and then turning away. "We can't waste time." She pulled off her gloves, turning them inside out so that one was wrapped inside the other, before tucking them both into the bag with the syringes. Then she put on a pair of earrings she'd found on the nightstand.

Peter pulled down the towel he'd come into the bathroom to grab in the first place, dried himself off, and then went to put on the tux. It wasn't as bad as he'd thought it might be—just a little tight across the shoulders, and of course, too short in the sleeves and legs. Still, not so much so that it wasn't halfway presentable. If he squinted, the two of them almost looked like they belonged at a presidential fundraising gala.

The only thing that didn't quite fit the image was Julia's frumpy canvas purse, but she refused to leave the used syringes and dirty gloves behind in the room. The tiny clutch that went with the sparkly dress wasn't even big enough for a tube of lipstick.

"Grab the invitation," she said, pointing to the gilded envelope on the desk.

Peter picked it up and slipped it halfway out, enough to read the fancy cursive lettering and confirm that it was, in fact, the invitation that they would need to get them into the banquet.

"Ready?" Julia asked.

"Ready as I'll ever be," he replied—faced with the prospect of a wildly mutating, potentially violent monster, a room full of rich, influential New Yorkers, and swarms of heavily armed federal agents. Not exactly his idea of a good time.

But he had no choice.

8

As Peter and Julia made their way down to the grand ballroom, he leaned heavily on her arm, favoring his good leg and keeping his eyes open for the slightest hint of an anomaly. Any rifts or shimmers, or anything that would indicate that they were on the right track. There was nothing.

Everything was frustratingly normal.

"What if the guy bailed?" Peter asked, leaning close to Julia's jeweled ear. "I mean, if he's loose on the streets of the city, we'll never find him."

"Let's just hope," Julia replied, "that his devotion to whatever crazy cause these people are into will keep him from straying too far from the original mission."

"Honestly," Peter said, "I don't even know why they're bothering. This country is way too backward to elect a black president, anyway. Maybe twenty years from now..."

"I guess even the remote possibility is enough to drive some people to extreme measures." Julia shrugged. "I never understood the point of fanaticism. Causes. Religion. All that. It's so arbitrary, so juvenile—like cliques in high school."

"I don't get it either," Peter said. "I certainly never fit in with any cliques."

There was a sudden burst of noise from the ballroom. Peter and Julia exchanged a concerned look, but relaxed when they realized it was cheering. They started hurrying toward the door.

There were bookend feds on either side as they approached. Two men, both white and middle-aged, and as similar as action figures. Standard issue spooks with steely gazes and clear spiral cords curling behind their ears.

"I hope we haven't missed the speech," Julia said in a breathy, girlish voice that sounded like someone else.

"No, ma'am," the fed on the right said, accepting the invitation Peter handed him and scanning it with a small, handheld device. His voice was so bland and without any regional affectations, that it might as well have been computer generated. "You're in time. It just started."

"Oh, my gosh, thank you," Julia said with a dazzling smile that was wasted on the dour fed who opened the door to let them in.

Inside, the opulent ballroom was older and much more baroque in design than the art deco pool area, all wedding cake molding and gilded cherubs and rococo chandeliers dripping with crystal. The guests who gathered around the tables were equally old and gilded, the men providing the age and the women the gilt. As they made their way to their numbered table, Peter realized that they were the youngest couple in the room by twenty years, easy. Excluding the staff, of course, and the muscle.

There were two other couples already seated at the table. To Peter's right was some kind of vaguely familiar power couple, Hollywood people but not actors. They were both in their fifties and both utterly absorbed in the screens of their respective phones.

To Peter's left sat a doddering oldster who looked asleep or possibly dead, and his formerly hot trophy wife, now sixty to his ninety. She smiled at Peter, her face a frozen rictus of botulinum injections and silicone filler, and then blatantly looked him up and down as if he were a fattening dessert and she was considering cheating on her diet.

He turned away, trying not to shudder visibly, and took Julia's hand, pressing it to his lips like a devout Catholic kissing a rosary to ward off evil.

Meanwhile, the presidential candidate was standing at a bunting-laden podium at the far end of the room, set up on a raised platform. He was well into his speech, and seemed relaxed and in good spirits. He clearly had no idea what was going on.

But he was also the one guy in the room who wouldn't suddenly mutate into a contagious monster, so Peter ignored him and started focusing on the crowd, searching the faces for anyone who looked out of place or nervous. Anyone who looked like they didn't feel so good.

He included the massive security in his sweep. It would be a real stretch for their terrorist to impersonate a fed, but given all of the other patently impossible things he'd seen today, he wasn't going to rule it out.

Everything seemed normal, the way it should be, until Julia gripped his arm and tipped her chin in the direction of a portly, red-haired waiter who was standing at the edge of the room, holding a pitcher of ice water and looking pale and sweaty.

"Think that might be our guy?" Peter whispered.

"We'll know soon," Julia said.

She drank down all of her water in a few quick gulps. Then, turning back and making sure that her overflowing cleavage was clearly visible, she caught the sweaty man's eye and raised her now-empty water glass.

He started toward her, weaving between the other tables.

"What are you going to do?" Peter hissed. "Stick him in the arm while he's pouring you a drink?"

Another man stopped the waiter en route, asking for a refill.

"I just want to get a closer look," Julia whispered through smiling teeth. "If he's infected, a distinctive ammonia-like odor should be detectable at close range."

The waiter ended up refilling glasses for the whole nearby table as Peter clenched his fists in his lap with anxious frustration.

"*Then* what?" he asked.

"Then I stick him in the arm while he's pouring the water," she replied.

Julia raised her glass again, to make sure the waiter hadn't forgotten her. He looked up, noticed her and nodded, trudging toward her like a child resigned to some punishment.

"Are you sure that's a good idea?" Peter asked. "Feds'll be all over you in a heartbeat if you try to pull a stunt like that."

She turned back toward Peter and opened her mouth to deliver a snappy retort, when the sound of breaking glass and splashing water whipped her head around.

The waiter had gone down beside the neighboring table, his body wracked with a violent seizure. In the time it took Peter to get to his feet, a ring of feds surrounded the convulsing man. Up on the stage, the presidential candidate trailed off, his brow furrowed by a practiced look of concern.

There was no time to think. Peter had to act and fast. He grabbed Julia's arm, pulled her to her feet, and shouldered his way through the concerned crowd.

"My wife is a doctor!" he called out in a clear, steady voice that sounded way more confident than he felt. "Please, let her through."

The two closest feds turned toward his voice, their broad shoulders parting like a gate.

"Who's a doctor?" the older of the two feds asked. He was a burly, sunburned man with thinning white hair. He turned to Julia. "You?"

"Yes, that's right," she said, seamlessly running with Peter's ruse as she got down one knee and opened her purse. "There's no reason to be alarmed. This man is clearly epileptic, and he's experiencing a severe grand mal seizure." She pulled out the antidote and syringe, raising it up and drawing out a dose. "An injection of a mild sedative will stop the muscle contractions and prevent accidental injury. It will also allow you to remove the patient safely to another location, so that the banquet can continue as planned.

"Hold him, please."

The two feds exchanged a look like they weren't entirely sold on Julia's suggestion. In the meanwhile, Peter could see strange, erratic movement underneath the man's uniform, as if his clothing was infested with some sort of vermin. The telltale lumps under his chin were starting to swell. Any minute now it would become horribly obvious—even to someone with no medical background—that this wasn't an ordinary epileptic seizure.

Julia paused, waiting for the feds to decide whether or not they would allow her to go ahead with the injection. It was like watching someone try to defuse a time bomb. His fists were clenched so hard, his fingers ached.

Blood began to ooze between the waiter's chattering teeth as he banged his head repeatedly against the glossy tile floor, eyes rolled up and unseeing.

"You," Julia said, indicated the younger of the two agents standing directly beside her. Her tone was clipped, authoritative. "Get something between his teeth before he bites his tongue off. You." She turned to the older fed. "Hold his head as still as you can, chin turned away. In his current state, the carotid artery will be our safest target."

The younger agent reacted unquestioningly to her barked instruction, grabbing a silver butter knife off a nearby table and wedging it between the waiter's bloody teeth.

But the older man hesitated.

"Now," Julia added, her tone calm and matter-of-fact, as if following her exact instructions was the only possible option.

Peter was about ready to shove the older agent aside and grab the waiter's head himself, but to his surprise, he didn't have to. The older guy gave a curt nod and did what Julia asked. If he noticed the swelling nodes under the waiter's chin, he chose not to mention them.

Julia deftly injected the waiter, depressing the plunger and emptying the syringe into his bloodstream. The twitching and spasming of his limbs began to slow immediately. The nodes in his neck pulsed erratically, like miniature dying hearts, then began to shrink. He let out a long, slow, shaky breath that whistled past the silver knife in his teeth.

Peter let out a matching breath, his own fists and tightly strung muscles starting to relax.

We did it. It was over.

That's when Peter noticed the female FBI agent who had checked them into the kitchen.

9

She was standing alone by an emergency exit near the far end of the raised platform, scanning the room.

Peter ducked down, feigning concern for the fallen waiter and tucking his own head into his shoulders like a turtle. If her sharp, searchlight gaze came to rest on either of them, he was certain she would recognize them as the two line cooks she'd allowed to pass earlier.

They would be screwed, and royally.

He reached down and gripped Julia's arm, probably harder than he intended.

"You're amazing, honey!" he said, leaning in to kiss her cheek and whispering in her ear. "But remember the kids. We need to go, *now*."

Julia nodded.

"Gentlemen," she said to the feds. "I'm sure you can handle things from here."

"No problem," the older agent replied, his attention focused on the waiter. "Thank you, doctor."

Julia stood, and Peter swiftly steered her around so that the two of them were facing away from the raised platform and the female agent. The presidential candidate had taken the mishap in stride, and was encouraging the guests to return to their seats so that he could continue talking about whatever people who want to run the country talked about.

Peter couldn't have cared less.

All he cared about was getting the two of them out of the hall before everyone else sat back down. While they were part of a milling crowd, they had a chance of escaping unnoticed. But once they were the only ones left standing, they might as well have had giant neon arrows floating around their heads.

Rabbit season…

Peter slung his arm around Julia's shoulders, leaning on her as he limped along and pressing his cheek close to hers as if whispering sweet nothings. Really he was just trying to hide his face.

The smell of her was just a bonus.

Peter dried his hair on a threadbare towel. The hotel they'd chosen, one of a generic chain designed for weekenders and people stuck overnight in the city, was a far cry from the opulence of the Ambassador. But what it lacked in amenities, it made up for in anonymity.

He wrapped another towel around his waist and left the steam of the bathroom to find Julia lying on the bed wrapped in a bathrobe. Though they had checked into separate rooms, neither of them wanted to be alone just now. They were both wired and exhausted after the Ambassador.

"You okay?" he asked.

She was idly flipping through the hotel's magazine, one of those touristy garbage publications that showed ads for local restaurants and boutiques that most of the hotel's patrons would either ignore or couldn't afford.

"I'm just trying to figure out what I'm going to do next." She put the magazine down and looked at Peter. "I've spent years on this cure. And now it's gone."

"I know it can't be easy," Peter said. "To have it stolen, to get duped, to see it used in a terrorist attack. That's not what you created it for. People died today, and I know that's not easy to think about."

She shrugged.

"That's not it," she said. "Yes, that's part of it, I suppose, but really, I just want to get back on track. I'm going to have to start over. God, Peter, what am I going to do?"

"Exactly that," he said. "Hey, the virus is gone, but they didn't take away what you know. You still have that. You can rebuild."

It was easy for him to say that. It wasn't his life's work. And he had more pressing concerns to address. He still had to figure out how he was going to get Big Eddie's money. *One thing at a time,* he thought, and he lay down on the bed next to her.

He touched her hair and she curled into him, her fingers running along his jawline. Since that night at Doctor Westerson's house, neither of them had made a move on each other. There were still some lingering doubts in Peter's mind about why she had decided to run out on him that morning, but they had been through so much today, and it had been so intense, that he just wanted a break for a bit.

A little time to forget himself.

He bent his head to kiss her, and his phone rang.

The sudden noise startled them both and they jerked away from each other. Peter grabbed the phone off his nightstand and looked at it. He didn't recognize the number, but didn't expect to. The phone was a burner he had picked up that morning, and supposedly no one had the number.

Tentatively, he answered.

"Peter, thank God you're all right," Bernard Stokes said the moment Peter put the phone to his ear. "I heard there was quite the kerfuffle at the Ambassador this afternoon."

"Stokes?" he said. "How'd you get this number? And why are you calling? This isn't exactly a secure line."

"A magician never reveals his secrets," Stokes replied, sounding pleased with himself. "Whatever you did, bravo. Considering that you're still alive, I'm assuming it all went well. However, you have another, much larger problem."

A pit started to form in his stomach. Was it Big Eddie? Had he tracked him to New York?

"How so?"

"The Englishman isn't finished. Once I heard about what happened at the Ambassador I assumed—rightly as it turns out—that there would be some online chatter. The same people have been talking all day, about another buy."

"Another buy, like today was a buy?"

"Sounds like," Stokes acknowledged. "It's couched in some ridiculously obtuse wording, but I think they're looking at another attack. Only much larger."

"How much larger?" Peter said.

"The last time they were talking about individual doses. This time there's talk about liters."

Peter's blood turned to ice.

"Do they say where?"

"Somewhere in the subway."

"That doesn't narrow it down much."

"Look, it's all very cryptic, so I'm doing what I can," Stokes said. "Do you know anything about"—he paused, tapping away at keys—"a tunnel at Atlantic Avenue?"

"The Atlantic Avenue station? That's down in Brooklyn."

"No, I don't think that's what they're talking about. They're saying something about unused track. That station's still used, isn't it?"

"As far as I know it is," Peter said.

He hadn't been down in Brooklyn in a long time, but that was a heavily trafficked area. They had taken the subway earlier that day, and with all the garbled messages about station and track closures being piped over the PA system, he would have expected to hear something if the station had been shut down.

"Could it be a different station?"

"Some of the messages are actually encrypted," Stokes said. "I'm trying to get into one of them to see if there's anything more concrete..." He went silent for a moment, and Peter could hear the clacking of a keyboard. "Here we go. 'Atlantic Avenue Tunnel.' No mention of a station, though."

There was something about the name that was triggering a memory.

"Hang on," he said. "I need to check something."

"Is there something I can do?" Julia asked, getting off of the bed.

"Yeah," Peter said. "Look up Atlantic Avenue Tunnel. Wait. No. Make it 'historic Atlantic Avenue Tunnel'."

She opened up the laptop they had brought with them from the lab, and typed it in.

"Here it is," she said, her eyes scanning a web page. "World's oldest subway tunnel. Built in 1844. Abandoned. Rediscovered in 1980. Goes under Atlantic from Boerum Place to Columbia Street. They do tours."

"Tours?"

"Looks like the next one isn't scheduled for another

couple of weeks. The entrance is a manhole in the middle of the intersection at Atlantic and Court Street."

"A manhole?"

"That's what it says," Julia said.

"Did you find it?" Stokes asked.

"Yeah," Peter said. At least he hoped they had found it. "It's an abandoned historical tunnel under Atlantic." Yet it seemed odd that the Englishman would try something so out of the way, in order to infect a lot of people. A subway station he could understand, but an abandoned tunnel? There was something here he wasn't seeing.

"When is this happening?" he asked.

"Tonight," Stokes said. "Nine o'clock."

Peter looked at his watch. Less than an hour. Not a lot of time to get over to Brooklyn, find this manhole, and stop the Englishman. And who knew what they might run into when they got there.

He weighed his options.

His first instinct was to leave. Take off and figure out what to do about Big Eddie. Call the police, maybe. Leave an anonymous tip. Yet he knew that wouldn't work. Even in a post-9/11 world, nobody would believe him—that there was a terrorist attack about to go down in an abandoned subway tunnel in Brooklyn. And even if they did, by the time they got anybody over there it might be too late.

No, if he didn't do this, nobody was going to do it.

"Anything else you can tell us?" Peter said.

"Be careful?"

"Thanks."

Peter bent down and reached under the bed, where he'd stashed a compact Sig-Sauer P228 that he had picked up in Bridgeport from a guy who owed him a favor. They had stopped on their way down from Hartford, and dropped a couple hundred dollars on it. It was probably stolen, even more likely used in a crime, but he hadn't had many options.

"I intend to," he added.

PART SIX

1

Julia and Peter got off the subway in Brooklyn at the modern Atlantic Avenue station, a few blocks from the old tunnel entrance. Though it had been years since he had been down this way, Peter remembered the streets well enough that a map wasn't necessary. It was a good six or seven blocks of tree-lined streets with red-brick and brownstone buildings.

Even though he didn't need a map, Peter had brought along the laptop. He might know his way around above the ground, but he needed to get a better picture of what awaited them below the surface.

They didn't have a lot of time, so as soon as they hit the street, he flagged down a taxi.

"Atlantic and Boerum," he said. "Quick as you can."

He wanted to get out a block before their destination, to give him an opportunity to scan the area and see if anyone stood out. Even if the Englishman was already down in the tunnels, he might have positioned someone outside as a sentry. If that was the case, Peter wanted to know it before he was spotted.

As requested, the cabbie stepped on it, weaving

through traffic like a Formula 1 driver, narrowly making it through several yellow lights. Within a matter of moments, however, they arrived at the requested intersection, only slightly the worse for wear.

Peter tipped the driver handsomely and they briskly covered the rest of the block. He scanned the street for anyone who looked out of place—a bum who seemed a little too clean, a cop who might be a little too attentive. He kept his hand in his jacket pocket and firmly on the pistol.

"Have you ever been down in the tunnel?" Julia said.

"I didn't even know it was there." He'd heard of lost subway tunnels in New York, many of them urban legends that didn't hold up to scrutiny. There were supposed to be dozens of them—some abandoned, others caved in, and some never even completed, but he hadn't heard of this particular one.

Peter was still trying to figure out how they were going to get the manhole open without attracting attention, when they came onto the intersection—and stopped dead. The Englishman had beaten them to it, all right, and he'd done it the right way. A power company truck was parked next to the open manhole, lights blinking, orange cones warding away traffic.

"Looks like we're late to the party," he said.

He took Julia's arm and pulled her into the shadows of the nearest apartment building. Then he glanced around, spotted a coffee shop, and pulled her toward it. Once inside, they ordered coffee and took two seats in the back. He pulled the laptop out of his knapsack, booted it up, and did some digging.

On the power company site he found some photos of the tunnel, along with a schematic showing the layout beneath the street. The truck was parked over the main entrance, but he spotted a small emergency exit, just a block or so away. Doing his best to memorize the map, he closed the laptop, put it back into the knapsack, and shrugged it onto his shoulders.

The ladder took them a long way down—the tunnel was deep beneath the street. It dropped them into a small chamber with a doorway at the far end. There were a couple of lights hung loosely on the wall, and Peter could see a dim glow coming from beneath the doorway that led to the tunnel. He kept Julia behind him, drew the Sig, and racked the slide as quietly as he could.

Cracking open the door, he peered through. A rickety set of stairs led down into an uneven tunnel with rough-hewn rock sides and an arched tile roof.

About twenty yards in, a lone man was stooped over the controls of a machine about the size of an industrial air-compressor, tweaking knobs, checking fittings. A series of wide hoses snaked out of its sides toward vents in the ceiling. He attached a propane tank to another hose in the side, and turned the valve.

"I think you can stop now," Peter said, stepping through the doorway and down the wooden steps, the Sig gripped in both hands.

"Oh, my dear boy, why would I want to do that?" the man said in an English accent. He didn't bother to turn. In answer, Peter fired a warning shot that echoed through the tunnel.

The man froze, stood slowly, and turned to face Peter and Julia.

"McCoy, right?" Peter said, motioning upward with the pistol. "Richard McCoy. Or is that just an alias?"

"One of many, I'm afraid," McCoy said, lifting his hands above his head. "And you're Peter Bishop."

"Bangkok," Peter said, coming off the final stair, Julia close behind him. Even in the poor light he was sure this was the same man he saw shot in Bangkok. His hair was different—cut short instead of the salt-and-pepper ponytail he was wearing in Thailand. The obnoxious Hawaiian shirt had been replaced with a sweater, peacoat, and jeans.

"You remember," McCoy said. "I'm flattered."

Now that he was closer Peter could make out more details of the device. The similarity to an air-compressor wasn't coincidental—that was part of it. But where he would have expected an intake filter, there was a hose leading to the propane tank, which didn't make sense, unless—

"That's the virus," Peter said.

"I put it into a nutrient suspension," McCoy said, sounding very pleased with himself. "Besides allowing it to be aerosolized, it helps the virus survive outside a host for up to six hours by reinforcing the viral shell with a protein polymer. One push of the button, and it all goes spewing out through those hoses."

"And you're going to spread it from here? A subway tunnel that hasn't seen a passenger in a hundred years?"

"I don't need passengers. This tunnel has ventilation shafts that lead out to the existing lines. Imagine all of the people who ride through Brooklyn on a daily basis. It only takes one infection. This will guarantee thousands. And do you know what the best thing is?" He opened one hand, showing a vial with a familiar-looking liquid inside. "I can make so much more."

"It won't take them long to trace it back here," Peter said. "Once that stuff hits people, you won't be able to move your equipment out of this tunnel. Everyone's going to be looking for anything even the least bit suspicious. They'll find the device. And then they'll find you."

"I don't think so. You see, I've taken steps," McCoy answered. "The base is packed with thermite. Once the machine has done its job, I'll activate the timer and run. Everything here will burn into slag. I'll go on my merry way, and do it all over again."

"Peter, don't let him distract you," Julia said, stepping up to his side. "Shoot him!" Peter frowned at that.

"Doctor Lachaux, it's wonderful to see you again," McCoy said. "Do you really want Peter to undo all of your hard work?"

"You're not trying to cure epilepsy," Peter said.

"Neither is she," McCoy countered. "Oh, peripherally, I suppose, but all of this? No, this is part of a master plan." He paused, and then continued. "You did know this was all her idea, didn't you? This, Bangkok, the chase in Hartford. All of it. She's been planning it for years."

"Like I'm going to believe anything you say," Peter replied.

"Look at her," McCoy said. "Doesn't she look familiar? Think back a few years. Your father's laboratory. A young woman who was interested in virology. The day your father's assistant died."

"Stop it! Peter, you need to stop him," Julia said, a note of panic appearing in her voice. "Shoot him *now*."

"What was the assistant's name?" the Englishman said. "Carla, wasn't it, Julia?"

"I said stop it!"

"Oh, how she burned."

Peter stood there, stunned. How could this man know what had happened in Walter's lab? Surely he couldn't have been there. And Julia... Peter turned to look at her. He imagined her younger, with glasses, different hair.

It all clicked.

"You were there," Peter said.

Julia grabbed the Sig from Peter's hand, shoving him to aside. She pointed the gun at McCoy, holding it in shaking hands.

"I'm sorry, Peter," she said. "You don't understand. You can't..."

"Julia, what the hell is going on?"

"It's complicated, Peter," she said, her eyes fixed straight ahead. "You wouldn't believe me."

"Oh, my," McCoy said. "Isn't this a pickle?"

"You shut up," Julia said. "You know what I want. Just put the vial on the ground, and back away from it."

"I'm afraid I can't do that," McCoy said. "If I move, they might shoot me." He nodded his head toward the main stairs leading into the tunnel. Peter hazarded a glance over his shoulder, and froze.

Big Eddie stepped down the stairs, carrying a nasty-looking .357. It was pointed at Peter's head. Little Eddie came close at his heels, a Benelli M4 semi-automatic shotgun gripped in his enormous hands. The wooden steps bowed under his weight.

2

"Skulking in sewers now, are you Bishop?" Big Eddie said. "It suits you."

"Listen, Eddie, you don't want to be here," Peter said. For a moment he thought about grabbing the gun and turning it on the Scotsman, but quickly discarded the idea. If he did, there was no way he or Julia would survive. So he didn't fight when Little Eddie shoved the barrel of his Benelli into his stomach. Big Eddie took the Sig out of Julia's hand and stuffed it into his waistband.

"Maybe I don't, maybe I do," he replied, and he turned toward the Englishman. "You the ponce that called me?"

"I am indeed," McCoy said, turning toward Peter. "He was becoming a thorn in my side, and I thought the two of you might want to catch up, perhaps revisit some past adventures." Big Eddie nodded at him, and McCoy lowered his hands. "Now, if you'll excuse me, I have work to do."

He placed the vial onto the control panel of the device, and went back to flipping switches.

"You've got to listen to me, Eddie," Peter said. "He's about to release a disease into the subway system, and it's going to kill a lot of people. We're all going to die."

"What, you think I'm gonna fall for that shite?" Big Eddie replied. "You're a great spinner of tales, Peter Bishop. Why don't you tell me the one I want to hear? Like the one that goes, 'Eddie, here's all that money I owe you, plus interest.' You know that one, don't you, Bishop? You've told it to me enough times, I figure you know it by heart."

"Look, Eddie, I'm not—"

"Shut it," Eddie said, pistol-whipping him with the .357. A white-hot flash of pain shot through the left side of his skull.

Peter knew Big Eddie wasn't going to let him walk out of this, so he didn't have much to lose—but he had everything to gain. He let his legs go out from under him, pitched toward the mobster, and made a grab for the Sig sticking out of his waistband. The two of them toppled to the ground.

Peter tugged at the Sig, but lost his grip. It clattered against the cracked pavement, bouncing into some shadows near the wall.

The pistol lost, Peter focused on keeping Big Eddie from shooting him with the cannon in his hand. He took an elbow to the face, but managed to dislodge Big Eddie's .357, sending the gun skittering across the uneven floor.

"Julia, get out of here," Peter yelled. "Get the cops!" He only hoped she'd be able to do so before Little Eddie knew what was happening.

But instead of running to the exit, she ran toward the discarded gun, scooped it up, and continued toward the Englishman. Little Eddie wouldn't open up on Peter as long as there was a chance he might hit his father, but there wasn't any such risk if he took a shot at Julia.

Momentarily distracted, Peter got Big Eddie's knee to the groin. The mobster shoved hard, pushing Peter away from him. He rolled on the floor, scrambled to stand up, and a wave of nausea swept through him.

It was over.

But he was damned if he was going to die lying down.

The shotgun roared in Little Eddie's hands, at the same time as Julia fired the .357. Gunshots so close together that Peter couldn't tell who was shooting at whom. It took him a stunned second to realize that he wasn't dead. Then he turned, and saw Little Eddie slump to the floor, his enormous girth turned into dead weight.

Big Eddie screamed and ran to his son.

Peter expected to find Julia dead, but instead she stood over McCoy with the .357 smoking in her hand. The Englishman lay face down on the ground, his back a meaty crater where Little Eddie's Benelli had blown a hole the size of a soccer ball. Peter blinked. In the dim light of the tunnel, the man's blood looked oddly silver.

"We need to call the police," he said. "Have them get a bomb squad down here. Disarm this thing."

"You go ahead and do that, Peter," she said, kicking the Benelli into the shadows of the tunnel, far out of Big Eddie's reach. "I'm not sticking around for it." She leveled the gun at his chest, moved to the control panel, and slipped the vial of virus into her pocket.

"I've got what I came for," she said.

"What are you doing?" he replied. But he thought he was beginning to understand.

"I'm sorry, Peter," she said. "I didn't expect any of this to happen. You have to believe me. If McCoy hadn't caught me outside of Doctor Westerson's house, none of this would have happened."

"You'd have gotten away scot-free."

"I would have, yes. And this time I will."

"You bitch," Big Eddie screamed. He held his dead

son, blood covering his hands, soaking into his clothes. Little Eddie's formerly pretty blue eyes stared sightless at the ceiling. "You killed my boy."

"Goodbye, Peter," she said. "Don't follow me. I don't want to have to kill you, too."

She started to back away from him.

Peter thought furiously, trying to find some way to get her to stop.

"The police will find out about the virus," he said. "They'll take it and they'll study it. And they'll make more of it. Do you want that out there in the world? Your life's work? You'll be a pariah, and somebody else will get the credit."

Julia paused, considering his words.

"You're right," she said. "It's too dangerous in the wrong hands."

"Exactly," Peter said. "Help me get rid of it. The police..."

"We don't need the police," she said, stepping over to the control panel and shoving McCoy's body out of the way. She examined the panel until she found the switch she was looking for—flipped it, and a readout showed five minutes. Then it began counting down. She reached under the panel, finding the wire leading to the switch, and yanked it out, rendering it useless.

"Julia, are you *insane*? You'll kill thousands of people."

"I'm not releasing the virus, Peter. You heard McCoy. This thing's wired with enough thermite to destroy it, and turn this whole place into slag. I'm leaving now. If you follow me I'll shoot you. When the countdown reaches three minutes you can leave. That should give both of us enough time to get out safely." She looked at Big Eddie crying over Little Eddie's corpse. "Even him."

She backed away again, and started up the stairs.

"At least answer me this," Peter said. "Is it true? What McCoy said? About Walter's lab? About Carla?"

She smiled at him, pausing at the doorway.

"A girl's got to have her secrets," she said, and she disappeared from sight.

Peter stopped himself from running after her. By the time he got up there she'd be long gone. Or she'd shoot him.

That was fine. He'd find her. He knew exactly where she was going.

Peter looked back at the device, the clock counting down the seconds. There was no way he'd get the switch re-wired in time to shut it off. And did he want to? This way, nobody else would get the virus, and thousands of people would be saved.

He gave it another ten seconds before heading up the stairs. As he stepped through the doorway, he heard Big Eddie's voice, bellowing behind him, followed by pounding footsteps. So he ran, taking the stairs two at a time and flying up the ladder like he had demons at his heels.

Worse than demons, he had Big Eddie.

When he popped up through the open manhole, Peter threw himself into the gutter, sliding behind a parked car as if he was stealing home base. Seconds later flames belched forth from the tunnel, and the ground lurched beneath him. He covered his head with his hands.

When he dared to sneak a look at the chaos in the street, he saw a crowd of anxious Brooklynites milling around the manhole. A pair of hipster Samaritans were trying to help a guy slumped against the power company truck. The guy's bald head was burned bright pink and there was a raccoon mask of soot on his furious face.

Big Eddie. Still alive and kicking, the hard old bastard. Luckily, he was distracted by the hipsters, giving Peter an opportunity to melt, unnoticed, into the crowd.

3

DUSK AT REIDEN LAKE.

It was an innocuous place, drowsy and lost in time. Not really big enough or scenic enough to attract out-of-state visitors. Mostly kids with nothing better to do, who wanted an unsupervised place to drink and make out, and the occasional lone older man in a splintery canoe who didn't really care that the fish were small and scarce.

The beach was narrow and rocky, the water murky and cold even in the summertime. A cracked rowboat had been abandoned belly-up on the far end of the beach. There were a few modest cabins clustered around the northern end, most of which seemed to be empty this time of year. If Peter remembered correctly, one of them belonged to some relative of his father—an uncle maybe.

But like all of Peter's memories of this place, it felt foggy and jarringly incomplete, as if he'd made it up or seen it on some television show. There was nothing about it that wasn't utterly mundane, yet it felt profoundly haunted, pregnant with mystery and secrets.

Like the scene of an unsolved murder.

I've got to stop reading so many cheap crime novels, he told himself.

Peter ditched the stolen car on the overlook and ran down to the beach. There was Julia, standing in the water up to her hips, a loaded syringe in her hand.

"Julia!" he called out.

She spun toward him, eyes wide.

"I thought you might follow me," she said.

"I had to," he said taking a step closer to the water. "I need to know what the hell is going on. What are you trying to do? You've done nothing but lie to me from the minute we met, and now I want some answers, dammit!"

"I understand," she said softly. "Of course you want answers. About your life. Your childhood. About why you feel so out of place, no matter where you go. We're alike in many ways, Peter. Outsiders. Strangers. Alone even in a crowded room. The difference is that you chose to run away and keep on running, even though no matter how far you run, you can never get away from your own head.

"Me, I chose to do something about it."

She leaned in, eyes glittering.

"You want to know who you really are, don't you?" she asked.

"I know who I am," Peter said.

"Do you?" she asked.

The question echoed, unanswered across the water. Peter clenched his fists.

Do I?

Of course he did. Why wouldn't he? There was never any doubt in his mind.

Except there was. A deeply rooted doubt, all tangled up in that strange time when he'd been so sick as a child. When things seemed to get so mixed up in his head, and everyone was acting like nothing was different when everything obviously was.

"What are you trying to tell me?" Peter asked, taking a step closer to the edge of the water.

"Let me *show* you," Julia replied.

She plunged the syringe into the crook of her arm. His hand jerked forward instinctively, then he stopped. It was too late.

Nothing happened for several seconds. The two of them just stood there in the cool, quiet evening while a single optimistic cricket and the soft lapping of the lake water against the shore provided the only soundtrack.

Then, something strange started to happen. The air behind her started to shimmer and split open like a wound. She turned toward this anomaly and let the syringe slip from her fingers.

"It's working!" she whispered.

"It's like what happened at the hotel," he said, squinting against the curious light. It was growing larger. "What is it?"

"The way home," she said, turning back to face him and extending her hand. "Come with me."

He looked down at her hand, and over at the pulsing gateway that seemed so alien, and yet at the same time so familiar. There was a cold coil of nausea beginning to churn in his belly, and he felt as if he was starting to lose his grip on what he thought was real. None of this was possible, yet it was happening before his disbelieving eyes. This, and of all the impossible things he'd witnessed over the past few days, left him feeling profoundly unsure.

He looked back at Julia's hand. Hadn't he been searching for answers his entire life? Could he live with himself if he turned away from the understanding he'd been craving all these years?

He unfisted his own right hand, and stretched it out toward her.

Just before they touched, he noticed something starting to happen to her hand. At first it was the proportions of her fingers that seemed slightly off. The index finger seemed too long, while the middle finger was too short and thick. The pinkie finger was age-spotted with the swollen knuckles of an older woman. She didn't seem to be mutating out of control like the virus's previous victims. She just seemed to be shifting into a strange jigsaw composite of different people.

Patches of her skin were dark while others were light. Some had freckles, or scars, or thick hair. When he looked up at her face, he was amazed and horrified to see a morphing kaleidoscope of varied features, both male and female.

"What?" she asked, her patchwork brows furrowed.

"I think—" he said, gesturing to his own face with a kind of inarticulate flapping. "I mean, something is..."

Before he could find the words to break it to her that she seemed to be transforming into a hundred different people at the same time, something started happening to that unnatural slash in the air behind her. It began clenching, tightening up and narrowing like reluctant lips.

She noticed the direction of his gaze and turned to look.

"No!" she cried.

Before Peter could process this new development, she flung herself through the shimmering rift.

Then she and the rift were gone.

4

Julia felt an uncanny power fluctuating and flowing through every inch of her body as she spun away from Peter and dove into the gateway. Everything seemed to turn inside out, thrusting her headfirst through a thousand improbable supernovas, all simultaneously.

Then she was suddenly plunged into chilly green water. Before she was able to orient herself and figure up from down in the murky shallows, rough hands gripped her arms and her clothes and hauled her, sputtering, to her feet.

She shook her head to clear it, and looked around at her saviors. They were a dead-eyed pair, pale and utterly expressionless. Both male and both in their mid-thirties, one blond and one dark. Unremarkable, except for their total lack of anything resembling human emotion.

There were two other people there, too. One was female and standing directly in front of Julia, knee deep in water. She was pretty, with wide-set dark eyes and honey-blond hair, but she was just as cold and inhuman as her male compatriots.

The other was a third male, with light hair and blue eyes, standing on the shore. All four were dressed in what looked like black military fatigues or maybe SWAT uniforms.

Are they soldiers of some sort? she wondered.

The blue-eyed man on the shore was the only one of the four wearing something that resembled a human expression. Unfortunately, it was a hostile smirk that didn't bode well for Julia.

Although everything looked just as it had before she entered the gateway, she had to assume that she'd made it through to the alternate universe that Doctor Bishop had written about in his journal. Peter was nowhere to be seen, and these grim soldiers were here in his place. But she hadn't been expecting this sort of welcome committee—or any welcome at all, for that matter—and her mind was racing, desperate to come up with something that would enable her to talk her way out of this situation.

That's when she noticed the skin of her arms was behaving strangely, flickering like a rapid-paced slideshow of different skin tones and textures. The virus wasn't supposed to have any mutagenic effects on an epileptic host, but an unexpected physical side effect of some kind was definitely occurring. It seemed odd that she didn't feel anything unusual, physically speaking, other than a slight adrenaline buzz. Could the fluctuations in her skin be hallucinations brought on by the symbiotic assimilation of the virus inside her brain?

But as fascinating as this effect might be, she had more pressing issues with which to deal.

"Who," she managed to whisper. "Who are you?"

The woman raised an unfamiliar gun and pointed it at Julia.

"Not in the head," the smirking man said. "The brain must remain intact."

The woman nodded, lowered her aim, and shot Julia in the heart.

Thomas Newton watched the subject sag lifelessly in the arms of the hybrid soldiers, bleeding out into the murky green water. He had a passing surge of discomfort, imagining contamination and rampant plague that might result from the viral load in the subject's blood.

But Jones had assured him that his newest re-engineered strain of the virus was neither as hearty nor as deadly as the first. It would die off within seconds of being exposed to the hostile environment outside the host organism's body.

"Get her into the cryo-freezer," he snapped. "Pronto."

The hybrid soldiers followed his command, hauling the still-shifting body ashore and carrying it quickly and efficiently to the back of the truck parked up on the bluff. The roll-up was open, the freezer ready and waiting to accept the specimen.

Newton couldn't imagine how something so obviously wild and unstable could really be the key to creating a new wave of fully organic shifters, soldiers that would outperform their current mechanical hybrids, and tip the balance in the war between the universes. After all, it was clear that the subject had been unable to control her shifting ability—indeed, she barely seemed aware that it was occurring.

His soldiers needed to be finely calibrated and perfectly controlled, able to pass without notice among their unsuspecting human targets. Still, he himself was just a foot soldier in this war, and it wasn't his place to question the orders of his superiors.

Once the body of the subject was interred in the cryo-freezer for transport to the lab, Newton closed the roll-up door on the back of the truck and rapped on it to signal the driver.

He watched without comment as the driver put the vehicle in gear and drove away.

⅄

Jones watched one of a bank of monitors on the desk. The image was of Reiden Lake through cameras he had installed to watch for Julia. He would be collecting them soon, since they were no longer needed, though it didn't much matter if he did. No one would find them, just as no one had found them in Bangkok, Hartford, the Ambassador Hotel, or in the Atlantic Avenue Tunnel beneath New York.

Of course, that last one hadn't needed to be collected. It was incinerated when the thermite destroyed everything in the tunnel. Just as he'd planned it.

Jones switched off the last of the monitors. As secret lairs went, this one wasn't so bad. He had everything he needed, and things were going according to plan. Oh, there were some adjustments he would need to make, but not many. With Doctor Lachaux's mutated brain in his possession, he had exactly what he needed to take his work further than anyone had dreamed.

A noise behind him caught his attention. He spun slowly in the office chair.

An electronic typewriter—a Selectric 251—hummed to life. The hammers began striking the crisp, white paper in the machine, yet there was no one at the keys. Well, no one on his side of the fence, at least. In the small mirror set up next to the typewriter, Jones could see the keys move. It was a fascinating process to observe.

Hit a key over there, make a letter over here. He watched the message take shape on the crisp, white paper in the machine. A message between worlds. He read the news, the import of it sinking in.

He smiled.

5

Another airport—the first place Peter went when he wasn't sure what to do next.

This particular one was New York's familiar JFK airport, and he sat slumped in a long row of uncomfortable seats facing the window, with a laptop balanced on his knees. He had been cleaning out the accumulated junk from one of his many email accounts, but found himself just staring at the screen, brain idling in a kind of dull, blurry neutral.

He was exhausted, wrung out like a washrag and weighed down with thorny, unanswered questions. The most pressing of which remained what the hell he was going to do about Big Eddie.

And he was all out of answers.

A new message appeared in his inbox, attracting his eye. It was from his old Iraqi friend and fixer Tarik. The subject was BIG FISH.

Hello my friend,

Please join me for another fishing trip. The big ones are jumping. Don't let them get away this time.

Meet up at the usual place for details.

— T.

A little fishing trip was just what he needed to put all this madness behind him, and if he was lucky, he'd score enough of a catch to get Big Eddie off his back for good.

Peter looked at his watch, then called up the schedule for Qatar Airways. He still had plenty of time to make the 4:30 flight to Baghdad. Shuffling through his various passports, he looked for the one that seemed the least dodgy out of the stack. He found one that didn't look too bad, and booked himself a seat in first class as Jack Johnson.

He closed the laptop and stood, stuffing it into his messenger bag. He turned toward the large screen that displayed the upcoming international departures, and spotted a man standing nearby, looking right at him.

The man was unremarkable, on the youngish side of middle-aged but dressed older in a high-end navy-blue suit and a subtle, pricy tie. His shoes were spotless and his eyes were small and shrewd behind wire-rimmed glasses. He could have been any ordinary businessman waiting for a flight back to the head office, but his interest in Peter was unmistakable.

He didn't smell like either a thug or a fed. Too well dressed and paunchy, with soft clean hands.

Peter couldn't decide if it would be wiser to shake this guy, or call him out, but in the end he didn't have to choose because the man came over to him.

"Peter Bishop?"

Peter narrowed his eyes but didn't respond.

"I have a business proposition for you," the man said.

He reached into an inner pocket and Peter flinched a little, even though he knew it was highly unlikely that the man had managed to bring a gun through airport security. Instead of a weapon, the man pulled out a thick envelope and handed it over. The envelope was unmarked except for an unfamiliar three-dimensional "M" logo in the upper-left corner.

Judging from the weight and shape of the envelope, it contained cash.

Lots of it.

The man had his interest now, that was for sure.

"My employer has authorized me to issue this advance, just for considering his offer. If you aren't interested, you can put that in your pocket and walk away right now, no explanation required. If you are interested, well, there's more where that came from. Plenty more."

"I'm listening," Peter said, slipping the envelope into his messenger bag. "But I have to catch a flight in two hours."

"We'll give you a ride in the company plane," the man said. "You can meet with my employer on the way to your destination."

"I'm not headed to Cleveland, you know," Peter said. "I'm flying international."

"We know where you're going, Mr. Bishop," the man said. "It's not a problem." He gestured to his left. "This way, please."

Peter frowned, still not entirely sure how to feel about this unexpected development. But he knew exactly how he felt about that envelope full of cash. And how Big Eddie would feel about it, too.

He followed the man in the navy-blue suit.

The man led him to a gate at the far end of the terminal. There was no one at the desk, and the door was closed, but the man just opened it and motioned for Peter to enter. No one seemed to notice, or object to what they were doing, but it still seemed strange and somehow wrong, like they were being naughty.

As they walked down the jetway, Peter could see a plane parked at the far end. It was larger than he had expected for a private jet—only slightly smaller than a standard commercial airliner. On the pristine white tail was the same logo he'd seen on the envelope full of cash.

When they reached the door of the plane, the man motioned for Peter to go ahead. As soon as he did so, he was greeted by a compact, clean-cut and very fit male flight attendant who looked more like a triathlete. The attendant shut the door behind Peter without comment, leaving the man in the navy-blue suit out on the jetway.

"Isn't he coming with us?" Peter asked, looking back over his shoulder at the sealed door and feeling a small flicker of anxiety in his belly.

"I'm afraid not," the flight attendant replied. "This way please, Mr. Bishop."

Peter walked into the body of the plane, which was richly appointed with roomy leather seats and wooden tables polished to a deep espresso finish. There were fresh flowers and tasteful lamps and even a long, plush couch, complete with silk throw pillows. The carpet beneath Peter's feet was as thick and soft as mink. The interior looked more like an expensive hotel lounge than any kind of vehicle.

There was nobody there except for Peter and the flight attendant, but he could see that there was an additional section in the rear of the plane—one that had been curtained off.

"So," Peter said, frowning, "where's this mysterious boss man I'm supposed to be meeting with?" He gestured toward the curtain. "In there?"

"You'll be joining him later," the flight attendant said. "Meanwhile, just relax and enjoy the ride."

Not sure of what else to do, Peter took a seat in

one of the big chairs. He looked around, then up at the flight attendant.

"Um," he said. "Don't I need a seatbelt?"

The man smiled like an indulgent parent.

"Not for this flight, Mr. Bishop," he said. "Can I offer you a drink before we take off?"

"Sure," Peter replied. "Make it bourbon."

"Ice?"

"Please."

The flight attendant nodded and disappeared behind the curtain.

The chair was perhaps the most comfortable seat Peter had ever been in, and it was kind of hard to maintain any level of anxiety when he felt so good.

I could get used to this kind of travel.

The flight attendant reappeared carrying a smoked glass tumbler with a single large, perfectly clear ice cube and a generous knock of rich amber liquid.

"Thanks," Peter said, taking the drink.

"Here's the control for the entertainment system," the flight attendant said, handing Peter a remote with more buttons than the dashboard of the plane. "Buzz me if you need anything."

"Okay, thanks," Peter said.

The attendant disappeared behind the curtain again, leaving Peter to his own devices. He set the remote on the table and took a sip of the bourbon. It was predictably fantastic—top shelf, like everything else on this plane—and added its own extra level of soporific comfort.

The plane started off down the runway just as Peter was finishing his drink. He set the empty glass down on the table, and within seconds the flight attendant magically appeared to snatch it up, and then disappeared with it as the plane started gathering speed for take-off.

The take-off was so smooth, Peter might not have even noticed he was airborne if his ears hadn't popped.

Now I can see why they don't need seatbelts.

He watched out the thick round window as the Manhattan skyline disappeared beneath the clouds, then started fiddling with the remote. A large screen slid silently up from the center of the table, displaying a dizzying array of entertainment options. Peter picked *Cursed*, a forgettable horror flick by the guy who had done *Nightmare on Elm Street*, and was sound asleep in his seat within minutes.

He woke with a start an unknown amount of time later, to a sickening volley of turbulence that shook the plane like an angry child. He gripped the armrests and looked out the window just in time to see a sizzling fork of lightning flash through the clouds inches from the metal hull.

"Jesus!" Peter said, involuntarily groping for a seatbelt, even though he knew there wasn't one. "Hey, flight attendant! What the hell is going on?"

The attendant appeared from behind the curtain wearing what looked like a crash helmet. He walked right past Peter to the front of the cabin, where he pulled down a folding seat and strapped himself in.

"Try to remain calm, Mr. Bishop," he said. "It will all be over in a few minutes."

Another nasty bump and the plane bounced from side to side, and then dropped steeply.

"Remain calm?" Peter asked. "Are you *crazy*?"

Instead of answering, the flight attendant pushed a button that caused a partition to slide out from the wall about three feet in front of him, sealing Peter into his section.

"What the hell?" Peter got up, fighting his way

across the pitching and shaking cabin to the partition and banging on it with his fist. It was solid metal and didn't budge. "What am I supposed to do?"

Another vertigo-inducing drop flung him backward into the mysterious curtain. To his dismay, he discovered another solid metal partition right on the other side, slamming into it and cracking his head hard enough to see red.

He was trapped and alone in this luxurious, high altitude coffin. Cursing himself for being suckered, he tried desperately to figure all the angles while trying to keep his feet under him.

What the hell is going on here? he fumed. He was supposed to have some sort of meeting, but there didn't seem to be anyone else on the plane. And why was he trapped like this? If it was an attempt to kill him, it was the most expensive, impractical, and unreliable assassination of all time. Might as well put snakes on the plane.

So what's this about?

All thoughts were erased from his mind as the plane went into a sudden, harrowing plunge that had Peter convinced they were about to crash into the freezing ocean. He was knocked off his feet as the cabin was engulfed in darkness, leaving the flickering emergency lights as the only illumination.

He lay there face down on the soft, expensive carpet with his arms thrown up over his head, waiting for the inevitable.

Then there was a blinding flash of white light…

…and just like that, it was over.

It wasn't that the plane had stabilized or leveled out. One second it was rocking like a ship on rough seas, and the next it was smooth as glass. The lights went back on, too. When Peter uncovered his face, the first thing that he saw was a pair of expensive black leather dress shoes, just inches from his nose.

He looked up and saw a tall, familiar-looking older man in a dark suit.

"Hello, Peter," the man said, extending a large, weathered hand to help him to his feet.

The man's resonant baritone voice was even more familiar, but he still couldn't seem to place him in any kind of context. He wanted to ask a thousand questions, but one came out first.

"Do I know you?"

The man smiled, dark eyes bright and sharp.

"We met when you were a child," the man said. "Shortly after your… miraculous recovery. My name is William Bell. I am an old colleague of your father."

Peter squinted at the older man, thinking now that he might have seen him while he was in Florida, but before he could nail down a solid, specific memory, he was distracted by the dawning realization that the interior of the cabin seemed *different*, in a hundred small ways.

The metal partitions were gone. The layout and position of the furniture was similar, yet subtly *off*. The color palette was still neutral, but with more cool tones than warm.

There were no flowers.

"Please," Bell said. "Have a seat."

The older man eased his body slowly down into one of the cushy leather chairs, and gestured to Peter to take one opposite him on the other side of the polished, blond wood table.

Peter sat and ran a finger over the surface. He was almost positive that the table had been dark wood when he first boarded the plane.

His sense of unease increased when an unfamiliar

female flight attendant appeared. She was slender and lovely, with a dark bob haircut and long brown legs flashing through the slit in her tight red skirt. He supposed she might just have been behind the curtain the whole time, but why?

And where was the male flight attendant, who he'd last seen strapped into a folding seat that was no longer there?

The woman carried a tray with coffee and all the accoutrements, which she set down on the table between them.

"Thank you, Fabianne," Bell said, filling a cup for himself and then a second one for Peter. "Cream or sugar?"

"I'm sorry," Peter said, pushing his fingers through his hair. He looked out the window. Nothing but infinite darkness. "I need a minute." Seconds later he asked, "What exactly is going on here? Why is everything... different?"

"I realize that this all seems somewhat unconventional," Bell said, sipping his black coffee. "But I assure you, everything will be explained in due time. In fact, I believe I have a lot of the answers you've been searching for most of your young life. But that's only a fringe benefit to the offer I'm prepared to make to you tonight."

Peter picked up the coffee cup and drank it black to buy time to think, even though he didn't really want any. His stomach was roiling with anxious acid and unanswered questions.

"I want you to work for me at Massive Dynamic, Peter," Bell said. "You see, under different circumstances, your father and I would have been partners in my current... endeavors. But certain weaknesses have unfortunately prevented that from happening. Weaknesses that you do not possess. You are smart, resourceful and flexible in your thinking, without being overly burdened by traditional morality. You could take your father's rightful place in this corporation.

"We are about to embark on an epic project that will change, well, at the risk of sounding overly dramatic, everything. I mean *everything*. But in any such project, I need men of vision on my team.

"I need men like you."

"But what kind of man *am* I?" Peter said doubtfully. "I'm nobody, Mr. Bell. I'm not a man of vision."

He wasn't, was he? Peter thought about that. Maybe it was time to stop running, stop trying to scam the world in one score after another. If he accepted, he'd have enough money to pay off Big Eddie, and then some.

Of course, money might not be enough anymore, now that Little Eddie was dead. No doubt the Scotsman blamed Peter for it. Probably better just to set that particular debt aside as unpayable.

At least with anything less than Peter's life.

"I've watched you, Peter," Bell said. "You're brilliant. You have a perception unlike anyone else. I know what you're capable of. After all, you are your father's son."

Peter bristled at that. Any thought of taking Bell's offer disappeared. Peter was a lot of things, but he was not *that*. Would never be that. He forced himself to relax, and loosen the hands he had balled into fists.

"No dice," he said. "I can't take the job."

There was a long silence, as Bell stared at him. Peter wondered what was going on behind those eyes.

"I won't deny that I'm disappointed," Bell said, and he asked, "Are you absolutely certain there's nothing I can do to change your mind?"

Peter shook his head.

"Look, I don't care what you say," he replied, "I don't want any part of this."

"Very well," Bell said, palms held out and open. "It's your choice."

He nodded very slightly—so imperceptibly that Peter might not have noticed it if Fabianne hadn't appeared beside him and jammed a hypodermic needle into the side of his neck.

When Peter woke up, he had a hangover the size of the *Titanic*, and felt as if he'd been dropped to the floor from a great height. His entire body felt bruised and achy. His head felt swollen and filled with metal shavings and broken glass. There was a weird taste in his mouth, like he'd been chewing on a cheap adhesive bandage.

He had absolutely no memory of what he had been drinking to get him into this sorry state.

What a waste of a good buzz.

He took quick stock of where he was. It was a crummy, generic hotel room that could have been anywhere in the world. Then he discovered that he didn't have time for a more comprehensive analysis that went beyond finding the toilet as quickly as possible.

He threw up for what felt like a year, his poor beaten body wringing itself out like a rag. Once that was done, he flushed the toilet and sat there for a few minutes with his cheek resting against the lip of the bathtub, taking stock of his body and mind.

Physically, he felt as if he'd been in—and lost—more than one fight, but he didn't seem to have any serious wounds or injuries. No broken bones. He did have an eight-hundred-pound gorilla of a headache. He also felt dehydrated as hell, but, even though he was sorely tempted, he didn't drink out of the tap, because he wasn't sure what country he was in.

Mentally, he wasn't in much better shape. The last thing he could remember was being in the airport in New York City, and getting the email from Tarik.

Baghdad? Am I in Baghdad?

A quick search around the small room confirmed this hunch, revealing a few rumpled maps, pamphlets, and tourist guides to the city. It also revealed the most beautiful thing he'd ever seen. A bottle of water with an Arabic label. He made short work of it, downing the entire bottle in two heroic swallows.

The phone rang, making him jump. The harsh jangling sound made him feel as if he was being attacked by rats, and he answered it more out of self-defense than the desire to actually speak to anyone.

"Yeah," he said, his voice a hoarse croak that he barely recognized.

"Peter, my friend!" It was Tarik. "I've been trying to reach you all morning. You sound like hell. Rough night last night, eh?"

"Apparently so," Peter replied, glancing across the room at his reflection in the mirror, and quickly looking away in shame. "But I've had worse. We still on?"

"We are on," Tarik said. "Meet me at the usual place in thirty minutes."

"Better make it forty-five," Peter said. "I need a little more time to put my head in a bucket of ice."

"You are too hard on yourself," Tarik said. "What you need is a good woman."

"What I need is a good score," Peter replied.

"Then get here as quickly as you can," Tarik said, "and you shall have it."

The phone went dead in Peter's hand.

He put the receiver back on the cradle and then slowly, gingerly began to pull himself together.

He showered and shaved and got himself into some semi-respectable clothes. He was sorting through his messenger bag to make sure he had everything he needed for the meeting, when he discovered an envelope full of cash tucked into a side pocket.

The envelope was entirely unmarked. The cash inside was nowhere near what he needed to get Big Eddie off his back, but it was certainly enough to keep him afloat while he hustled up a more substantial score.

He must have had an even more interesting night than he had thought.

Downstairs in the cramped and seedy hotel lobby, Peter fumbled for his sunglasses before daring to venture out into the unforgiving Iraqi sun. As he did so, the clerk furtively motioned to him over the desk.

The fellow was a scrawny scrap of an old man who couldn't have been more than five foot two and had a face like a mummified child. His name was—if Peter's addled brain was remembering correctly—Walid, and he could be counted on to keep his mouth shut, in return for a few extra dinar. Which was the reason Peter always stayed at this miserable excuse for a hotel when he was in town for business.

Somehow, that deeply ingrained force of habit had steered him here, despite his blacked-out state the night before.

"*Ahalan,*" Peter said, ambling casually over to the desk. "What's up, Wally?"

"A tall, blond American woman was looking for you," Walid said, leaning in and speaking without moving his thin, stubbled lips. "She said she was FBI. I told her you were out."

"Good man," Peter replied, slipping a few American bills into Walid's bony hand.

The last thing in the world he needed was the damn FBI sniffing around his business. His instinct told him to cut and run, but he couldn't afford to pass up an opportunity to get Big Eddie off his back. He needed to shake this hungover fog and bring his "A" game, or the gangster was going to be the least of his worries.

He put on his sunglasses, and walked out of the hotel.

ACKNOWLEDGEMENTS

The author would like to thank Al Guthrie, Steve Saffel, Noreen O'Toole, Anna Songco, Lisa Fitzpatrick, Nick Landau, Vivian Cheung, Alice Nightingale, Natalie Laverick, Angela Park, Rob Chiappetta, Glen Whitman, Joel Wyman, Nathan Long, and Stephen Blackmoore.

ABOUT THE AUTHOR

Christa Faust is the author of a variety of media tie-ins and novelizations for properties such as the *Fringe* trilogy, *Supernatural*, *Final Destination*, and *Snakes on a Plane*. She also writes hardboiled crime novels, including the Edgar Award-nominated *Money Shot*, *Choke Hold*, and the Butch Fatale series. She lives in Los Angeles. Her website is christafaust.net.